"Herr Marx! It's a — — — — — to the ground!"
Moosic shouted.

Marx was about ten feet from Sandoval, and at the noise and yell he froze and turned to look back in utter confusion. Sandoval reached into his pants and pulled out a gun, while behind Moosic, in the alley, two strange figures ran out into the light. Two figures out of nightmare.

They seemed to be almost like living statues, black all over, although they seemed to wear nothing except the time belts, their skin or whatever it was that was glistening like polished black metal. Their features were gargoylelike, the stuff of nightmares in any age. Both had automatic rifles in their hands.

DOWNTIMING THE NIGHT SIDE

Look for these other TOR books by Jack L. Chalker

JACK L. CHALKER
DOWNTIMING
THE NIGHT SIDE

A TOM DOHERTY ASSOCIATES BOOK

DOWNTIMING THE NIGHT SIDE

Copyright © 1985 by Jack L. Chalker

First printing: May 1985

A TOR Book

Published by Tom Doherty Associates
8-10 West 36 Street
New York, N.Y. 10018

Cover art by Norma Segrelles

ISBN: 0-812-53288-0
CAN. ED.: 0-812-53289-9

Printed in the United States of America

To all those time travelers who came before:
H. G. Wells, Jack Williamson, Murray Leinster,
Robert A. Heinlein, Randall Garrett, and Fritz Leiber
most notably; and also to the one among all others
who inspires my plots:
Niccolo Machiavelli

PROLOGUE

It was with mounting frustration that the computers and the experts who controlled them were well primed for nuclear defense, laser defense, outright invasion from space, and all the other exotic ways in which the enemy might inflict damage, yet not totally effective against the slingshot.

Somewhere a siren sounded, and soon a cacophony of electronic warning bells went off throughout the defense complex. Technicians put down whatever they were doing and scurried to their situation boards, but there was little for them to do even with danger approaching. The computers could handle things much faster than they, and all they could do was watch and worry and check the status of the defense systems.

"Incoming!" somebody shouted needlessly. "Oh, my God! Look at that board!"

The main situation screen showed it now: more blips of various sizes than any of them could count, all coming in in a wide pattern. Two blips, however, were enormous.

"What the hell are they shooting now? *Planets?*" somebody else muttered, the awed question carrying in the sudden silence of the room, now that the warning signals had been cut off.

It was a meteor storm like they had never seen before—tens of thousands of chunks of space junk and debris with only one thing in common—all were at least large enough to survive entry into Earth's atmosphere. Nor was this a random swarm. Like the rest, it had started out around

Jupiter, with the great space tugs of the enemy forming them up and shooting them around with vast energy beams the defenders could only envy, using the gravity of the big planet to whip them around and send them in a predetermined spread inwards to the Earth.

This group had also been particularly well placed; they would strike within a relatively small area a quarter of a million kilometers square. Small, considering the enormous task of grouping such shots so that they would hit the planet at all; enormous, if you had to defend that area against such a rockfall.

A few hundred well-placed missiles would have done the job, but Earth was long out of missiles for this or any other use. Still, millions of ground-based laser cannon and other such defenses would get the majority of them, but at a tremendous cost in energy. The computers were also forced to target the largest meteors with the majority of weaponry, since to allow them to hit intact would be disaster, but this had the multiple effect of breaking them up into hordes of smaller rocks, and there would not be enough weapons to spare for them and the others.

"Mostly Indian Ocean," somebody said, relieved, "but parts of East Africa are going to get creamed anyway."

In the midst of the tension, a tall, lean man with flowing blond hair watched, sighed, and shook his head. He was not very old, but his gaunt frame, slightly bent, and his drawn face, lined and worn, made him appear much older than he actually was. He turned and stalked out of the situation room, taking the elevator up five flights to the Command Headquarters level. The sentries barely gave him a glance, so well known was he on the level, and he walked up to the secretary's desk with a steady, determined gait.

"I wish to see the Chairman at once," he told the secretary, who nodded and pressed a small intercom button.

"Colonel Benoni is here," the secretary said crisply.

There was a muffled response, and he turned to the tall, blond man again. "He'll see you now."

Benoni nodded and walked around the desk to a large sliding door. This time the sentries checked his full I.D. as did the scan machines, despite the fact that they knew him. The Chairman trusted no one, and even inside Benoni knew he'd be under computer-controlled defense mechanisms that would evaluate his every move and mood and would make their own decisions as to whether or not he was a threat to the Chairman. It wasn't that Benoni didn't mind—he just didn't give a damn.

Max Shumb, Chairman of the Leadership Council of the Democratic Motherworld, was a handsome man in his middle years, the kind of man age helped rather than hurt. He sat behind his huge, U-shaped desk looking over some papers and didn't immediately acknowledge the colonel's entrance. Benoni, however, knew just what to do, and took the comfortable chair opposite the desk and waited.

The Chairman looked up at him, nodded, and put down the papers, but he did not smile. "Well, Eric, we were lucky this time."

Benoni nodded. "But perhaps not next time, and certainly not the time after that."

Shumb sighed. "You'd think they'd run out of rocks at the rate they send them here." He stared straight at the officer. "The project isn't working. They've countered you at every turn. If anything, we're slightly worse off than we were. We have to have the energy you're bleeding away, Eric."

"It won't matter. That's why you approved the project to begin with. Little by little the defenses break down. Before we began, we had an optimistic estimate that they would be able to invade within nine years at current rates. I have cost you perhaps a year, certainly no more than two. You could not shut down anyway. If they win, it's the only exit available."

Shumb did not attempt to rebut the truth. He spent too

much of his time doing that as a politician. "I assume you're here for permission to make another try."

"We've run this through the computers and it looks most promising. Because it does not directly involve us, merely pushes certain period people in our direction, it might not be obvious that it is us at all. The degree of change is enormous in our favor, yet incredibly subtle. There is even the possibility that there would be no revolution, no war at all. We would be all one big, happy family—under Earth's control. And your line remains constant. It will be a far different situation, but you will still be in control."

"I'll check it against my own computers on that. Still, I hesitate. Perhaps one more major operation is all we can stand. Two at the most. This last attack is a harbinger of things to come. Next time it might be Europe, or North America, or eastern China. Sooner or later it *will* be."

"Run your computations. It's worth a shot. As you say, tomorrow it might be here. Surely it is better to try for it all than rule over . . . *this*. Is it not?"

"If it wasn't, I'd never have permitted you to do this in the first place. Still, after all this time, I am not clear about your own motives in all this."

"You know the rules. I can live as myself only in prehistory or at the reality point. I've had enough of primordial dawn, and I have no love for the Outworlders. I prefer an unsullied humanity. If I am to live here, and not under them, then you must win. That is all there is to it."

I wonder, . . . Shumb couldn't help thinking. He'd never liked nor trusted this strange man, who was of no time or place at all. Trust had never been one of the Chairman's strong points. Finally he said, "I'll run it through myself and let you know."

The colonel got up, stiffened, and saluted. "That's all I can ask, sir," he responded, then pivoted and walked out of the office. He went immediately to make the preparations and check the final calculations. He already knew full well that it would be approved, and to what strange paths it would lead, the number of lives it would change, and cost—and create. He knew, in fact, exactly where it would lead him, but he did not know what he would find there.

MAIN LINE 236.6
THE CALVERT CLIFFS, MARYLAND,
U.S.A.

It was not an imposing structure, rather low, as nuclear power plants went, and sprawling across the tops of the great wide cliffs that were filled with the fossil remains of forgotten seas and looked down at the wide Patuxent River as it flowed towards Chesapeake Bay. The whole plant had been white once, but age and weather had taken its toll, and it was now a grimier gray than the sea gulls that continually circled and squawked around the cliffs.

Most nuclear power plants, including this one, were obsolete now, too expensive and dangerous to maintain. The people around the site, for the most part, and those throughout the state continued to believe that this hulking dinosaur, this monument to the misplaced, golden-age optimism of the past, supplied much of their power, but, in fact, it supplied none at all—and had not for years. And yet, so complete was the fiction that families down for a warm weekend to swim and hunt fossils still often wound up going up to the visitor's center and getting the Gas and Electric Company's spiel on the wonders and safety of nuclear energy in general and this plant in particular.

He reflected on this as he cleared the gate to the employees' parking lot and drove through the massive fence that surrounded not only the lot but the true access to the plant. He couldn't help but wonder what it was like to collect money week after week telling cheery, convincing lies to a gullible public.

The big security system had been put in ostensibly to

protect the plant from anti-nuclear protesters, of which there were still legions, and also because a Naval Reserve unit had been set up on a part of the grounds to deal with nuclear power and waste. In point of fact, the whole thing was a cover so good it should not, perhaps, have amazed him that it had lasted this long and was this complete. So complete, in fact, that here he was, pulling into a parking space and preparing for a few weeks of orientation before becoming chief of security for the installation, and, as of right now, he himself hadn't the slightest idea what they really were doing here.

He knew the problems, though. Only a month earlier a crack Air Force security team had managed to get in and literally take over the place, despite all the elaborate precautions. That had cost the previous security chief his job, and when those whom the National Security Agency's computers said were best qualified for the job were given complex plans and blueprints and asked to pinpoint holes and suggest better security measures. Within the limits of security, he'd apparently done the best job. A jump to GS-17 came with it, so he'd accepted the post when it was offered even though he had no idea at the time where or what the place really was. When he'd discovered that it was barely two hours south of his current job at the NSA, he'd been delighted.

What would come today was the less than delightful prelude. Today he'd have to meet with Joe Riggs, the man he was replacing, and with Riggs' very proud staff. It would be an awkward time. He paused a moment to savor the bright, fresh June air off the water, then walked up to the unimposing door simply marked "Employees Only! Warning! Unauthorized Personnel Not Permitted Beyond This Point! Badges and I.D. Required!" *That* was an understatement.

He opened the unlocked door and stepped into a relatively small chamber that seemed to have no exit. The door closed behind him and he could hear a *chunk!* as special security bolts shot into place. The chamber was lit with only a small, bare light bulb, but he could see the security cameras and the speaker in the ceiling. Somewhere, perhaps in back of the speaker, would be a canister of knockout gas.

"Name, purpose, and today's password, please," came a crisp woman's voice through the speaker.

"Moosic, Ronald Carlisle, new Security Director. Abalone is no worse than baloney."

There was a moment's hesitation, then a section of steel wall slid back far enough for him to pass through. He stepped out of the chamber and the door slid shut again behind him. He was now in a hallway lined with heavy armor plate for six feet up from the floor, then thick security mesh from there to the high ceiling. Cut into the metal plate were three security windows, such as you might find at a drive-in bank. He went up to the first one and saw a man in a Marine uniform sitting behind three-inch thick glass staring back at him. A small drawer slid out. "Place your I.D. and security badge code in the drawer," he was instructed.

He did as ordered, then waited until the drawer opened again with a small card in it and a tiny inkpad. "Thumbprints where indicated," the bored Marine told him. Again he did as instructed. The clerk took all of the material, fed it into a computer console, and waited. After a short time, the computer flashed something to him and a tiny drawer opened. The Marine removed a badge, checked it against the thumbprints and checked the photo against the face he was seeing, then fed it back through the drawer.

He looked at the badge, similar to the one he'd used at NSA, with its holographic picture and basic information, then clipped it on. He knew that this badge had a tremendous amount of information encoded within its plastic structure. Computer security would read that card by laser hundreds, perhaps thousands of times as he moved through the complex. Doors would or wouldn't open, and defenses would or would not be triggered, depending on what the card said in its unique code. None of these badges ever left this building. You picked it up on the way in; you turned it in on the way out. In fact, there would be other areas requiring different badges with different codes, all premanufactured for the authorized wearer alone. Each time you turned in one badge, you picked up the next.

He walked down the rest of the corridor and found that the door at the end slid back for him. He walked through and entered a modern-looking office setup, very military but very familiar to him. He'd worked at NSA for nine years and was used to such things.

A pudgy, gray-haired man in a brown, rumpled-looking suit waited for him, then came up to him and stuck out his hand. "You're Moosic, I guess. I'm Riggs."

He took the other's hand and shook it. "Sorry we have to meet like this," he responded.

"No, you're not. Not really," Riggs responded in a casual tone, without any trace of bitterness. "Not any more than I was when I took over the same way. It's no big deal. I'll be bumped to an eighteen, push papers for two years, then retire with over thirty. Short of running for President, it's about as high as I ever expected to get anyway. Come on—I'll show you around the place."

They walked back through the central office area. Three corridors branched off the room, each of which was guarded by a very mean-looking Marine with a semiautomatic rifle. Moosic looked around and noted also the cameras and professionally concealed trap doors in the ceiling. Anyone who made it even this far would still be under constant observation by people able to take action. It was impressive, but it made the Air Force penetration even more so. As they stood near a corridor entryway, each of them inserting his gold photo I.D. into a computer and waiting for the red ones to appear in the slot at the bottom, the newcomer said as much.

"No place is totally securable," Riggs replied. "You can say they were pros with some inside information, but any enemy trying the same thing will have those advantages as well. The big hole in the end was the centralized control of security within this installation, as I'm sure you know. If you got in, you could get out."

Moosic nodded. "That's the first priority now. Central control will have a permanent override elsewhere, connected directly to this place. We received funding for it." He didn't mention that it would take ten weeks to install even the basics, six months before it could be fully tested and operational. Riggs no longer had a need to know that sort of thing.

They got their red tags and went on down the corridor. "This place is as bad as Fort Meade," the newcomer remarked as they passed Marine after Marine, computer check and trap after computer check and trap. "Maybe it's about time you told me what we do here."

Riggs chuckled. "They didn't tell you, huh? Well, it wouldn't matter. Nobody would believe it anyway, not even if we let the Washington *Post* in and they made it a page-one cover story. You know this plant doesn't generate any public electricity?"

Moosic nodded. "I figured that out from the problem they handed me and a close look at the place. But it's in full operation."

"Oh, yeah. More than ever. Close to a hundred percent capacity. It takes one *hell* of a lot of juice to send people back in time."

Ron Moosic stopped dead. "To . . . what?"

Riggs stopped, turned, and looked highly amused. Moosic had the uneasy feeling he was having his leg pulled. "Come on—seriously."

"Oh, I'm serious. I just get a kick out of seeing anybody's face when I tell 'em that. Come on down to the lab levels and I'll see if anybody's free enough to show you the works."

*   *   *

Dr. Aaron Silverberg was a big bear of a man with a wild lion's mane of snow-white hair and penetrating black eyes. He was not only physically imposing; he had that deep-down egotism that assumed that everybody he met had not only heard of him but was also awestruck at his very presence. Ron Moosic, of course, had never heard of him before in his life.

"To tell you how we happened on it would take far too long," the chief scientist told him. "It was the usual— one of those accidents that happened when some folks were doing something totally unrelated. Basically, a few odd random particles in the big accelerator out west consistently arrived before they left when you did things just so. Only a few quadrillionths of a second, of course, but it shouldn't have been possible at all. The first thought was that something had finally broken the speed limit—the speed of light. Later, using various shieldings, we found that light had nothing at all to do with it. The damned things arrived before they left, that's all. Knocked causality into a cocked hat all at once. For those of us who knew about it, it was more gut-wrenching than if God wearing a long beard and flowing robes had parted the heavens in front of us."

Over the next half-hour Moosic spent a good deal of time looking at evidence of trips back in time, mostly photographs and small objects. There were already a huge number of more elaborate things—a tape of one of the Lincoln-Douglas debates, several of tavern conversations between Franklin and Jefferson as well as many others of the founding fathers, and others recording personages who'd lived even earlier. The earliest was an eavesdropped argument between an incensed Christopher Columbus and the refitter of the *Santa Maria*, or so he was assured. He spoke no Spanish, let alone fifteenth-century Aragonese with a thick, equally archaic Italian accent.

"Funny," Silverberg commented. "Nobody ever plays

Franklin with a New England accent, although he came from Boston, not Philadelphia, and nobody ever gave Jefferson that hill country twang he really has. Had. Whatever. Napoleon had a silly voice and never lost his Corsican accent. If they'd had television back then, he'd never have made it in politics."

Moosic just shook his head in wonder, still not quite believing all this. "I find it all impossible to accept. What *was* was, that's all. You can't recapture a moment that's past."

"And so I was raised to believe. As the poor two-dimensional creature in Abbott's Flatland could not accept depth, so we cannot accept but a single perspective of time. In a way, it's like motion. We know we're in motion because of a lot of phenomena and reference points. We move in relation to something else. Yet the Earth is now turning at around twenty-five thousand miles per hour and we can't feel it. It's going around the sun at an even greater speed, and we can't feel or sense that, either. The sun, in turn, is going around the galactic center, and so on. Since all that is around us, including us, is moving at the same speed and in the same way, we cannot sense that motion and speed relative to us. Since we are going forward in time, all of us at the same rate and everything else around, we cannot really relate to time in any way except as the progress of one moment to the next. But it's all there—the past is forever. We are immortal, Mr. Moosic. We exist forever frozen in our past moments."

"But time is . . . immutable."

"Oh, so? Even before we knew that it was not so. Einstein showed it. Time is relative to mass and velocity. The closer you approach the speed of light, the slower your time is relative to the universe. Time also gives way around areas of heavy gravity—suns, to a small extent, and black holes to an enormous extent. No, it's not the fact that time is malleable that is the stunner. Apply enough power, it seems, and time will finally give. Rather, the shock is that time exists as a continuum, a series of events running in a continuous stream from the Big Bang all the way to the future. How far we don't know—we can't figure out how to go into the future relative to our own time. It may be possible that far future scientists can go past today, but we cannot. But the past record is there, and it is not merely a record: it's a reality. Now you understand the need for security."

He nodded, stunned. "You could send an army back and have it pop up out of nowhere."

"*Bah!* You're hopeless! Mr. Moosic, you will never send an army back in time. We need the entire capacity of this power plant, which is capable of supplying the energy needs of roughly ten million people, just to send four people back a century, and the further back you go, the more power is required. To get one human being back to 1445 would require our total output. That and to sustain him there, anyway, for any period of time. Beyond that the energy requirements get so enormous that we've estimated that just to send one person back to the first century A.D. would require every single bit of power this nation could generate for three solid weeks."

"But for only, say, a week back? Surely—"

"No, no. It's impossible. Physics is still physics and natural law is still natural law. Just as nothing is permitted past the speed of light, no one is permitted to coexist at any point in the past where he already exists. It just won't do it. In fact, it won't do it within a decade of your birth date. Why we haven't any idea."

He thought about it, trying to accept it at least for argument's sake. "A decade. Then you could go back and live past the time you were born."

"No. Not exactly, that is. You *could* go back, yes, but by that time you wouldn't be you anymore. Nature does resist tampering. We made that discovery the first time out. You're back there, and you don't fit. Time then *makes* you fit. It is far easier and more efficient to integrate you into that present you're now in than it is to change all time. It creates a curious niche for you. It adjusts a very small thing in what we call the time frame so that you were born and raised there. In a way, it's very handy. Go back to fifteenth-century France and you'll find yourself thinking in the local language and dialect and generally knowing your way around. Only the massive energy link, a lifeline of sorts, between here and there keeps you from being completely absorbed. Unfortunately, the longer you are there, the more energy is required to sustain you. It's in some way related to the subject's age, although we haven't gotten the exact ratio. It requires more energy to send an older person back than a younger. Someone up to about the age of fifty we can generally sustain back there for the number of time-frame days equal to half his age. How old are you?"

"Forty-one," he told the scientist.

"Yes, so we could safely send you back for a period of twenty days with an adequate safety margin. Over fifty, it accelerates like mad. It's simply not safe."

"What happens, then, if you overstay your welcome? Don't come back within that margin?"

"Then the energy required to retrieve you would exceed our capacity. The line would break. You would literally be integrated into that past time as that created person, eventually with no memories or traces that you were not native to that time and place. And if that was, say, 1820, we could not later rescue you. You could not go forward of your own present—1820—and even if there *was* a way, we would retrieve someone else, not you. Someone, incidentally, invariably minor and unlikely to change any events. We learned our lesson the hard way."

"You've lost someone, then?"

He nodded, "An expert in Renaissance history and culture, who was also a valuable agent when he attended East European conferences, which is why he was one of the few scholars we allowed to downtime personally. He was forty-six when he went back the first time, and he stayed two weeks. Later, he needed a follow-up, so we sent him back again—and lost him. The clock, we learned, starts when you arrive the first time, and it does not reset if you return again. He, and we, assumed at the time that he had two weeks a trip. He didn't. So he's there now, for all time, a meek, mild Franciscan monk in a monastery in northern Italy, a pudgy little Italian native of the time. To give you a final idea of how absolute absorption is, Dr. Small was also black—in our time.''

Ron Moosic whistled. "So then how do you get the recordings and pictures?''

"They tend to have a stronger sense of shape and substance, being inanimate. We've discovered that recorders and the like can be retained for almost the safety period. Weapons, on the other hand, tend to be absorbed into period weapons rather quickly. One supposes that a battery-powered recorder has a minimal chance of affecting history, while a new weapon or something else of that sort could do a great deal of damage. *Why* and *how* such judgments are made by nature we don't know at all. Why is the speed of light so absolute even time must bend before it? We don't know. It just *is*, that's all.''

"Still, the old saw about going back and killing your own father before he met your mother still holds. How can you do that and still exist? And if you didn't exist, you couldn't go back.''

"But you *could*. We haven't actually had a test, but this absorption phenomenon seems designed mostly to counter that sort of thing. In theory, you would in fact cease to exist in the present as soon as you committed the deed, which would snap your energy link. You would then become, immediately, this wholly new personality, this created individual. Joe would become time-frame John, and it would be John, not Joe, who shot the man who would have become Joe's father. Of course, John would create a ripple that would then wipe out Joe, or so we believe, but the deed would still be done.''

"It would seem, then, that there's very little to worry about in all this," Moosic commented. "The only real risk is to our time traveler, not our present."

Silverberg sighed. "That, alas, is not entirely true. The time mechanism itself, for example, is rather bulky, much like a space suit. You don't need it where you're going, but you need it to keep you alive until you get there. That can fall into other hands with potentially disastrous results, as you might understand. We can take precautions on that. But for the active period in the time frame, you—the present you—are still in control. During that period, particularly in the early stages of it, you are a walking potential disaster. The fact that it was John, not Joe, who shot Joe's father does not make Joe's father any less dead. We haven't yet tested it because of the dangers and unpredictability, but we suspect that if causality is challenged, in the same way light speed is challenged, then something has to give, and what gives will be time.

"We suspect, in general, a minimal disruption—if you kill Hitler, someone will arise who is substantially the same and formed by the same sort of hatreds and prejudices. If Joe's father had sired three children in the present track, those children would still be born—to a different father, but one rather similar to the first. But there are key figures in key places at key times who might be irreplaceable. Would a Second Continental Congress without John Adams ever have declared independence? Would we have won the Battle of Saratoga and gotten French and Spanish allies if Arnold had been killed earlier? What would a contemporary Britain be like without a Churchill, or a U.S. without Roosevelt? *That* is why the Nobel prizes must be unawarded and this installation protected. I would rather have it melt down than have proof of what we have here leak out.''

Moosic nodded. "I think I see. So somebody *could* change things."

"We believe so. The best model we have begins with the Big Bang. With all of the rest of creation, a time wave is created as a continuous stream. It might be an anomaly, might be necessary to keep everything else stable, but there it is. Think of it as a thick glob of paint on a sheet of glass. It runs down the glass, when we tilt it, at a slow and steady speed. The edge is where time is now, still running down so long as everything else is expanding, but the paint trail it left is still there. The edge, where we are now, is the sum of that trail. Alter that trail, and you will start a ripple that will run down to catch up with the leading edge. The math is rather esoteric, but the ripple will run at ten times the edge rate primarily because it's smaller. If it's a tiny ripple, it may resolve things and die out quickly. A big wave, though—it would change the sum of the world."

Moosic had a sudden, uneasy thought. "What about others? Would we even know if, say, the Soviets had a project like this? They're doing fusion research now."

"No, there's no way of knowing. Of *ever* knowing. A time war would be the most frightening thing of all. However, it would still be badly limited in several respects. It would require enormous power. It would require a country insane enough or desperate enough to risk its own lot on a new roll of the dice. And it would certainly involve few participants in any event, participants who would be limited to a small amount of time in any frame to accomplish much at all. The Soviets are our opponents. They are not mad, which is why we are all still here. Neither are the current Germans, Japanese, Chinese, or others capable of such a project. It is only the fear that someone else is doing it that keeps us funded at all, so expensive is this operation. We spend a lot of time trying to convince them that there *is* military potential, when actually there is not. But we don't know, of course. And so long as NSA's very budget is classified, we can continue to get the money. You keep us out of unfriendly hands.''

''I'll try,'' Ron Moosic assured him, shaking his head and feeling far more worried now than when he'd walked in the door. This was a bit much to digest, even after a career in high-tech environments. In a sense, there was more unsettling business going on here than at the Pentagon and Kremlin war rooms. Here, just one well-meaning scientist could obliterate all that was constant in the world. A social experimenter would be even worse.

''That's who we fear the most,'' Riggs agreed. ''The Air Force boys showed it wasn't impossible to infiltrate here, but it's pretty near so. On the other hand, how do you *really* get into a guy's head when he's being considered for downtiming?''

''Downtiming?''

''That's what we call it, since you can't seem to go uptime from here in any way except the way we're doing it—one second at a time. You see, the big problem is that the boys here are mostly technical types. It's a crew over at NSA that looks around for candidates for research and approves 'em before they even know about this place. The weed-out's pretty extensive, but you can go only so far without spilling the beans about the place. Then, of course, they get the full treatment—drugs, lie detectors, you name it. We try as hard as we can to make sure that nobody goes into the chamber if they have even the remotest impulse to do anything but observe.''

''But nothing's perfect,'' Moosic noted. ''Even the sanest of us has sudden impulses and urges. Until that person goes back there, you can't know for sure.''

''Yep. And there are ways to beat the system—any system. It's a constant worry. That's why we don't let any professional historians go back at all. After all that, they're told we have a way of *observing* and even sometimes *recording* the past. They give us the targets, and then we send one of our agents back. They have romance in their souls but no stake in the actual work and not enough professional background to know just what wrong button to push. They know, too, that one false move and we can nightside them—cut them off in the past.''

"But this nightsiding, as you call it, wouldn't prevent them from doing something. It would only mean they couldn't profit by it.''

He nodded. ''That's about it. It's a chance we have to take.''

Ron Moosic stared at the man. ''Why?''

Riggs chuckled. ''Because, throughout history, you can't uninvent something. Oh, you can suppress it for a while, but it's funny that lots of discoveries of the same thing seem to happen around the same time, whenever the technology of the world will allow it.''

"The Greeks invented the steam engine but didn't do anything with it,'' the younger man pointed out.

"That they did—but they invented it in a closed society that kept their discoveries not only from non-Greeks but from the bulk of their own people. Silverberg will go on and on telling you that science is a collective and not really an individual sport these days. Oh, sure, Einstein dreamed up all that stuff on his own—but did he, really? Or did he take a lot of stuff discovered and discussed by a bunch of scientists in a lot of countries and put it all together to see something they missed? What if Einstein didn't have a way to get that stuff from the others? No mass-produced books, no international postal system, no way to know what all those guys were thinking or finding out? And even if he did—what if all Einstein's theories were written down on paper and filed away in one spot in just a single hand-written book? Who'd know it to make use of it, except by accident? The Greeks had that kind of problem. Lots of brains working, but nobody telling anybody else. Not like now. This whole project can be traced to a hundred different teams working in half a dozen countries on different stuff. Let just one word leak out that we're doing this and others can put the same information together through mass communications, computer searches, and stuff like that.

"With Einstein and the others to build on, almost every one of the major countries in World War II was working on the A-bomb. We just got there first. Now everybody's got the damned things. A couple of dozen countries so poor they keep their people in starvation still have computer-guided smart missiles, and everybody and his brother has something in orbit now. The Russians have an accelerator at least up to ours. They'll eventually get the same results we did, if they haven't already. So much power and so many people are required for something even this size that eventually there'll be a leak, others will get on the track, and it'll be a real mess. We better know all the rules of this thing backwards, forwards, and sideways, or we're gonna be up shit creek when the time ripple comes along and wipes out you and me and maybe the whole damned Constitution."

"Nice thought. I'm not sure I even like the idea that I know it now. Even without this job, it's going to make sleeping a lot harder."

"Tell me about it. The only thing I can tell you is to think of the thing just like the H-bomb and all the other things out there that can cripple or kill us. It's just another in a long line of threats, just another doomsday weapon. It's so complicated and so expensive it probably won't be the one that gets us, anyway."

Some comfort, Moosic thought sourly. He wondered how long it would take him to grow as cynical and pessimistic as Riggs, then considered it from the other man's point of view. Too long, he decided. Riggs had, in fact, the only way of really living with this.

"I guess you should meet the security staff now," Riggs suggested. "That'll give you a picture of the whole layout."

Moosic nodded. "I guess we—"

At that moment the lights went out, then came back on again, and there were shouts, screams, and the sound of muffled explosions. Bells and sirens went off all over the place. Riggs recovered quickly and ran out the door, Moosic at his heels. They made it through a screaming mass to the central area. There were bodies all over the place, and the smell of gas, but the bodies were all office and Marine personnel. Areas of the ceiling were bubbling, smoking masses occasionally dripping ooze onto the floor as they smoldered and gave off foul smells.

"Somebody's going for the chamber!" Riggs shouted, drawing his pistol and moving off down a corridor that should have blocked their entrance. No passes were necessary now, though—the computer terminal was another smoldering mass of fused metal and plastic.

Moosic recognized it as the corridor he'd come from only a few minutes earlier, the one that led to Silverberg's offices and the time chamber.

A bunch of uniformed and plainclothes security officers were near the elevator. They saw Riggs and rushed up to him, all talking at once. With a mighty roar of "Quiet!" he got them settled, then picked one to tell him the story.

"Four of 'em," said Conkling, the middle-aged uniformed man picked as the spokesman. "They knew the exact locations of *everything*, Joe! Everything! They had the password, knew the right names, and when the door slid open for the one who came into the entrance, the other three blew open the outer door. By that time, that first one had set off a mess of gas bombs from someplace. None of 'em had any masks I could see, but one whiff and you died while they walked through it cool as can be. They had some kind of gun that worked like a bazooka one minute and shot gas the next."

"What about the gas in the reception area?"

"Didn't bother 'em. They shot everybody up, then fried all the ceiling weapons with some type of laser gun. I tell you, Joe, I never saw weapons like that before from *any* country! Never! Right outa Buck Rogers.''

"How many of 'em did *we* get?"

"Uh—none of 'em, Joe. They all got down here—and, so help me, the damned elevator *opened* for 'em just like they had the pass and the combination. Took 'em down and stuck there."

Riggs nodded and turned to Moosic. "Inside job."

The younger man nodded. "All the way. Any way down there other than by this thing?"

"There's a stairway, but the panels are designed only to open from the other side."

"So were ours. Let's blow them or get whatever it takes to blow them. I assume the whole level below was gassed?"

"Knockout type. Real strong—six to eight hours. But if it didn't get them up here, it sure won't down there."

"Maybe not," Moosic responded, "but it'll get *everybody else* down there. You can't tell me they can work all that stuff down there without anybody except their inside man."

"Hardly. The computer alone would freeze up without five different operators at five different locations, each of whom knows only part of the code. And one of those operators is at the end of a special phone line topside and a mile from here."

"Then we either wait for them or go after them. The Air Force thing is one way, but with the commotion they caused getting down there's no way out short of hostages, and those they've got."

Riggs took complete charge. He ordered various security personnel to make certain all exits were blocked with heavy firepower, ordered another to establish an external command post, and still others to report to NSA and Pentagon higher-ups. Finally he put a heavy firepower team at the only stairway exit, and it proceeded to line the area with enough explosive to bring down the entire wing. Nobody was going to get out *that* way without Riggs' personal permission.

Then they walked back to the security command center, which hadn't been taken or touched. It had been the key to the Air Force team's success, but these people hadn't touched it. They obviously had no intention of coming back out this way—or they wanted it intact for reasons of their own.

The command center was impressive, with its masses of monitors and one whole wall showing a complete schematic of the entire installation, even the public parts, parking lots and roads, along with lights indicating the location of cameras, mikes, and defensive equipment. Much of the board was flashing bright red.

The security personnel inside the center had remained at their posts, but it was clear that they were bewildered and frustrated. They had been attacked in a manner that the installation was designed to thwart, and the invaders had simply marched right through.

A crisp, professional-looking woman with gray hair sat at the master controls and barely looked up as Riggs and Moosic entered.

"Hey, Marge? What's the story?" Riggs called.

"Twenty-four dead, thirteen critical, about forty more with minors, give or take," she responded. "They're immune to all our gasses and pretty cold-blooded. I'll put them up on number six for you over there. Three men, one woman. No makes yet, but give us time."

Riggs and Moosic went over to one of the monitor banks. A screen flickered and came on, then a whole series, showing every room below. Most had unconscious forms lying about, a sea of limp forms in lab whites. In the central control chamber, though, the four were clearly visible. No—not four. Five. "Who's that other one?" Moosic asked.

Riggs ordered a zoom. She was in her late twenties or early thirties, short, fat, and dumpy, with big horn-rimmed glasses, the lenses of which looked like the bottoms of Coke bottles.

"Karen Cline," Riggs told him. "There's our insider. My career was already shot to hell, but I'll still retire. Somebody back at the Palace is going to swing for this."

Moosic looked at the woman. "What's her rank?"

"Oh, she's a top-grade physicist. I don't know how they got to her, though. Conservative family, workaholic, and don't let her looks fool you. She's slept with so many guys they need a separate computer just to keep track of them. Just goes to show you."

"Got a make on two of them," Marge called from the command console. "The young, good-looking boy is Roberto Sandoval, twenty-eight, born in Ponce, Puerto Rico. The girl's Christine Austin-Venneman, twenty-four, born in Oakland, California."

"Terrific," Riggs muttered. Christine Austin-Venneman was the daughter of one of the country's most prominent liberal Congressmen, a very popular and powerful man. Her mother was the heir to a fairly large fortune based on natural gas, and had always felt guilty about it. If there was a liberal cause, she was in the forefront of it and usually much of the bankroll behind it. Christine had been on forty protest marches for twenty causes in half the states in the union before she was five.

"More on Sandoval," Marge reported. "Father unknown, mother a committed FALN member and revolutionary Trotskyite, trained in Cuba and Libya years ago. His mother was killed three years ago when a bomb she was working on blew up her and her safe house in Washington. Sandoval is suspected of being involved in several robberies and bombings, mostly in the New York area, since that time. Since Austin-Venneman's mother organized the March on the U.N. for the Liberation of Puerto Rico from Colonialism last year, we can guess how the two got together."

Both security men nodded absently. The figures below seemed in no hurry, but all had nasty-looking weapons, except for Cline, and were making a methodical check of the area, room by room. A small status line at the bottom of each monitor indicated that gas had been released throughout the complex and that the elevator and stairway doors were sealed.

Ron Moosic just stared at them and felt helpless. His first day on the job and *this* happened. He looked at the status line again and noticed that there were two small blinking areas in it on the right. "What are they?" he asked Riggs.

"The area is far too dangerous to risk. Those are last-resort items. There is enough explosive in the walls to fry and liquefy the whole lower complex. They're on a fail-safe mechanism, though. We can fire them, but we can't arm them. Only the President or the collective Joint Chiefs can do that. If the left one stops blinking, it means the system is armed and at our discretion. If both go solid, we have twenty minutes to clear out, or so they told us."

At that moment the left one stopped blinking.

TIMELY DECISIONS

Ron Moosic suddenly felt like the President faced with Armageddon on the day of his inaugural. He didn't even know the names of most of these people or the way to the nearest men's room, yet here he was, facing what might quickly become the shortest job he'd ever had.

Riggs looked over at him. "Well? What do you think?"

I think I want to know the location of the men's room, he thought sourly, but aloud he said, "You say there's no way they can operate the time machine or whatever from down there?"

Riggs nodded. "There's no bypassing that outside code, and nobody down there or even up here knows what it is."

Moosic sighed. "Then all you've got here, when all is said and done, is a classic hostage situation. Sooner or later they'll threaten to shoot the hostages one by one if we don't come up with the code, but if *we* blow it we just as surely kill them all. They've trapped themselves, and even if they eventually go suicidal, we're no worse off than if we push their button. I'd say let's string 'em along and work at getting them. They have the counters for a lot of the nasty stuff, but they still have to get air down there from somewhere."

"It's all super-filtered stuff from its own buried source. No way to get a man in there. Still—I'll get a team working on tapping into it. We already have one working on bypassing the stairway seals. If we can just buy enough time, we can puke 'em to death. There's some pretty nasty

32

stuff near here I can get my hands on, stuff that's absorbed by the skin and pretty ugly, but stuff with an antidote. I agree.''

Riggs left to issue the proper set of commands, leaving Moosic alone to watch the monitors and think. He didn't like to think much right now, but he *did* feel a little bit more comfortable with a classical hostage situation. He watched the tiny figures on the monitors and tried to figure out just what they were doing.

Ron Moosic hadn't started out to be a cop, not even the kind of high-tech one he wound up being. His great-grandfather had come to the eastern Pennsylvania coal mines when that area was flourishing. The family name then was thirty-seven letters long and pure Georgian—the one south of Russia, not the one south of South Carolina. The old boy had heard that if you didn't Americanize your name, the immigration boys would, so he looked at a map of where the Immigration Society had written he'd be living and saw, near Scranton, a little town that sounded reasonable to him, and he'd written in the name Moosic with no understanding of the jokes his descendants would have to bear because of it.

Ron's father had also worked in the mines, and the boy had grown up in the small town of Shamokin, Pennsylvania, a town whose biggest claim to fame was the largest slag heap in North America. It towered over the town, and it was on fire all the time. Still, it was a nice town in which to grow up, large enough for all the civilized amenities and small enough not to have many of civilization's biggest penalties. One penalty for a miner was always injury, though, and his father had been hauled out of the mine when Ron was still small. A loader had backed into him, crushing him between it and the wall of coal. He'd lived a few more years, a permanent invalid with a strong spirit and sense of life, but complications finally took him when Ron was just eleven.

Vic Moosic had been a big bear of a man, with bright

eyes and walrus moustache. He looked a little like all those pictures of another Georgian, Joe Stalin, and always had claimed to be related to the Soviet dictator. "Old Joe got all the meanness," he often said. Later, when Vic's son needed an exhaustive security check, it was found that the Moosic family was not even originally Georgian, but rather Uzbeck. Young Ron had always rather liked the idea of being an Uzbeck. Nobody else he'd ever met could make that claim.

Insurance and the union helped out a little—his mother had needed it, with six kids ranging from ages seven to fourteen—but they were not a wealthy family. His older brothers had gone into the mines, but he had not. He'd always been more intellectual and reclusive than his brothers and sisters, but he'd worshipped his father and his father had understood his peculiarities. "You're not like them," Vic kept telling him. "You got the family brains, boy. Don't go into the mines. Find a way out. You'll be the first one."

And he *had* found the way. It was called the U.S. Air Force, and it offered a smart, young high school graduate free college for a set number of years of service. He'd majored in geography at Penn State, with a minor in computer science, and done pretty well. The Air Force, at least, thought highly of him, and after graduation they assigned him to intelligence work.

It sounded romantic, but it wasn't. Nuts-and-bolts stuff, mostly—cryptography, aerial photo interpretation, that sort of thing. Still, at the end of twelve years he was thirty, a major, and on the right career track. He also, along the way, met and married Barbara.

He never quite came to grips with splitting up. At the start, she'd been pretty and sexy and had a desire to see the world. She was a college graduate, but was never really on his intellectual level, something he knew from the start. Well, maybe that was unfair, but she read very little and watched a lot of TV, and she seemed to have not the slightest curiosity about his work, although he really couldn't have told her anything specific anyway. She wanted kids, and he did, too, but after three miscarriages, the last of which almost killed her, the doctors told them that she could never have them. She'd changed after that, although he'd told her that it didn't make any difference to him. Somehow, she seemed to blame *him* for her enforced barrenness, although it was clearly the fault of no one. Her irrationality became progressively worse and painful to him. It was his fault she could not bear children, yet somehow this made her, in her own eyes, less a woman, and she dreamed up all sorts of paranoid fantasies that he was having affairs all over the place. She became increasingly bitter, and frigid.

Ultimately, he'd given up, inventing excuses not to be home, and, eventually, he'd had an affair. She never knew for sure, but when you're accused of something incessantly, you don't incur a penalty for really doing it. Ultimately, they'd had a final blow-up, and that had been that. The temporary alimony she'd been awarded had stopped three years ago, with the last check going to an address in San Francisco, and he had no idea where she was or what she was doing now.

The funny thing was, he still loved her—or, rather, he loved the woman he'd married and hated what she'd become. He'd been faithful to her through all the good years, and if she'd accepted things, he'd have remained so, or at least he liked to believe he would have. He'd certainly had a series of strictly physical affairs since, but he found it impossible to get really close to another woman. He wanted some permanence, perhaps even a kid or two before he was too old to see them grow up, but he couldn't take the plunge again. He was, he knew, just too afraid that it might all happen again, and that would be more than he could stand.

Shortly after the divorce, he'd been posted to the NSA. He owed the Air Force no more service, and it didn't take much genius to realize that he could take on the same sort of jobs permanently at a much higher pay level than the Air Force would give him, with all his service time counting towards government seniority and retirement. Despite a lot of pleading, he resigned from the service and took on a permanent job as a civilian. Within a year he did the usual, joining a reserve unit at Andrews, hiking pay and benefits still further. It was the way the government game was played, and he played it pretty well.

Not that things were any more romantic at the National Security Agency. The massive complex, about halfway between Baltimore and Washington, was the real nerve center of U.S. Intelligence, happy to let the CIA take the publicity and the heat. Still, what it was was mostly dull, plodding, boring work, the biggest challenge being to sift through the enormous amounts of information pouring in at all times for things that seemed important or worth following up. Computers made it possible, but it still came down to the human element at the end. The tens of thousands of NSA agents employed there were, in fact, a highly paid infantry forever trying to take the paperwork hill—and losing.

And now, thanks to some boredom and the ability to solve complex topological puzzles that were security problems, here he was, staring down at somebody else's failure.

"One of them's calling for negotiations," the woman at the control panel called out. "What do you want to do? Mr. Riggs is topside now, talking to the National Security Advisor."

"Put it on here, if you can," Moosic instructed her. "I'll talk to him."

It was Sandoval, his handsome face and large, dark eyes telling the world how he got so many women to commit treason for him.

Somebody came over and showed Moosic how to work

the intercom. "Ron Moosic here, Sandoval. Let's hear it."

The revolutionary could not repress a snicker. "*Moo*sic?" He turned to Cline, the traitor within. "Who's he?"

She shrugged. "Never heard of him."

"All right. Who are you, *Moo*-sic?"

A little edge. Not much, but something. "I'm the Security Director for this station."

"That's Riggs."

"I'm *his* boss. I'm the man who decides if we can evacuate this place and I'm the man who can push the button that will make it a big blob of bubbling goo."

"You wouldn't do it. Not with all these hostages here. Not with the brains you'd melt with us, and the money."

"Riggs wouldn't do it, maybe. *I would*. And I already have the presidential authority. I don't know those people down there, so it's not as hard for me. Sort of like a bomber pilot who never sees who his bombs land on. I *do* know we were closing down this place and moving to a better one with more power, so we don't lose there. Nobody down there is irreplaceable, either." He checked the monitors and saw the drawn faces and nervous glances among the others there. He had drained them of their self-confidence, and that was a victory. Now it was time to drop a little sugar in the vinegar.

"Still, there's no reason for any more people to get killed than already have been," he went on. "I can wait a while. And while I wait, maybe you can explain to me why you went to all this trouble to seal yourself in with no exit."

"There's an exit," Sandoval came back, sounding a little more confident now. "You know it and I know it. You can blow us up, yes, but you cannot cut our power, not within the next twelve hours. If you attempt to break in or pour some agent through the air system, I assure you all down here will be dead. We are committed to victory or death, *Moo*-sic. We all live, or we all die. The hostages are simply a wall between you and us. We intend to bargain. I suggest you call Admiral Jeeter and tell him to check his mail today. When you have done so, we will talk again."

Jeeter was the current head of NSA. Ordinarily, the man would be impossible for someone on Moosic's level to reach, but he had a suspicion that today the call would be put right through.

He was right, at least as far as the admiral's executive secretary. When the conversation was relayed, the secretary, himself a Marine colonel, instituted a frantic search for everything that had come in addressed to the admiral. It took very little time, surprisingly, to find it. It had been delivered by express mail.

Within another ten minutes, the admiral himself was on the phone. "It's a massive file," he told Moosic. "Still, it's only parts of things. Enough. It's selections from almost every major research paper relating to the project. It's almost inconceivable that we could be penetrated to this degree."

"Is it just the files?"

"No, there's a note. It points out that these are merely photostats and that they are one among hundreds of sets. They assure me that none of them have been sent anywhere yet, but that they will be mailed to just about every newspaper and foreign government if we don't give in to their demands. Even if it's no more than this, it'll blow the whole thing wide open!"

"I assume you'll try the trackdown of the accomplices. In the meantime, what do you want me to do here?"

"Keep this line open. I'll go downstairs and patch in to where I can see and hear everything in the lab. We'll hear what they want; then it'll be up to the President and the NSC whether or not we give it to 'em."

Moosic nodded to himself, sighed, and turned back to the monitor board and opened communication. He wouldn't wait for the admiral—whatever he said and did was al-

ready being recorded, and he knew that there would be a
lot of calls for the old boy to make before he made it down
to a situation room.

"So our little letter was received?" Sandoval said smugly.
"I assume they do not like it much."

"You know they don't. But we can't afford to believe
you haven't already mailed them or that you might not just
let us know where most of them are while sending one or
two elsewhere to do the most damage."

"To whom would I send it through the back door?
Russia? Czarist pigs masquerading as Communist liberators!
China? Half of China doesn't even have the electricity to
run its villages, let alone power this. No, my offer is
genuine. You will not be able to stop it from being made
public. Public, not secret. But if we get what we want,
you will receive all the copies—every one. This I swear on
my mother's grave."

Ron Moosic sighed, glad it wasn't *his* choice. He didn't
believe the oily revolutionary, but if the alternative was
taking a chance he was being honest for once or just letting
it all come out—which would be the best chance?

"Your demands aren't for me to decide, as you must
know, but you tell 'em to me and they'll also be reaching
the ones who *do* decide," he told the revolutionaries below.

"We have looked in the chamber and found three time
suits. Dr. Cline has told us that there are but four, and one
is in use. Very well. We will need to use them. I am told
that sending three back will strain things, but that two will
be no problem. The codes will be given. We will go back,
while my associates here make certain you do not break in
and cut our cords, as it were. However, once back there,
you still will not know where the hundreds of other copies
are. Only I know that. I will return in ten days and tell
you. I will have no choice—I must return here or cease to
exist. If I do not tell you within fourteen days from nine
o'clock this morning, all of them will be sent."

He thought about it. "Then you don't go. You could

have anything at all happen to you back there, stuff way beyond our control."

"It could," he admitted, "but I go or no deal. You will have to take some chances. If you press that button and blow us up, some cover story will have to hit the papers, causing the material to be sent immediately. We have your bosses by the balls, *Moo*-sic. And they know it."

The bosses knew it. It was a heavy decision, and the debate was not yet over, but clearly they were in the mood for a deal if one could be struck. Security, in particular, argued for it, confident that they could find and plug the leak, and equally confident that there was very little the two could really do downtime. The military had the opposite opinion, wondering if such a highly planned and thought-out infiltration could be so easily dismissed. Crazy radicals might be sent back with no real risk, but these people were extremely well-prepared. Whatever change they were going to attempt to make, it was argued, had already been computer-tested and found to have a high probability of success.

Most of the hostages had been hauled into a central office complex early in the attack, and most were now awakening to bad headaches and the sight of Stillman's and Bettancourt's submachine guns pointing at them.

Moosic noted that Riggs had not returned and that everyone now was deferring to him. He hoped the security man was working on the break-in and not strung up someplace.

"All right, boys and girls, they're willing to listen," he told them, keeping the calm tone of someone in control at all times. In truth, he hadn't had any time to really think about his position, but he was still more than a little scared at the potential down there. He honestly didn't know if he had the guts to press that button if it came to that—but the invaders and his bosses thought he would, and for now that would do. "They want to know exactly when and where you want to go."

"London, England; September 20, 1875," Sandoval responded.

Moosic frowned. Not only was this the first indication that one could travel in space while traveling in time; it was also a totally puzzling combination. Why there at that particular date?

The National Security Agency had the finest and most complex computers the world had known up to that time, and they came up with a lot of small things and even some major figures in and around that time and place, but nothing that would significantly alter the time-line, particularly when correlated with the known ideology and goals of the radicals. In fact, man and machine could find only one correlation that made any sense at all.

"On September 20, 1875," the admiral told him, "Karl Marx arrived back at his home in London from a mineral bath treatment at Karlsbad. Unless they're so convoluted we can't follow their thought processes, it's the only event on record that fits."

"They want to consult with Marx?" Moosic responded, puzzled.

"We doubt it. The best idea we can come up with is that they want to give the time machine to Marx. We think that they've had no better luck than we on what could be changed to make their goals close. So, they have the machine and the means—why not give it to the man whose ideas they profess?"

The security man thought it over. In a way, it made a perverted kind of sense. Particularly if you were a committed radical getting more and more disgusted and disillusioned with the progress of your goals. In all but rhetoric, nationalism had triumphed over ideology long ago. The Russians always sounded like Communists but acted like Russians had always acted, as did the Chinese and others. The true believers had been systematically purged or assassinated, from Trotsky down to Maurice Bishop in Grenada—by the very states and systems they'd established.

The radicals below were no stooges of Russia; they were true believers. Not only their statements but also their intelligence files and psychological profiles proved it.

Ron Moosic sighed. "All right, I'll buy it. I assume this has already gone to the President and the NSC. What do they say?"

"Our computer models indicate no particular danger. They're not going to meet the man they imagine, but rather a nineteenth-century philosopher very much a product of his times. Still, there's a risk. There's always a risk. Joe Riggs tells me that they've bypassed virtually all of the systems at this point. One of his teams has managed to tap into the system and reduce the available power to the time chamber itself. Still, we'll have a two-hundred-year range to deal with if they really have some other date in mind. If they know this much, they might know how to bypass and go remote on the suits."

"Bypass?"

"It was built in as a safety factor after we lost that fellow back in the Middle Ages. If you know you're going, you can boost yourself out of there into one other time frame without severing the automatic connection. It'll save your ass until the automatics on this end can bring you back. They'll have a second chance once they're where they say they want to be, although travel in space will be severely restricted."

"Then we can't afford to let them go. Simple as that."

"Maybe not. We've proposed to let them go, all right, but doing a little funny business ourselves. The time-space coordinates change every moment, and they're continually updated. That update is partially through a satellite link with the Naval Observatory. We have proposed, and they have tentatively agreed to, a little alteration. Instead of getting the atomic clock, they'll be plugged into one of our computers. Let's send them back to September 10, 1875—ten days early. The suits will have a low charge, and won't be able to boost immediately. That'll give us a week or more to get back there and track them down, as well as work on this end to trace their accomplices. We think it's worth the risk.''

Moosic thought it over. "But we'll have to get in there pretty quickly to go after them," he noted, "and that's not going to be bloodless. Then we'll have to have these time suits or whatever they are available for us. I assume they're going to destroy what they don't use."

"That's where they have us, of course. There are two spares, but they are both down for repairs right now. That leaves the one on the man now downtime, and he's due back on automatics at six tomorrow morning. That means we have to convince them to go now, then deal with the remaining ones by whatever means we have to use and regardless of costs. Cline knows when that other one comes back, too.''

The security man frowned. "That gives us less than eighteen hours. Why not just cut the power to them when they go back?''

"Because they'd still have those few days of grace to do whatever mischief they wanted before they got absorbed. We must know what they do, where they go, all of it. And even if we cut 'em off, restore power two weeks from now, and send somebody back, I'm told that the newcomer will re-energize their suits anyway. Don't ask me how—I'm not a physicist.''

Ron Moosic sighed. ''And this was supposed to be my first day on the job.''

A MATTER OF PERFECT TIMING

Dr. Aaron Silverberg was anything but pleased. On the one hand, he felt he had the biggest hangover a human could bear; on the other, his baby was in the hands of kidnappers and one of the nannies was telling them what to do.

Still, he led Sandoval, Austin-Venneman, and Cline back to the time chamber and its control center. The center itself was behind massive multiple sheets of lead-impregnated glass. A single operator's chair was in the center, surrounded by an inverted crescent-shaped control panel with myriad instruments and controls as well as a number of differently colored telephones.

Christine Austin-Venneman, who'd been fairly quiet during much of the takeover but who'd also looked from the start like the kid turned loose in the candy store, looked around. "Wow!" she said in a soft, deep voice. "This looks like the bridge of a spaceship!"

"Or the supervisor of a telephone exchange," Sandoval responded, less awed. In point of fact, it looked far less exotic than he'd imagined and he felt somewhat let down. "Everything is controlled from here?" This was addressed to Silverberg. Cline, obviously, was there to make sure he didn't trip anybody up.

Silverberg sighed and tried to keep himself erect. His head was killing him, the aftereffects of the gas. He also felt somewhat frustrated; he could not understand how Karen could be with these people, but they had made talking to her impossible. Still, she avoided his glances.

"Nothing whatever is controlled from here," the scientist told them. "It is exactly what its name implies—a command center. The director sits here and gives the orders necessary to accomplish the mission. He cannot initiate, only abort. The instruments confirm that all is as it should be, nothing more."

Sandoval went over and peered through the dark glass. The time chamber itself was quite small, no more than a dozen feet square, and unimpressive. There was an airlock-like door to one side, and then the chamber itself, a barren and featureless box of a room. The walls, ceiling, and floor were all made out of a single material and looked cast as a whole. The material itself was smooth and featureless.

Sandoval turned. "Where are the time suits?"

Silverberg sat down in the chair with a groan and held his head. The weapons came up, but he waved them away with a gesture. "I do not care if you shoot or not. I did not have your handy filters stuck up my nose and my head is splitting. Shooting me would be a mercy."

"I'll show you," Cline said, and Sandoval looked over at Austin-Venneman. "Go with her and get them. Bring them here," he ordered.

Silverberg lay back in the chair and breathed deeply for a few moments. He seemed to feel a little better. "What do you hope to accomplish by all this?" he asked the terrorist. "I mean, no matter what, you have to accept much of what is done here on trust. Karen is the only one who knows anything at all about the proper things to monitor, and she must sleep. I still expect them to blow us all up the moment we begin, anyway—although, I must admit, with this head I am not sure it would not be a mercy to me."

"We have confidence in the plan. We know we will go back to the right place and time."

"So confident! Even I am never *that* confident!" Silverberg's brows lowered. "Unless—it has already been confirmed?"

"I think if you want to live, you won't go any deeper into that, Doctor," Sandoval responded nervously.

It took three trips for the women to bring in the suits. They looked very much like the spacesuits worn by astronauts, all made of some fine, silvery, mesh-like material. The helmets were airtight. Each contained a backpack air supply and a front pack consisting of instrumentation, which told the status of the air and other suit systems, and also a meter series with small, recessed pentometers above each meter. Cline checked each one of them. "This suit's a bit large, but has a four-hour air supply and a fully charged power pack," she told them. "This second one might just fit Chris, but has a little under three hours of air and a ninety percent charge. Enough to get you both where you want to go. The third one fits you like a glove, Roberto, but has only an hour-and-a-half's worth of oxygen and a sixty percent charge."

With Chris covering the doctor, who, despite some romantic notions, was in no condition to try much of anything even if *he* had the gun, Sandoval tried on the large suit. It was clear even without the helmet that the fit was ridiculous, and with that helmet he would barely be able to balance himself. "No use," he muttered. "It'll have to be the other one."

Dr. Karen Cline sighed. "Yes, I agree. But you haven't much reserve. You'll be O.K. for the trip, but if you have to make a boost, it'll be touch and go."

"We are traveling in time!" Sandoval exclaimed. "Why do we need much at all?"

"Time is relative. All other things being equal, time breaks first, so you'll go back. But the journey takes time because it requires a steady power supply. Inside the suit, it'll take time to get there at the same rate as power is being supplied. To 1875, it'll take, oh, forty minutes or so. Once there, the reality of the suit is the only link you'll have with the present. The suit must be kept energized from here, using full power, or you'll nightside. That means we can't add anything once you're on your way. The internal suit charge will remain at where it was when you left, minus the power required to get you there. Even then, it'll deteriorate as time will try and throw it out. The effect is progressive. Twelve days is all it's safe for Chris, fourteen for you, in any one time slot. And we have to hold this installation for the exact same amount of time you spend back there, because we can only send power at the normal clock rate."

"In other words, the shorter the better," Sandoval said. "Well, I depend on you. All of you. You know the stakes."

Sandoval quickly got into his suit, then took the rifle while his companion donned hers. "Get Clarence in here," he ordered, and Cline left.

Silverberg was feeling much better. "I'm curious—just what *are* the stakes?"

"The future of humanity on the face of Earth, and I do not mean that as a metaphorical or idealistic statement," the terrorist replied. "If we fail, humanity will be wiped out to the last man, woman, and child. I don't just believe this, Doctor—I *know* it."

The big black man entered the command center, followed by Cline. He grinned when he saw the two dressed in the suits. "Buck Rogers, huh?"

"Don't get funny. Are you sure John can handle that mob alone?"

Stillman nodded. "They're pussycats with bad headaches. Still, they'll be trouble later on. I wish we didn't need 'em as hostages."

"We're depending on you to keep this place operating and secure until we return, even if it's two weeks," Sandoval told him. "There's food down here, enough to last if you ration it, in the little cafeteria."

"Plenty of locks, too. Don't worry about it, Roberto. These dudes didn't even trust *themselves.*"

"Then I think we had best be at our business as quickly as possible," the terrorist leader told them. The two suited people followed Karen Cline out of the command center. Soon Silverberg and Stillman saw the inner door open and the three of them enter the time chamber. First the woman, then the man, kneeled down so that the scientist could fasten their helmets and activate their internal systems. Soon she exited the room, leaving the pair there alone, and returned to the command console.

"Doctor, will you handle this or shall I?" she asked him. "I would prefer that you do it, for safety's sake. Remember, all our lives depend on you doing it exactly right."

Silverberg chuckled dryly. "Do you really think they gave the enabling command?"

"They gave it. Either that or we are all going to be very dead very fast. It doesn't matter to me, Doctor. I'm dead, no matter what. But I wouldn't like to see you and a lot of the others, a lot of my friends, die as well." She seemed on the verge of hysteria, and that made him more nervous than the big man with the gun. Clearly, Karen Cline was having a hell of a fight between what she saw as her duty to her friends and associates and her resolve to see it through. He wished he had more time to work on her.

"I'll do it," he told her. "And I'll do it straight. We're still pretty much on automatics because of Jamie, but I assume you've already fed the instructions into the computers."

She nodded. "I made them up and tested them weeks ago. The code is Auer, comma, Geib, comma, Bebel, comma, Liebknecht."

"*That* you'd better input. I might make some terrible spelling error. The rest I will do."

Quickly she went over to the keyboard on the side of the

control panel and typed in the passwords. The board came alive.

"Just what's gonna happen?" Stillman wanted to know.

"They'll just . . . disappear in there," Cline told him. "Or so it will seem to us. Actually, we're going to keep going and they're going to stand still."

"Huh?"

"I'll try and explain it later. All right, Doctor—we've got limited air and power on one of those suits. Let's do it."

Silverberg shrugged and turned to the console. The sequence and number of controls he changed, punched, pulled, pushed, or otherwise manipulated seemed enormous. Stillman couldn't follow any of it and turned to Cline. "You sure he's doing it right?"

"He's doing it right; don't worry. Most of it is security, anyway. The whole operation's computerized and, as I said, *I* did that. If he does anything wrong, they just won't go anywhere."

An alarm buzzer sounded, making the big man jump. "What's that?"

"Warning to clear the area. Here they go!"

Suddenly the walls blazed with light, and the two figures inside clasped metallic gloved hands. Beams of energy, beams nearly too bright to look at even through the shielding, shot out and enveloped the two. There was a sudden burst of light from where they stood, and then all of the energy seemed to flow into that spot, as if swallowed by some great mouth. In a moment, all was normal again—except that the time chamber was empty.

"They're away!" came the call over every security frequency. Ron Moosic held his breath and just watched and waited. It was now or never—with the two dangerous ones separated and only one man, no matter how crazed, with the bulk of the hostages.

"Stairway doors are open!" came a cool, professional voice. "We are going on down."

"We're on top of the elevator," said another voice, equally calm. "On your mark we'll enter."

"Now!" came the not so calm voice of John Riggs.

The operation was handled with surprising quiet and determined professionalism. The cameras had shown that the terrorists had constructed a makeshift barricade at the base of the stairway door, not so much to keep out anyone who reached that level but to make one hell of a clatter when they did so. The elevator, however, was not so well guarded. It was designed to have its door open if held by its stop on a floor, and it was not in full view of anyone at this point. At the start, there had been two holding the hostages, one in the hallway and one covering the central working area, but now both the traitorous Dr. Cline and Stillman were still in the command center, while two were downtiming and no longer a direct threat, and Bettancourt was alone with the hostages. Nobody could see the elevator area, and three well-armed, black-clad agents slipped into the car.

Quickly they took up positions to cover one another in the hallway, and one crept silently down the hall towards the stairway door. This route took him directly past the open door in which Bettancourt lounged with the surviving staff, but all areas were covered by cameras and all of the agents had earpieces connecting them with Riggs and Moosic. It was rather easy to time the quick dart past the door under those circumstances.

The agent heard the voices of Stillman and Cline, and hurried to remove the debris piled up against the access door. It could not be blocked with desks or other heavy objects, since it opened in towards the stairwell.

A small horde of similarly clad agents came through and quickly took up positions to cover all avenues of entrance or escape. Two agents took positions on either side of the door to the hostage room, while others stood poised at the entrance to the command center. They were prepared to move immediately if Cline or Stillman came out and discovered them, but now they waited until the cameras, which the terrorists had left intact to demonstrate their control, told them when Bettancourt would be most vulnerable.

They didn't have long to wait. The big terrorist grew annoyed at a woman sobbing in the back, got up from his perch atop a desk, and started to walk back to the small crowd, snarling, "Shut that bitch up or I'll shut her up for good!" At that point his full back was to the door, and Riggs shouted, "Kill him!" through the agents' earpieces.

The two agents converged as one, and pulled their triggers. The semi-automatics were well silenced—there was a muffled sound like furniture being pulled across a floor, and Bettancourt went down, his back a bloody mess. He never even knew he'd been had.

The hostages began shouting and screaming, and this brought Stillman out of the command center, gun at the ready, moving fast enough that he went right past the agents flanking the door. When he saw what he was facing, he tried to bring up his rifle, but he was quickly cut down.

At the same time, the two flanking the door entered the command center to see a surprised-looking Dr. Cline and an equally surprised Silverberg staring back at them in amazement. Cline was clearly not armed, but she suddenly looked stricken, then cried, *"No!"*, and popped something into her mouth. They reached her almost immediately, but it was too late. The pill was designed for a very quick death.

Silverberg rose from the chair and looked over at the two agents checking the limp form, and he shook his head sadly in bewilderment. "Why?" he asked softly, of no one in particular. "In God's name, what would drive someone to *this?*"

*   *   *

It took far less time to clean up the mess than to try to sort out what had happened and why. Teams of specialists interrogated the surviving staff workers, who were then hustled off to secure medical facilities, but on the work level there were no physically wounded people—all were either alive or dead. Admiral Jeeter had come down personally in a helicopter to discuss the final stages.

Silverberg had refused all attempts to get him to leave, although he patiently gave his account and his reactions to the clean-up team. With Moosic and Riggs, he went through the command center instrumentation checks and established what he could.

"There's no question that the two of them went downtime," he told the security men, "although they seem to have missed their target by a matter of ten days. Ten days early, I would think."

Riggs nodded. "We were able to create a power drain, operating on the theory that it's Marx they want to see."

The physicist sat back and thought for a moment. "I see. So they are now faced with the choice of waiting ten days or returning here. They destroyed the spare suit here, so I assume that you intend to use the one coming back tomorrow morning to go and get them."

"That is precisely the plan," Jeeter replied. "How soon can the other suit be charged up enough for a try?"

Silverberg went over to the time suit that remained crumpled on the floor and, with the help of Riggs, pulled it out to its full length and examined it. "The electrical system on this one is shot to hell, but if we have any luck at all in this business, we might salvage the power pack. I would get this up to technical services in a hurry, gentlemen. If we can salvage that much, then we might be able to insert the batteries from this one into the returning suit. It would be a jury-rig, but it might work. If so, we could turn around in, oh, six or seven hours. If not, we would have to wait for the other suit to recharge, and that would cost three or four days."

"Too long," the admiral told him. "Six hours I can sweat out, but no more." He gave the instructions to his aides to get the suit upstairs in a hurry. "This equipment— you're certain we can't just pull the plug on them?"

"We could, but they would still have their two weeks, and if we break off the power, we will have no way to monitor them. They could cause a great ripple, perhaps change everything, and we would never even know they did it. Not that it would do us much good to know, but at least we might be able to rest easy if we detect *no* ripple," the scientist responded. "No, I would let them go."

"Then I have no choice but to send somebody back," said the admiral. "I'm going to have enough grief from this without being accused of letting them get away with this. Besides, there is something unsettling about this whole operation, far more than the penetration."

Silverberg nodded. "Yes, I think I know what you mean. They acted like they *knew* the outcome in advance. What could convert dear Karen to such dedicated fanaticism? Surely she had every background check, was under near constant surveillance, passed lie-detector tests—all that, as we all have. I am not saying that she couldn't somehow fool the system, but she seemed genuinely torn here. She was acting against every instinct, every shred of decency or humanity she felt, yet she felt such conviction that she not only went through with it but died rather than face interrogation and reveal anything. She would have cracked."

"That's the most unsettling part, Doctor," Ron Moosic put in. "I got the same impression of her, just watching her in the monitors. It took a supreme act of will for her to go through with what she did. I have to agree that she would have cracked—and anybody good enough to fool *all* the security we have wouldn't have cracked under any conditions. Sandoval said to me that what was at stake was the survival of the human race. At the time, I passed it off as radical rhetoric, but maybe he meant it."

Jeeter looked worried. "You mean that this isn't the only time project?"

Silverberg thought it over. "I think it is—now. But suppose, Admiral, that 'now' isn't really 'now.' We've gone through this in theory for the past few years, you know. Suppose the leading edge of time isn't right now, but some time in the future? How far? Ten years? Fifty? Five hundred? With cheaper energy, perhaps from sources we don't even understand at present, and better technology. . . ." He paused a moment. "No, that wouldn't make sense. If that were true, then they would do their own temporal dirty work, not depend on some silly radicals."

"But suppose there wasn't cheap energy," Moosic said, picking up Silverberg's reasoning. "Suppose, in fact, there was less. A future civilization on the ropes, able to send one or two people into the past but not far enough to do what had to be done. You said you were limited to a few hundred years. Maybe they are, too. But able to come back far enough and with enough proof—and enough records of who might pull something like this off—to convince these people to do whatever they had to."

The scientist grew excited. "Yes! Yes! Perhaps a few survivors of some atomic holocaust, using their version of this project, perhaps this very project, to come back and convince these people that only they can halt the extinction of mankind. What sort of proof we may never know, but it would explain your security leak, Admiral. I assume our computer records will be uploaded someday into new generations of computers. They might only have had to call up this day to get everything from the security measures to the passwords. What little minutiae they couldn't know, Karen would."

Jeeter shook his head in amazement. "Are you telling me we should let them go and do whatever it is they intend doing?"

"Perhaps we should," Silverberg replied. "But perhaps we are just whistling in the dark on this, too."

"I can't take that sort of gamble, and you know it. Somebody is going back and getting those clowns. I wouldn't trust that kind of mind with the future of my cat, let alone the human race."

Ron Moosic sat back and considered the arguments, and realized that he sided with the admiral. Roberto Sandoval was no savior of mankind; he was a cold-blooded killer. His girlfriend was a limousine radical, with no more concept of the proletariat than Marie Antoinette, and seemed vacuous to boot. Even granting his original speculation, those people of the future would have been faced with a dilemma. The best people to get into this place, and take it, and get back in time, were hardly the best people to trust once they'd done it. On the other hand, from a purely pragmatic standpoint, they'd compromised about as much as they could. If their agents didn't get in, the rest wouldn't matter, and if they were faced with certain death, they had nothing to lose.

"Have you thought about who's going back after them, Admiral?" Riggs wanted to know. His tone indicated clearly that he was *not* volunteering.

Jeeter looked at Silverberg, who shrugged. "My agents are the test-pilot type," the scientist said. "They might be best in tracking the two down, but they would hardly be a match for Sandoval when the showdown came."

"I guess it's the CIA's baby, considering it's London," Riggs noted.

"But this is *our* project," the admiral reminded him. "They left here in our . . . vehicle . . . and they are legally still here, tied to that machine. If you want to pull legalisms, it's the FBI's baby, but I wouldn't want to pull somebody in to do it. No, it's NSA's job, and specifically NSA Security's." He looked over at Ron Moosic. "You're the new boy on the block here, but I was very impressed with your handling of the entire situation, and so was the President. Do you think, if push came to shove, you could shoot them down in cold blood?"

Ron Moosic was shocked. This level of involvement, after all he'd been through, was not something he'd considered at all. He was tired and pretty much spent. "I don't know, Admiral," he managed. "I just don't know."

"Your record's good; your psychiatric profile is excellent, and you have some background and feel for history. You're single, childless, and haven't been very close to your surviving family. I cannot and will not force you to go, but I *am* asking you. The suggestion came right from the National Security Council. We just don't have any time to tap somebody, brief them fully, and send them back cold."

"I'm pretty cold, too," Moosic reminded him. "Until this morning, I didn't have any idea this place existed or that what it did was possible. I'm still not sure I believe it." But, even as he protested, he knew that he would go. He was always the one who volunteered to do the things that had to be done, even when he knew somebody else alway got the credit and he always got the blame. But—to go back in time, to really visit the London of Victorian England. . . .

If he refused, they would find somebody, perhaps one of the agents long experienced at this station. He, of course, would never know the result—and the admiral knew that he understood. His career, the entire rest of his life, depended on this decision.

"If I can get some background, and some sleep, I'll give it a try," he said at last. The admiral smiled in satisfaction; Riggs smiled in relief.

DOWNTIMING THE MAIN LINE

Ron Moosic had a brief time to eat and relax before they were ready. The cuisine wasn't the greatest, being mostly hot dogs and microwaved soup, which made him wonder about whether those old movies showing condemned prisoners eating lavish feasts were just fantasy.

Somebody had brought down copies of the Baltimore *Sun* and Washington *Post,* and the lead stories in both were, at the very least, amusing. It seemed some Cuban-financed radicals shot their way into and briefly took over the Calvert Cliffs Nuclear Generating Station with the avowed purpose of causing a nuclear meltdown as a protest against U.S. policy—there was even a "manifesto" from the radicals, allegedly given to authorities after the bloody takeover—and that all of them were subsequently killed by federal and state security forces. All of them were named, and named correctly. Only Dr. Karen Cline was not listed as among them; instead, her name appeared among the plant workers who died in the onslaught.

They had allowed some reporters and photographers in to photograph the upstairs carnage, and it shocked, as it was intended to, while giving away nothing. Interviews with hostage survivors, however, were carefully controlled, and while he couldn't tell, he suspected that none of the people interviewed were actually people held down there. It was, nonetheless, a compelling and convincing story. There was even mention of a "low-level secret Defense Department project" at the site, which served to allow security to be clamped where it was needed and which explained the large number of federal officers and military personnel involved.

He almost believed it himself, although he knew that at least two of those radicals were not dead, but simply away somewhere, or somewhen. To him, there was still an air of unreality about it all that he couldn't shake. Not the invasion and its aftermath, that was something he could at least accept, if not understand. To travel back in time, to actually change the past—that was the problem, and quite possibly the root cause of his accepting the assignment. To be convinced, he would have to see for himself, and were he to say no to this, he'd never really believe it.

Dr. Aaron Silverberg looked tired, but he was going to see it through, at least until Moosic was back. Then, perhaps, he would allow himself the luxury of sleep. He'd tried on the couch in his office earlier and hadn't been able to, and his body screamed at him.

"The suit will be a bit snug, but it will fit," the scientist assured him. "We've had someone doing adjustments on it. The batteries transferred nicely and took a good quick charge to boot, so you will be going with over ninety percent of full power, which is more than they've got. The instruments show that they are now still in 1875, in London, and by this time they must know that the date is off. They have chosen to wait, it appears, and that is to our advantage. However, they are now in phase with the time frame, and that puts time at risk."

"You'd better tell me what that all means," the agent suggested. "What's this 'phase' business?"

"Let's start from the beginning. First of all, everything is in motion—Earth, solar system, galaxy, whatever. Remember our paint sliding down the glass? Each moment that the paint has passed over the glass is a real place, a physical point. What we do is put the brakes on you, so to speak. *You* remain motionless relative to here and now, and we slide past. Now you are, so to speak, out of phase with time. A gentle nudge, and you move from this frozen spot in time back along the temporal paint smear. A slight lateral nudge, and we wait for the point where you and the universe are both where we want you to be. Presto! You are in London, because the spinning Earth, the rotation, and solar movement have been calculated. When you are where and when we want you, we keep sufficient power to maintain you in that spot. Your motion and the motion of the time stream become identical. However, as long as you are in the suit and in the direct energy field, you will remain out of phase. You are not moving relative to point X, so time is standing still relative to you."

"Clear as mud, but I think I have the general idea. I'm stuck in the moment, with everything frozen. Can I move around?"

"Not in the suit. So, the first thing you do is check your gauges here and make certain you are, indeed, where and when you are supposed to be. Our people have already gone over how to read and reset them?"

He nodded. "That's simple arithmetic."

"Good. Then you remove the suit, and you will find that you have some mobility. You will begin to accelerate relative to the Earth's normal time speed. This can be disorienting, so prepare for it. You will have more than four hours to find some place to hide the suit. That is a tricky part, and we can only make vague suggestions on it. Remember, though, that the suit's power pack is quite heavy; the suit's systems will not be bothered by water or other routine elements, and sinking it tied to a small rope such as the one in the utility pouch works well."

He nodded. "We've been through all that."

"All right. Eventually, you will become somewhat ill. You will pass out—and awaken in phase. This is the easy part. You will, quite literally, be someone else. That someone can be very old or very young, male or female, but it will be someone rather insignificant and ordinary, and with a past. However, *you* will be in control. At the start it will be easy and fun. As the days pass, however, you will find it slightly but progressively more difficult to retain control. The other you, the new you, will become more real to you, while your own self will erode in little bits. That is where you will have an advantage. At your age, you will be able to remain in control longer than they. In nine more days, they will be hard-pressed to remain themselves, while you should have all your wits about you.''

"Wait a minute! Are you telling me that I might come out a *woman?*''

"It's quite common, really, although there seems to be no rule on it. It's actually quite logical. In most of the past, women had less power and position and, therefore, were the least likely to make a major change.''

Moosic had another worry, almost as pressing as who he'd become. "This is going to make things nearly impossible for me,'' he pointed out. "I don't know who I'm looking for, or what. They may not even know each other. Both of 'em could be kids, or they might be fifty years old. If we're wrong about Marx being their objective, there's no real way I can find them.''

"That's true. But I don't think we have to worry about that so much. The passwords used for their program were related to Marx's work of the time frame. Four German communists of the period, I think someone said. No, it's Marx all right. You've memorized the pertinent details?''

"As much as we can guess is pertinent. I *still* think it's impossible, though.''

"If it is, you've gained an experience I would love to have and it will have cost you nothing. At fifteen days, simply go back and put on the suit, and it will automatically bring you back. You will be your normal self once more, and the richer for the adventure. But I am convinced that anything important enough to cause even a minor ripple in time will be obvious. If you can see it, you can stop it. The odds there favor you. Time is always on the side of the least change."

"I hope you're right," he said worriedly. "Well—let's get on with it."

They stripped him naked so he'd fit in the suit better. It didn't matter, he was told—the only artifacts he would need would be carried in a pouch in the suit. Time, adjusting to his unnatural presence, would provide whatever else was necessary.

Even so, he had to be helped just to walk in the thing. The airlock looked even more imposing and final as it opened for him. The room itself was as cold and barren as it had looked from the command center, and the nature of the lighting made even the super-insulated glass panel before him seem dark and featureless, although he knew Silverberg and several technicians off-duty at the time of the invasion were there, checking on everything.

Silverberg had feared that Cline had somehow fouled up the computer programs. They all checked out O.K., but, taking no chances, he bypassed them and tied into computers with backup programming at the NSA's headquarters at Ft. Meade.

Two white-clad technicians fastened on the space helmet, turned on the internal systems and checked them, then closed the seals. He had done it three times without them, of course, since he'd have to do it on his own to get back, but this was the first time out and they could check all the mechanical and electrical systems better than he.

Now he could hear nothing but his own breathing, which seemed nervous and labored to his ears. The suits contained no communications gear, since that would add to the anachronism of the suit itself and, of course, because there was no one really to communicate with to any purpose.

He was perspiring profusely, despite the small air conditioning unit in the suit. He turned his head and could barely make out that the airlock had been closed and the signal light on the door was now red. With the suit pressurized, the chamber became a near-perfect vacuum. There was no sense in expending already precious energy by also transporting back a lot of surrounding air.

Come on, come on, you bastards! he thought nervously. *Let's get this over with!* He suddenly had the urge to back out, to hold up his hands and make for the airlock controls. *This is insane!* his mind shouted at him. *How the hell did I get myself into this mess, anyway?*

The room filled with a blinding light. The photosensors in the faceplate snapped on, but he could see nothing. Suddenly he felt a mild vertigo, as if he were falling— falling, but in slow motion—like Alice down the rabbit hole. He tried to move, but the suit was locked into position. All he could see, and that tempered by the tremendous faceplate filters, was the blinding nothingness, the awful sun that seemed all around him. Still, beyond that, there was only the sound of his breathing and that feeling of falling, ever so slowly. . . .

It seemed an interminable journey. The relative time clock in his helmet clicked off the seconds and the minutes, but no matter how fast it went, it seemed agonizingly slow. Faces, their voices from his past, seemed to form in his mind like ghosts and whisper to him.

"Your father would be so proud of you!" his mother whispered to him. *"One of his sons an officer, for Jesus' sake! The only one who'll not kill himself in the mines. . . ."*

"So there you go again," Barbara chided him, sounding thoroughly disgusted. *"Always volunteering, always sticking your neck out! And for what? Nobody'll ever know, and your bosses will take all the credit, even if it works. Why are you always everybody's sucker?"*

"All I wanted was some love and some understanding!" he heard himself shouting. *"Just somebody to care about me as much as I cared about them!"*

"Nobody gives a damn about you," Barbara snarled

back. *"Nobody in this whole fucking, stinking world ever gives a damn about anybody but themselves in the end! Well, maybe it's time I started joining the garbage!"*

Why me? he wondered. *Why did they stick me in this job?* But he knew the answer. He was the most expendable dependable they had. Living alone in a tiny apartment, drowning himself in his work, no social life to speak of. As the admiral had pointed out, he hadn't even talked with his family in almost a year, except to send up some gifts around Christmas and beg off the family gathering. Work, you know. . . . Important work. . . .

Pop another frozen dinner in the microwave and take a couple of drinks while it cooks. . . .

"Who's cooking now, Moo-sic? Who's floatin' in the middle of nowheres with the sun all around? Who's got to pee and can't never get to the potty? . . ."

They never told him it would be like this. . . .

Expendable, dependable; expendable, dependable. . . .

Suddenly the photosensors flipped off with a dramatic *click,* and the blinding light was gone, replaced with a ghostly gray. He checked his instruments and they said, as near as he could remember, that he'd arrived. The relative time clock kept going, and the system gauges continued to supply air and some cooling, but all else had stopped. The destination LEDs were flashing now, telling him to get on with it.

For a moment, he couldn't. It wasn't that he didn't want to reach up and throw the proper switches, only that he was suddenly overcome with a massive fear that it hadn't worked, that he would release it all in a vacuum, that to take off that helmet was to die. He hoped that the two bastards that had brought him here had undergone a similar fear, but he suspected not. Sandoval was too much the fanatic and Austin-Venneman too much the airhead.

He steeled himself, reached up, and punched the release buttons. There was a mild hissing sound, and he felt the suit deflate and seem to cling to him. He reached up and removed the helmet. All was still, and surprisingly chilly, but there was air he could breathe.

He decided that freezing was better than remaining in the suit, and removed it. There was no wind, no air movement of any kind except his own breath. He had been warned about this period, and moved with purpose. He was caught right now in a moment, a single slice of time. His body could breathe the air in that slice, but he had to keep moving, for other air would not rush in to replace it.

He bundled up the suit and looked around. What he had taken for a gray nothingness seemed instead to be a dense, sooty fog. He was near water, that was for sure, and walked down a rocky path to where it seemed to be.

There was no sound at all that he didn't make, no movement, nothing. The water looked choppy, what he could see of it, but the scene was frozen. Only he could make waves in such a still life.

He made his way along the bank to a massive stone outcrop and realized, with some surprise, that what he was seeing was the main support of a bridge. He looked under it, and saw that there was no real foothold there under the arch itself. Quickly he removed the rope and small hammer from the suit, then attached the rope to the suit itself, which had a small hook for that purpose. Slowly he eased the suit into the water and then pushed it a bit under the bridge. It continued under his momentum until the rope became taut, and he took the end, which had a small piton attached, and hammered the thing into the rock just below the water line. He knew the suit would not sink until time caught up, but it made him nervous to look at it all the same. The pouch it had, like its power pack, was watertight, which was important. He would have need to return to this spot when things returned to "normal," if there now was any such thing.

Satisfied he had done what he could do, he got up and walked back up the bank to the top of the river wall. The fog was so thick it cut visibly to the bone, but it certainly was not night. Early morning, he guessed. Early morning on Saturday, September 11, 1875. . . .

He had wondered why he couldn't just travel back to a point in time just before the two would have appeared, still fresh and vulnerable in their silver suits, but it had to do with the limitation of the equipment. If they had had a second time chamber, it might have been possible—but to the same period, with people already downtime, the computers simply could not handle it all. He had to live within their relative time frame, and that was that.

He had to keep moving, both for warmth and because any time he stood still he grew quickly short of breath. The streets were gaslit, but shed little light on the gloom, which was not only wet but also incredibly dirty.

He came suddenly upon a frozen tableau—two men: one dressed in the uniform of a Victorian policeman, complete with rounded hat and billy club; the other, a middle-aged man in shabby-looking tweeds: both of them frozen stiff in some sort of argument. Just behind the fellow in tweed, a nasty-looking bulldog was frozen, its left hind leg raised.

He resisted the temptation to play games with the two, to pick their pockets or push the policeman's hat down over his eyes. He'd been told that no matter what he did, the *next* time frame and all subsequent ones would not be changed, so whatever he did would be unnoticed and undone. That was something of a relief now, since he knew that if *he* could barely resist it, the two he was after certainly could not. Time was not easily trifled with, although it could be done. Certainly, two people were here, someplace, dreaming of doing just that. How nice it would be if he could find them while still in this phase. That, however, was impossible. The variations in the motions of the bodies of the universe were such that it was miraculous that the project could even get him to London; landing someone in the same spot a day later was simply impossible.

Still, he walked quickly, partly to keep warm and partly

to get to know a little of this area. Normal time agents—
how quickly this had become "normal" in his mind!
—received weeks of briefing on the time and place they
would visit, often months. He had been sent in cold, the
only justification being that anyone else sent would have to
go cold, too. The small amount of time he'd had had been
spent in learning the operation of the suit and the specifics
of this time-travel medium.

That brought him back towards the river in something of
a panic, and he spent some time walking along it, trying to
find that certain area of the bridge again. How long had he
been walking? How far had he gone? Was this the Thames,
or some other body of water? How many bridges crossed
the Thames, anyway? And did they all have cobblestone
sea walls and stone arches?

As he ran along the path beside the river, he was barely
aware of a whistling sound, faint at first, but growing
steadily louder. Finally it became so pervasive that it shocked
him out of his panic and redirected his mind to the unknown,
new danger. He stopped, and it seemed all around him.
Vaguely he was aware that he was breathing normally,
despite the fact that he was standing still, and that a breeze
was chilling his sweat-soaked body.

Abruptly he was hit by a trememdous dizzy spell that
brought him crashing to the ground. He tried to rise, but
the nausea wracked him while the terrible whistling sound
became unbearable. He was abruptly in the worst agony of
his life, and it became too much to bear. He passed out.

Alfie Jenkins awoke coughing. He often did, particularly during times of heavy fog. He got up from his
makeshift bed of straw and crudely fashioned wood framing.
After a bit the coughing stopped, at least for a while, and
he was able to take in some deep breaths and get awake.
From far off, the bells tolled six, and he knew at least that
his personal clock hadn't failed him. Somehow, he always

woke up at six, no matter what the previous day and night had been like.

He struggled to put on his well-worn shoes and tattered jacket that he'd found discarded in somebody's rubbish, then pushed a bit against the board held only by one nail and peered out into the street. All clear, it looked like. He squeezed out and made certain the board fell naturally back in place. The old stable hadn't been used in months, but it was still owned by somebody and he'd rather they not find out they had a boarder.

The neighborhood, down by the old docks, could be called a slum only by someone with extreme charity, but he knew it as an old friend and liked the fact that he felt so free and comfortable in an area where the coppers went around in pairs and most adults would avoid unless there was a bright sun on a clear day.

He ducked into an old warehouse through a broken ground-level window and heard the rats scuttling away, wary of the unknown intruder. He treated them with respect, but they didn't particularly bother him unless one crept into his "home" and bit him in the night, as had happened.

The warehouse was as abandoned as his stable, but it had something most of the other buildings accessible to him lacked—a working pump. The thing screeched an awful racket when used, the sound reverberating through the large, empty building, but it was the one chance he took each time. In the two years he'd lived this existence he'd never been found out, and he knew more exits than any investigator could. He was good, he was, and smart, too. He hadn't stayed long in that hole of an orphan asylum where they'd put him after his mum had died of consumption. His father, she'd said, had been a seafaring man, but he'd never known that man and never would. Mum hadn't even been sure which of the dozen or so seamen it had been, anyway.

His life now was luxury compared to that asylum. Up at six, some cruddy mess they called porridge for breakfast, then off to the woolen factory promptly at seven. Twelve hours a day, and if you made your quota, the asylum got the two quid a week the company paid. If you didn't, you got beaten real bad. All by stern men who seemed to really think they were doing their best for the "poor, unfortunate children."

Well, he'd foxed them. Lit out one Sunday in the middle of church, when they couldn't do very much. Back up to where things never changed much from when he played here as a kid. He wasn't no kid anymore. He was past thirteen.

Finished with his drink and wash-up, he relieved himself in a corner and then scrambled back out again. Breakfast was first on his mind, thanks to old Mrs. Carter paying him a few shillings to clean up the pub from the previous night's rowdiness. He wasn't sure if Mrs. Carter suspected his existence or just filled in the blanks to suit herself, but he didn't mind. They didn't ask no questions in this area.

It was a very routine morning for Alfie Jenkins in every respect but one. Instead of the usual hustling over by the market, he had to go down to the river.

Ron Moosic could waste no time in finding that time suit. It had a lot of period money—and a pistol.

MAIN LINE 351.1
LONDON, ENGLAND

There was a strangeness about this temporal existence he now lived. For one thing, he knew intellectually that, until this morning, there had never been such a person as Alfie Jenkins, at least not the one he now was. Time had adjusted to accommodate his alien presence by creating the boy by some process not understood.

There were natural laws, Silverberg had explained, that we knew nothing about, and this appeared to be in the arcane field of probability mathematics. He had created a ripple in the time stream by appearing where he should not be, but in this case it was a backward ripple, flowing the shortest possible rearward distance to find the point where Alfie Jenkins might have been conceived or, perhaps, had been stillborn. A minor probability had been changed, and he now existed and, in fact, had now and forever afterwards *always* existed. But time had not been indiscriminate in its creation; it had created the first individual to fit all the time and place criteria who had the least possibility of interacting to cause a forward ripple.

There were millions of Alfie Jenkinses in the past and present and, probably, the future as well. The legions of those who might as well have never lived. But now Jenkins *did* live, and he was subject to the same randomness in his subsequent existence as anyone else born into this time and place and situation. There were no guarantees now, any more than Ron Moosic had had in his own life and time.

The experience, the dual personality, was odd but nonetheless clear to both parties. Alfie was Alfie, and would act and react as Alfie, but Ron Moosic was there as well, sharing Alfie's body and his memories and sensations, although it was by no means clear that the reverse was true. Still, Alfie knew he was there and regarded him as a distinct and separate individual, one whose important and romantic mission appealed to the boy. Moosic made suggestions, but mostly he remained along for the ride, letting Alfie be himself. He knew, though, that he could take control, if he wished, simply by willing it.

The sunlight burned off some of the industrial smog, but it was still thick and ugly even in the full light of day. It was almost ten o'clock by the time Alfie had finished his chores, gotten his shilling and breakfast, and was able to be on his way. It didn't take very long, though, to find the path and the bridge. Apparently, location was specific in this time business—the bridge was very near Alfie's lair. Much more difficult was getting down there and doing the business unobserved. The streets, deserted in the early morning darkness, were now alive with traffic and pedestrians.

Ron Moosic took it all in with a feeling of awe. The hansom cabs clattered across the bridge, and peddlers with horse-drawn carts went this way and that. The dress styles seemed archaic, but really not that much different in the details than his own time, at least insofar as men were concerned. Women were extremely well covered from neck to ground, with most of the dresses appearing to have been made to hide almost any physical attributes.

The atmosphere was certainly big-city cosmopolitan, with lots of people of all sorts going this way and that on countless unknown errands, while the *physical* atmosphere was a mixture of garbage-like smells and foul industrial odors. To most, perhaps all, of the people, the sights and sounds and smells were normal and taken for granted. To Moosic, it was not at all that romantic or pleasant, despite his awe and excitement.

This was, after all, the London of Sherlock Holmes, of Disraeli and Gladstone, Victoria and the British Empire near the height of its glory. Holmes might not really be here, but Doyle was, somewhere, and probably Wilde, perhaps Kipling, Lewis Carroll and Robert Browning. Winston Churchill was a year old; Albert Einstein, whose work would eventually lead to Moosic being where he was, hadn't even been born yet.

And in nine days, up in the northwest part of the city, at 41 Maitland Park Crescent, Karl Marx would be returning home from the continent.

There was simply no way to gain access to the bridge in broad daylight, so he abandoned it for now and allowed Alfie to have his own way. The boy was a streetwise thief, panhandler, and hustler of the first order. He was well known to a number of people of all ages from the docks up to Whitechapel, and he wasn't the only young boy working the streets. Moosic watched with growing admiration as the boy hustled anyone who looked like a soft touch, slickly grabbing an apple from a fruit stand almost in full view of the suspicious and nasty-looking proprietor, and getting a few pennies for helping a vegetable merchant bring out more stock.

It was an active, and educational, day for the time traveler, a day that would normally not have ended with darkness but did this time. Alfie went back to his "digs" to catch a catnap, knowing that he had to get down to that bridge when things quieted down once more.

It was not, in fact, until the bells chimed two that he risked going back down there. The fog had closed in even more, making sight almost totally useless, which was fine for Moosic and all right with Alfie, too. He didn't need to see much in this neighborhood. Only the boy's occasional coughing spasms caused any problems at all.

Getting down to the right spot was no problem, and even though occasional boat whistles could be heard as the commerce of a big city continued, there was no chance anyone could see him down there in this fog. The river helped, of course, to make it so dense. Away from here, in the better neighborhoods, it was probably rather pleasant.

Alfie, however, was not Ron Moosic. The suit was extremely heavy, and it seemed as if he was never going to be able to haul it up and close. Going into the water was out of the question; Alfie couldn't swim, and Moosic was not all that certain he could manage the boy's unfamiliar frame. Still, he was almost willing to take the chance after repeated tries to pull the suit in had failed.

Finally, though, with one last mighty effort, the boy managed a mighty heave and the helmet broke the surface. It still took some tying-off of the rope and a lot of breathers before it was within his grasp.

Quickly the seals were broken and he removed the precious pouch from the outside. The pocket was then reclosed and sealed, and the suit eased back into the water once more, where it sank quickly from sight.

Alfie hurried now, clutching the precious cache with both hands, and made it back to his hiding place in no time. Although he was nearly done in by the night's work, both he and Moosic were not about to nod back off without seeing the contents of the pouch.

"Cor!" Alfie swore as he looked at the most familiar of the contents. "It's a bloomin' fortune!"

Well, it wasn't that, but it was the amount of pre-1875 notes they could round up on short notice. Fortunately, this period was one of those in which some research project was ongoing, and they had accumulated a small store of such material to help with the work. While very little from the future could go back and remain unchanged, things could be brought *forward,* including currency. Then, as now, a little ageless gold or gems could be converted into cash rather easily in London.

There was, in fact, more than two hundred pounds in the pouch, mostly in small bills. That was a year's wages to many in this period of time, and men had been killed for far less. Additionally, there was a small map of London of the period and a short dossier on what was known of Marx and his neighborhood and friends. There was also a small .32 caliber pistol of the era, along with a box of twenty-five cartridges.

Alfie was almost overcome with the sight of all that money, more than he had ever seen in his whole life or expected to see. The pistol provided an almost equal thrill, one that Moosic wasn't sure he liked. Still, the boy was exhausted from his night's work and finally succumbed to sleep.

Moosic abandoned any ideas of tracking down the two fugitives ahead of time. Just being Alfie had convinced him of the futility of that task. He used the time well, though, first making some judicious purchases to get the boy in better clothes. There was really no way for a thirteen-year-old to take a room at a hotel or rooming house without arousing suspicion, and Alfie's manners and dialect were a dead giveaway that no cover story could be really convincing. There was something to remaining cautious and, particularly, not arousing suspicion at the sight of sudden wealth. In *his* neighborhood, it would have meant death; in the better ones, it would raise questions as to its source. Still, by using the small bills one at a time and never showing the money in the same place, it was convertible. Far more so, in fact, than if he'd had no money at all to work with.

Sandoval and his girlfriend had nothing of this sort when they had traveled back to this time and place. That put him a jump ahead.

There was also the advantage that no one really took much notice of a young cleanly dressed man when he boarded the horse-drawn omnibuses or walked through various neighborhoods by day.

Forty-one Maitland Park Crescent, N.W., was easy to find with the map and some exploration. It was a nondescript three-story, gray frame house—Moosic thought it Victorian, until he realized the ridiculousness of that term in 1875—that was, nonetheless, a large and comfortable single dwelling in a peaceful, middle-class neighborhood. Moosic was enough of a cynic to think that this was one of the ironies of the founders of Communism. Somewhere in Britain, Engels, the millionaire industrialist, was financing the Communist movement while living what could only be thought of by a twentieth-century mind as the *Playboy* philosophy. Marx, the middle-class German, descendant of a line of rabbis, college-educated and devoted to intellectual pursuits, lived in a house the London proletariat could only dream about, although it was certainly no mansion and no luxurious abode in any sense of that word, and took frequent trips to Karlsbad to take the mineral bath ''cure'' far beyond the means of the working man.

Later, this man's work would be modified by the upper-middle-class born and bred Russian son of a school superintendent who would call himself Lenin and the upper-middle-class librarian in Hunan, Mao Tse Tung.

These men all sincerely believed they were revolutionizing the world for the poorest and the most downtrodden of humanity. Marx, who loved children as a group and class of their own, had been horrified by the child labor and the terrible factory conditions. They had all been, at least to some extent, and Marx totally, devoted to removing the mass of the proletariat from these inhuman, near-slavery conditions.

Let them spend more than a week in the body and mind and existence of Alfie Jenkins, Moosic thought sourly. It would make them all more dedicated than ever to their goals, certainly, but perhaps it would also add true understanding of just what it was like to be the lowest of the low in a class-oriented society. That had been the basic problem and the reason for the perversion of the noble ideals of men like Marx, after all. It was an intellectual problem, or a problem dealt with out of guilt in the way many rich men became champions of the poor, but these were human beings in the individual sense as well as the faceless "masses." How could they know, or really understand, what it was like to be an Alfie Jenkins?

When you reduced the millions of Alfies of the world to a faceless class, the "masses" or the "proletariat," you dehumanized them. None of the leaders, the intellectuals and the politicians who acted at or near the top of and in the name of the "dictatorship of the proletariat," had anything really in common with the Alfies, not really. Nor had Ron Moosic, no matter his truly proletarian background and upbringing, although he was certainly far closer to the Alfies than the Marxes and the Lenins.

Nobody had ever tried a "dictatorship of the proletariat," and nobody ever would. Many, of course, established that in name, but it always turned out to be a "dictatorship *for* the proletariat," not of or by it. When the proletariat objected, the proletariat was forced back in its place—for its own good, of course. For the good of the masses, the proletariat, the downtrodden of the world.

Of course.

Moosic was reminded of a tour of Versailles he'd taken while posted to NATO during his Air Force years. In back of the magnificent palace had been a peasant village, with peasant houses and small gardens. It was not a true peasant village, but rather an antiseptic recreation of an eighteenth-century French aristocrat's concept of what a peasant village was like. They used to go there, the guide told them, and put on "peasant garb" and play at being peasants, the better to get the "feel" for the people. The masses. But when Marie Antionette, who used to lead such playing, was faced with the concept of starvation, she had not been able to conceive of it.

And the leaders of the dictatorship of the proletariat collected fancy cars and lived in lavish apartments and brought their children up in much the same manner as royalty had raised their own. *They* believed in the ultimate socialist dream; they couldn't understand why the Alfie Jenkinses of the world could not.

"Why, let them eat cake, then!"

Sandoval was here, someplace. Had probably already stood where Alfie Jenkins now stood, looking over the house. He was a true proletarian and a true believer in the dream. In the revolution he'd fight to win, the rulers he would put in power would make sure he was the first to be shot. In the meantime, he was fed at their direction by the guilt money of the Austin-Vennemans of the world, the Engelses of the late twentieth century.

Who had sent them here, with such perfect intelligence, and on what mission? Did it, in fact, center on that house over there, so innocent and calm? It had to. It just *had* to.

Alfie Jenkins had never heard of Karl Marx.

The assimilation process was so insidious he really was only slightly aware of it. Still, he was beginning to dream Alfie's dreams, beginning to think more and more Alfie's way. Slowly, but quite progressively, he was beginning to merge with the mind and soul of the boy.

It hadn't hit him at all until, in the late afternoon of September 19, he'd taken out the dossier one last time to look through it and had found considerable trouble in reading it.

Alfie, of course, was illiterate.

The problem scared him, and set his mind to wondering. Just how much had he begun to become the street urchin whose body he wore? It was beginning to be very difficult to separate the two of them, and he was still well within his "safety margin," according to the time project's formula. The two revolutionaries had a far narrower margin. Austin-Venneman would reach the critical point by the twenty-second; Sandoval on the twenty-fourth. Within a day or so after that point, they would become more the personalities they now were than their old selves; they would not go back of their own free will.

Both had to know and understand that, all the more because what was happening to him must be happening with even more force to them. He was convinced that they would waste no time once they had their objective where they wanted him. If, in fact, Marx was their objective, they would attempt a visit on the afternoon or evening of the twentieth; of that he was certain. If the old boy was too tired and fatigued to see them, well, all the better. Callers late on the twentieth who were turned away and then returned the next day would certainly be prime suspects. Stuffing a leather pouch with sandwiches and a water bottle, he was determined to camp out within sight of 41 Maitland Crescent from early on the twentieth until—well, until as long as it took.

The waiting was the most difficult thing. Stakeouts were dull, boring work of the worst kind, not the sort of romantic cops-and-robbers business most people thought of when they thought of police work. At the start, he and Alfie had been distinctly separate personalities, but now it was hard to tell where one left off and the other began. He chafed with the impatience of a thirteen-year-old and found distraction in small games satisfying only for a brief while.

The house, however, was not bereft of activity, for it was clear that something was up. Many times he saw the squat, rotund figure of Helene Demuth, the Marx family's devoted housekeeper who looked the very model of the quintessential German nannie, rushing to and fro, airing out rugs and cleaning up inside and out.

But the tip-off that they were expecting something important was the occasional appearance of Jenny, Marx's wife, who was in extreme ill health and had not been seen on any of the earlier forays when he'd "cased" the place. She looked very old and very tired. Seen, too, was the pretty but frail-looking Eleanor "Tussy" Marx, an aspiring actress who usually went with her father to the continent but had not this trip. Unseen was the truly frail and sickly daughter Jenny, but he had no doubt that all were working hard to get things just right for the homecoming.

As the day wore on, the sky darkened and a light rain began. He had never felt so miserable or so bored out of his mind. Every time a cab had clattered past, he'd gotten his hopes up, but it was well after the city clocks chimed four that one of them came up the street and stopped in front of the gray frame house.

The driver, a fat, jolly-looking man, jumped down with surprising agility and opened the door on the curb side, away from the watcher's view, first helping someone out of the cab and then unloading the luggage. Moosic decided on a more open approach and actually crossed the street and walked right by, seeing the cabbie and Helene Demuth struggling with a large trunk while another figure was already on the porch, affectionately greeting his wife and youngest daughter.

It didn't pay to stop and stare, but Moosic's impression was of a surprisingly slender man of medium height who gave the impression of youth and great strength, despite a flowing white beard and shoulder-length white hair; he was dressed in a dark brown suit. Although appearing quite wrinkled, he was highly emotional and his joy at being home and with his loved ones was obviously genuine. It was a touching, very human scene glimpsed in passing, one that caused Moosic some unease, and he was surprised by that.

Somehow, Karl Marx had never been a real person, a real human being. He'd always been a face on the Kremlin wall during parades, a posed statue in the history books. Up until now, Alfie's London had been a real place, but in an exotic sort of way, like visiting some remote island country in the Pacific or an ancient village in the heart of Europe. Now, suddenly, this was Karl Marx—the *real* one—looking and acting very human and very ordinary and yet unexpectedly warm, no longer a symbol or a stiff historical photograph, but real. The discomfort seemed irrational, but somehow very human in and of itself. We do not expect our myths and our symbols to be ordinary people.

He crossed the street and went around the block, coming back to his inconspicuous stakeout spot diagonally across the street. He was aware that he'd taken a chance now, since anyone else watching the house might well recognize that the same boy had just gone to some lengths to wind up in the same spot as he'd started, but he was only mildly concerned. The quarries had no reason to believe that they were being stalked. As far as they knew, their confederates had destroyed the other suits, even if later taken.

The luggage was inside now, the cabbie paid, and the hansom cab, pulled by a gray sorrel, went on down the street and back into the mainstream of London traffic. It grew dark as he continued his watch, but still no one had passed who seemed inordinately interested in the house or its occupants. Still, he was certain they would come tonight—at least one of them, anyway. Their time was quickly running out, and having been dealt the unexpected ten-day delay, they could not afford to miss him by chancing a meeting the next day. The twenty-first was a Tuesday, and certainly Marx, who'd been out of the country for a couple of months, would have many errands and catch-ups to do, perhaps a multitude of visitors and appointments. If Marx was indeed their quarry, and they still had their wits and will about them, they had barely thirty-six hours to do whatever they had gone to all this trouble to do.

He was getting tired, though, and getting resigned to the idea that he would have to get some sleep if he were to resume the stakeout the next day, when a horse and wagon came up the street. The gas lamps were far apart in the block, but as the wagon passed by, he stared at the driver, a rumpled-looking man of middle-age dressed in well-worn and baggy gray coat and trousers. He appeared to be some kind of street peddler, although what, if anything, the wagon contained was not clear, and he was certainly

nondescript, although a bit out of place in this neighborhood at this time of night. Still, he would have rated only
a passing glance, except for the fact that he had come by
twenty minutes or so earlier from the same direction.

The man in the wagon had circled the block.

The first time through, Moosic hadn't paid him any
more attention than any of the others, although Maitland
was short and off the main track and hadn't had a huge
amount of traffic, but he still remembered him.

Beyond a few local residents, a strolling bobby, and the
lamplighter, there hadn't been much foot traffic, either,
but just as the man with the wagon reached the end and
turned right out of sight, another figure came from that
direction and began walking up the street.

She was a plain-looking and weary woman with short-
cropped hair and a long, light blue dress that had obviously been patched almost to death—obviously a woman
of the lower class. A factory seamstress, or perhaps a hired
cleaning woman for one of the houses—that would be
about the highest she could have been. Her age was
indeterminate, anywhere from eighteen to the mid-thirties.
It was that kind of face and walk.

Concealed in the shadows and by the bushes of Number
38 Maitland, he remained unseen to her, but his eyes followed her intently. As she walked past Number 41, she
paused for a moment and looked at the house, then around
the street. His heart quickened, and, almost without thinking,
he guided his hand to the revolver in his bag.

After a moment, she continued to walk up the street to
the other end, young eyes with far too much knowledge in
them tracing her way. He knew what he expected next,
and waited for it.

It took the man with the cart only ten minutes to turn
back in and start up the street, but as he passed the first
gas lamp, it was clear that he and the woman had been
satisfied. She now rode next to him on the seat, looking
warily around. Either they were taking few chances or,

even after all this time in assimilation, old habits were hard to break.

They seemed confident at last, though, and the man reined in his horse in front of Marx's house, got down, then helped the woman down, although she clearly didn't need such help. They looked more like father and daughter than anything else, and might well have been, Moosic realized. Still, he was pretty sure that they were also, originally, something quite different.

He resisted the urge to confront them immediately. There was no way to tell if either or both were armed, but they were both bigger than he. Short of shooting them down cold, on Marx's front lawn, there was no way to do it safely here.

Abruptly he realized that shooting them cold was exactly what the admiral and the others who'd sent him here expected him to do. Worse, they were right—here, on this deserted and dark street, well-placed shots would do the deed and allow him a good opportunity for a getaway. There was no knowledge of fingerprints in 1875 that would stand up in court, so he could just shoot, drop the revolver, and make his getaway. Find the time suit, and off he would go to his own time.

They were on the porch now, ready to knock. He made his way across the street on silent feet, crept around the rear of their wagon, and, using the shadows, approached very close to the house. The man gripped the woman's hand in a rather familiar gesture, but they hadn't yet knocked. He stepped out, still unseen, grasping the pistol with both hands. . . .

The man turned the bell on the front door. In a few moments the door opened, and Helene Demuth was there, framed by the interior light.

"*Ja?* Vat is it dat you vant?"

"Horace Whiting's the name, mum, and this is me daughter Maggie. We'd like a word or two with Dr. Marx, if it be all right with him."

"It is *not* all right at all!" Demuth huffed. "He's been home only a few hours and is very tired. Any business you haff vith him can vait until the morrow." She said this in a tone that indicated there was no business she could conceive of that Marx might have with such as these.

"Will you just do the courtesy of givin' this note to 'im, if you please, mum. Then, if he won't see us, we'll go away and wait until tomorrow."

She looked at them hesitantly, and with disdain, but she took the note. "Very vell. You vill vait here!" And then she closed the door firmly in their faces.

There's still time, Moosic told himself, but he couldn't make his finger close on the trigger. He knew who they were, and what they were, but he could not bring himself to shoot them down coldly in the back. He slipped back into the shadows.

"D'ya think he'll take the bait, luv?" the man asked worriedly.

"We cum this far, 'e's got to," she replied. "We're so far gone now we either git in ta see 'im or we 'av t' risk another jomp. Another day 'ere and I won't remember 'ow."

The man scratched his head. "I ain't so sure I want ta. I'm in trouble now jes' rememberin' that other one. I kind of loike who I be."

With a shock, Moosic realized that time had played a cruel joke on the couple. Not only had it made the lovers father and daughter, it was Austin-Venneman who was the father and Sandoval the daughter!

He only hoped that Marx would refuse to see them. If so, *then* he could confront them. Then—when there was no chance of hitting anyone else.

The door opened, and Demuth was back. She still regarded the pair as she would a month-old dead fish. "He'll see you," she told them with her tone making no bones about how she regarded the decision. "Come into the living room. He vill be down in a minute."

They entered, and the door shut, leaving Ron Moosic outside and his quarry inside with the man who was the object of it all. He cursed to himself that he'd let the golden opportunity slip away, that he'd given them license to do damage, by his own failure to be as cold-blooded as they.

"But it wouldn't be sportin'," his Alfie part seemed to say. *"If we did it that way, we'd be just like them, wouldn't we?"*

To beat them, you often had to be like them, he reflected sourly. But he wasn't like them, and never had been. Not yet.

The living room was on the first floor in front of the house, and the curtains were only partly drawn. Stealthily he crept up onto the porch and made his way to below one of the windows. Both were raised an inch or so to allow some air to circulate, and he could hear, and occasionally risk seeing, what was going on. That is, if the beat cop didn't come around and catch him first.

Karl Marx was a striking figure in person. Although thin, he had an athlete's build and broad shoulders that gave the impression of great mass and strength. His carriage was strong and upright, the body of a much younger man than his fifty-seven years. It was clear that his trip had done him much good; he looked excellent for any age.

He had a large brow framed by curly, white locks that reached to his powerful shoulders, a snow-white beard that flowed deep down, and brown eyes that sparkled with warmth and intelligence from underneath black, bushy eyebrows. The eyes, in fact, were a giveaway that did not generally reveal itself in photographs. They were warm, human, emotional eyes, highly expressive and penetrating at one and the same time. He was full of what the Greek called *charisma*—both visitors involuntarily stood up and waited in awed silence when he entered the room, not just from politeness but from the strength and magnetic power he radiated without doing or saying a thing.

He had changed into informal black pants, a white shirt, and had obviously thrown on an old smoking jacket for the visitors.

If Marx more than lived up to what the visitors expected to see, they certainly lived up to Helene Demuth's description in his own mind. In his hand he held the envelope they had handed to the housekeeper, its top now torn open. "So," he said in an orator's baritone that more than fit his striking appearance, "vat in hell is the meaning of this?" He held up the envelope and shook it for emphasis.

His speech was heavily accented, and somewhat hesitant. Although he spoke, read, and wrote a half-dozen languages with ease, it was clear that he was not blessed with the translator's talent of thinking in the tongue he was using. Everything, although extremely quickly, was translated into German in his mind and then back again when he spoke.

"If y' please, sir," said the woman, "that is, as y' must know, the title and first few pages of yer rev'lut'nary book in the French and Russian tongues, along with some words from a letter y' haven't yet mailed to yer Russian friend."

"I am vell avare of the content, young lady," Marx responded coldly. "I vish to know how it is possible for you to know a letter I am writing still, and vhy somevun vould to the trouble go of printing up pages of books not yet published. Und Russian, yet! Ven it is possible to Russian publish, they vill still be too stupid to read it!"

"They're for real, sir," she assured him, somewhat shocked by his rather anti-Russian scorn. "It was the only way to show you we ain't what we seem, sir."

The massive brows came down. They were all still standing. "Und, just vat 'ain't' you, then?" he responded scornfully.

She blushed, feeling ashamed of her dialect. In point of

fact, it was taking an extreme amount of will to take the lead in this conversation at all. Her upbringing and background was as deferential and passive as Sandoval's had been commanding and assertive. Clearly, whatever laws of time there were had moved hardest on Roberto Sandoval, to quench his fanatical personality and impulsive amorality. Time had contrived to make it difficult for someone to make tiny ripples even if they desired to make great waves. There was clearly a war of wills going on between what time had imposed and the strong-willed fanatic who'd stop at nothing—and, to Moosic's surprise and grudging respect, Roberto Sandoval was winning. Clearly, whoever had planned this had chosen well indeed—but, then, why the empty-headed accomplice?

The beat cop came down the street at this moment, causing the listener to have to move away and crouch flat in the darkness to avoid being seen. The cop stopped by the wagon and inspected it warily, then looked right at the Marx household. For a few precious minutes Moosic dared not move, fearful that the cop would come up to the house to see just who would be visiting in that kind of vehicle at this time of the evening. Indeed, the cop seemed to be mulling over whether or not to do just that. Moosic prayed that he would not, for there was no clear exit off the porch without coming into full view of the cop, and he was certain to be spotted now—him with a revolver in his pocket!

The bobby finally decided on a middle approach, walking on down the street but walking with frequent glances back at the cart and horse. Clearly, he was not going to go far until he saw the owners.

The cop finally was far enough down to allow him to cautiously return to his listening post. He had no idea what had gone on in the few minutes he'd missed, but clearly Sandoval had been convincing.

". . . You must understand," Marx was saying, "that vat you say is true is the one total und horrible negation of my laws. If a device truly exists that can make changes in history, und such a device vould be qvite naturally in the hands of the capitalists, then the revolutionary process may be postponed indefinitely, even cancelled out after the fact! This is horrible, horrible! It is the same as if you came to a professor of physics und let go of an apple und it floats up to the ceiling!''

"It is exactly the point," the woman responded, still in that lower class accent but with the grammar now seeming to smooth out. "The weapons of our toime can kill all livin' things on Earth. The capitalists, then, must fall from within. But this—this is eternal slavery or the end of 'umanity!''

So that was it. More than enough to convince the committed, although it still didn't explain Karen Cline.

"Ja, ja. Or ve haff a time var, vith history obeying vatever laws one side makes up that the other cannot see.''

"We can destroy the place, kill the scientists, but it'll do no good," Sandoval told him. "They know 'ow. They'll just build another bigger and better. So we busted in and brung the suits t'you.''

Moosic felt a shock run through him, and he almost cursed aloud. The two time suits were in the wagon! All he had to do was steal them or get at them long enough to destroy them and this would all be over! He looked back out at the street—and saw that damned copper standing over near where he'd hid out all day. "Alfie" calculated the odds, and decided there wasn't a chance in hell of getting to that wagon and getting away with it unless he killed the copper. Just after that, all hell would break loose anyway.

So easy—it could have been so *easy*. If he'd shot the pair, that would have been the end of it, and only the guilty would have suffered. If he'd known, or guessed, that the suits were in the cart, he could have easily made off with it between the time they entered the house and the time the beat cop showed up, with nobody dead. Now, there was an innocent life at stake—and he couldn't take that kind of chance. It was a long shot, sure, but killing the cop might change things worse than letting this run its course.

No chance to do it easy now. He waited for the cop to saunter on down the block once more, and then, when the coast seemed clear, he stood up and drew the revolver. He was standing just outside the living room window, which was chest-high at its base and had no screen this time of year. He peered in, saw the two radicals seated on a couch against the wall to his right, while Marx sat in an over-stuffed armchair facing them. Steeling himself, he measured his moves and then counted down in his mind.

Suddenly he pushed up on the window and stuck the revolver inside. "All roite!" he commanded in Alfie's less than elegant voice. "Everybody just stay still! This gun's loaded and I know 'ow to use it!"

The three in the room froze, and it was Marx who dared the first move. "Now vat is dis?" he roared. "Who vould stick a gun in my parlor?" He was clearly more angry than scared.

Being as careful as possible, he got a leg over the sill and slipped into the room. "You moite call me the toime coppers, Doctor Marx. Just stand easy—I got no business with you, only wit' them what're tryin' to choinge what is."

The woman whose form hid Roberto Sandoval looked crushed. "So they didn't hold on even for a day."

"No," he told them. "You killed a lot of people, but we killed 'em all that you left. Don'cha remember me, ducky? *Moo*-sic?"

Both of the radicals blanched at the name, even the old man who was almost too far gone into the time frame. The one man they couldn't scare. The one man who'd scared *them*.

"Who is this person?" Marx wanted to know.

"An American capitalist agent," Sandoval told him. " 'Is job is to make sure it *stays* theirs."

"So vat vill you do? Shoot them and fade away?" Marx asked him calmly.

"No. We're just all going out to that wagon. You, too, sir, Oi'm afraid. Everybody in front of me. Nobody needs to be 'urt in the least."

"'E's gonna shoot up the suits!" Sandoval exclaimed, understanding it all. "Leave us 'ere all stuck good'n proper!"

He gestured with the revolver. "All roite, let's get it over with. All of you, up and out. Oi don't wanna shoot nobody, but Oi will if Oi hav'ta. Now—*move!* And no tricks! Just all noice and pleasant-loike."

They stood up, and even Marx looked hesitant. Alone, Moosic guessed, he might have tried something, but with his family in the house this was no time to make a move.

They walked out into the hallway leading to the double door, and he followed, eyes on them. As he walked through the doorway into the hall, someone suddenly made a grab for him from the side. Powerful hands grabbed his arm, but so hard and sudden was the grab that the pistol discharged—once—then he was on the floor and Helene Demuth was on top of him. The pistol fired three more times before she got it away, screaming and banging his head against the floor. He was unconscious before the cop reached the porch.

OF ANGELS AND DEMONS

Medical science had progressed only a small amount from the Middle Ages by 1875. It *was* true that physicians were now true scientists and knew a great deal. The trouble was, they also couldn't do very much more about it than their Aristotelian forebears could with their leeches and bad humors. All doctors really knew in 1875 was how futile all that old stuff was.

He was mostly in a coma—a strange dreamlike state that produced few dreams and mostly only a sense of floating, with occasional snatches of an unreal reality. The prison surgeons were not exactly in the forefront of medical skills and research, either, but they were competent and did what they could. He was aware, at times, of people flitting about and even discussing him, and once or twice it seemed like some people were asking him questions, but he could neither make out the questions nor form an answer.

When he finally did regain consciousness, he wished he hadn't. The doctors and nurses were hard and cold and could do little except load him with morphia for the pain. They would answer no questions. Within a few hours of coming out of it, though, there appeared a young man in a neat business suit who asked many and would answer some.

"I am Inspector Skinner of Scotland Yard," he told the patient, who listened through a drugged haze that still didn't quite blot out the pain, "I think you should give some answers."

"Uh—'ow long 'ave Oi been here?" he croaked.

"You've been in a coma almost seven days," the inspector told him. "The old woman did a job on you, she did."

Seven days. That would make this the twenty-seventh of September. He tried to think about why that was important, but couldn't quite manage it.

"Now, then," continued the detective, "I think it's time for a statement of sorts." He took out a fountain pen and a small notebook. "First of all, I've told you who I am. What's *your* name?"

"Alfie," he rasped. "Alfie Jenkins."

"How old are you, Alfie?"

"Dunno. Never got to countin'."

The inspector nodded. "Do you remember last Monday night?"

He thought back. Something. . . . Some kind of shooting. "It's all kinda dim."

"You shot two people, Alfie. You broke into a man's home and shot him and a guest of his. You remember that?"

Alfie nodded, getting a little handle on what had happened, although still somewhat confused as to why. "Didn't mean to shoot nobody. The old hag grabbed me gun."

He nodded. "Nevertheless, you broke into the house and you brought the gun. You understand that, don't you?"

Alfie managed a nod. "Yes, sir. 'Ow are they—the two wot got shot, that is?"

"Dead, Alfie. Both dead."

Somewhere in the back of his mind something screamed, *My god! I just killed Karl Marx!*

"The old peddler lingered on for a few days, but it was just too great a shock to his system."

Things were coming back to him now, in little bits and pieces. "The old boy 'ad a daughter. Wot's 'appened to 'er?"

"They say she fled screaming in panic. Got on the cart and went. We haven't found her as yet, but we're looking."

He felt totally lost and alone. Worse, after all that, *he* might swing for murder or be sentenced to life in prison, which was as sure a death to somebody like him. Marx was dead, and at *his* hand. History had been changed. And the important one had gotten away and was now—where and when? At least it answered one big question, that of why Sandoval had brought the woman along. He needed somebody to wear the suit to get it back—for Marx.

As the intellectual part of him stirred in response to the questions, it found itself being pushed back, almost as if under attack. It took a supreme effort just to bring those thoughts up, and they were fading almost as they were made. The combined effect of the morphia and the additional seven days were having full effect. Not that it mattered, of course. He was in a prison hospital somewhere in London, with no real hope of ever getting out in time to reach the suit. He had mucked up everything with his failure to act coldly and decisively, and now the villain was free to roam again, while he faced a short and unhappy future as Alfie Jenkins.

"Wot—wot'll 'appen to me now?" he asked plaintively, knowing the answer.

"Ordinarily, you would stand trial as an adult because of the seriousness of the offense, and you know what that result would be. There are mobs outside the prison demanding that they be allowed to save the Queen the expense. Doctor Marx, you know, was a famous and well-loved man."

"Oi'd 'eard that, sir."

"However, you may be lucky here. There is no liking for making a big trial with a roaring crowd that could become a circus or, worse, a scene for rioting and violence. You're quite ill, Alfie. Did you know that?"

"Just a cough, sir."

"It's far more than that. You have a very bad lung disease. We can do little for it. Do you understand that?"

He managed a nod, feeling oddly better at the news. It beat hanging—maybe.

The inspector sighed, put away his pen and notebook, and looked down at him. "Just rest and relax, Alfie. You'll not come to trial while gravely ill—we'll see to that."

After the inspector left, he thought it over as much as he was able to do so. They expected him to die here. It would be better for everybody if he did, in fact. Marx wanted revolutions, he remembered, and he was smart enough to see that Her Majesty's government wanted none of that here, no symbol to rally everyone against.

With that thought, he drifted back into sleep.

"Wake up," a woman's hushed voice said from somewhere near. He felt hands gently shake him, and when he stirred and opened his eyes, he frowned, thinking the vision a dream.

She had a chubby, freckled face and hair cut very short, like they used to cut the boys' hair at the orphan asylum. She was dressed entirely in some strange black body-garment that looked like dull leather but was soft, like cloth. Around her waist was a thick, black, belt-like contraption that seemed more like a misplaced horse collar, but had a bunch of red lights on it, both on top and around her middle. The tight-fitting garment emphasized her chubbiness, and was not very complimentary. A pair of goggles sat atop her head, ready to be pulled down at a moment's notice.

"'Ho're you? Some kind of prison nurse?"

"No," she whispered, "and keep your voice down. Time is very short, and the amount of power required to allow me to be here without assimilation is enormous."

He was in great pain, but much of the morphia had worn off, allowing the Moosic personality a little latitude. He mustered all his will to force himself forward, reminding himself that Sandoval had done it. "You—you are from the future." It was a statement, not a question.

"In a way, yes. I've brought you something you need desperately, but you'll have to move fast. Can you make it out of bed?"

"Oi . . . think so." He tried and, with her help, got to a shaky standing position. It was then that he saw it, there on the floor. "The toime suit!" he breathed.

He sat back on the bed and she helped him into it. It was enormous for the body of Alfie Jenkins, far too large to be practical, and he said so.

"Don't worry. Once you punch out, it'll be O.K., and both Alfie and Ron will live. Understand?"

He nodded dully.

"The power pack is on full-charge now—I did it before coming here. And I've set it for the correct time and place. There is still a chance of catching Sandoval."

"But 'istory—it's already changed."

"Very little. Marx would have died in a few years anyway, and all his important work was done. He was killed by a boy in the pay of anti-Communists, a boy who then escaped from gaol. That's all the change. Now—helmet on. Check the pouch when you arrive. And remember—Sandoval's power is nearly gone. He's landed a hundred miles from his goal. You can beat him there. Now—seal and go!"

"But wait! Just 'ho *are* you?"

But the seal snapped in place and he was in silence, although nearly swimming in the suit. If he stood up, he knew he'd sink below and out of the helmet, so he didn't try. The mysterious woman reached out and touched the suit activation switches.

Reality faded. The suit's anti-glare shield snapped on, and all around was blinding light. He was falling again, falling through time and space. . . .

The journey this time was the same in all physical

respects, but not for the man himself. Suddenly he felt the cramping and pinching of the suit once more and realized, with a start, that he was Ron Moosic once again in form.

Mentally, the trip was stranger. Slowly, ever so slowly, the personality of Alfie Jenkins came to equal status with his own. There was a period of terrible confusion in his mind, as he lost all true orientation of self. It was a strange, indescribable feeling of being, at one and the same time, not a rider in someone else's head, but two people simultaneously.

Now, rapidly, the elements of Alfie Jenkins' life and personality began to merge with his own. The process was strange and total, and he realized, with a shock, that he was *still* Alfie Jenkins, would always be Alfie, but only a part, only a small part. . . .

He knew, intellectually, that this would change him, perhaps in subtle ways, but in a permanent fashion. He also realized that he would not really be aware of that change, that the new whole would be natural and normal and right for him.

This was something Silverberg and the others had not warned him about. Lives created could be absorbed, but not destroyed once they were real. And yet, now that he thought of it, it was logical. And, somewhere, he knew, Alfie Jenkins was free and happy at last. . . .

But where—and when—was he going now?

After Sandoval, that was clear. And, for now, that was enough. Still, he couldn't help but wonder about this fourth player in the game and why she had come to him and helped him. He wished he'd had more of his wits about him and had been able to ask more questions. It was quite certain she was on his side, and the simplicity of her time mechanism, compared to the bulky suit he wore, made it certain that she was from some future time. So the "leading edge" of the time stream was not his own origin time, but rather farther into the future. How far ahead? he wondered. Or did that matter as much as the fact that she seemed definitely on his side. An enemy of any sort would have let him rot. Still, if someone from the future was assisting him, that presupposed a fifth player in the game. Perhaps the one that initiated all this? The one that converted Dr. Cline? But, if that were so, why had they needed the help of some radicals from the past at all? Why not just go back with their superior equipment and do it themselves? Questions, always more questions, and no one to get the answers from.

For now, it would have to be enough to know that history's alteration had been a mere ripple, of no major consequence in the long run, no matter how much pain and sorrow he'd caused Marx's innocent family. And he could still complete the mission.

This time I won't hesitate to shoot for a moment, Sandoval, he swore.

The falling sensation stopped, and he felt himself fall forward onto solid ground. He had forgotten that he'd left in a more or less sitting position. This time it was also night, but the area looked quite different from England. Releasing the seals on the suit, he was also relieved to find that it was relatively warm. He couldn't help wondering what happened when his naked self was forced out into a sub-zero February for a couple of hours, with no fire able to warm him.

The instruments on the suit indicated a charge at still well over ninety percent, which meant he couldn't have come far. The month and year he could make out by simple subtraction, but the geographic coordinates were beyond him.

The time was some point in June, 1841. The closeness of the date surprised him. Silverberg had said something about a "twenty year window," which would cover Alfie, barely, but hardly the girl who had been Sandoval. Clearly, the scientist had been wrong—or the date the mysterious woman had set for him was wrong. That latter worried him, but only a little. He had more than enough power to get home now, and all he had to do was set the controls to zero. Perhaps, he surmised, it was not a flat twenty years but an individual thing. Running into the twenty-year barrier in one case would cause the scientists to clamp down a limit and accept it. In his time, after all, time travel was in its earliest stages.

Perhaps those who'd coached Sandoval had more experience.

He spent a little time scouting the area. It was a city, certainly, old but not very large. It was immediately evident by the signs that it was in Germany, but he had no knowledge of German and so couldn't get more than vague information. Certainly the central square contained some relatively tall buildings for the time, at least one of which rose six stories to a flat-topped pyramidal structure that went up perhaps two or three more. The centerpiece to the square was an ornate European fountain which looked ancient even for 1841, but it still functioned.

To one side of town was a mammoth structure that made even the medieval fountain seem new. A massive structure of weathered stone, it was clearly an ancient city gate, with portals to pass two-way mounted traffic, two levels on top of the portals, and two towers, one the same height as the rest of the structure, the other with yet an additional story on it. He really didn't recall them being much in Germany, but damned if the thing didn't look kind of ancient Roman. It stood majestically in the middle of the roadway, with incongruous German-style buildings adjoining its taller tower on one side and a park on the other.

He was conscious of the press of time now, and he searched frantically for some place to hide the suit. He finally decided on a heap of rubble very near the Roman gate. The stones were fairly easy to move and replace, not likely to be quickly disturbed, and the ruin itself was a proper landmark. Still, it was a major undertaking to get the cavity made, the suit put in, then covered to his nervous eye. This time, if possible, he'd do what the radicals had done in 1875 and retrieve the suit as soon as possible.

He was still positioning and repositioning stones when he felt the nausea and dizziness strike him. In a matter of minutes he'd passed out.

Holger Neumann had been born in Trier in 1805, which made him thirty-six now. He was the only child of an attorney with a small local practice, and he'd been rather spoiled early on. His father had been something of a wimp at home, and it was his mother who dominated almost everything either one of them said or did. He'd gone to good schools and received a solid middle-class education, but, despite his father's hopes, he found the law did not appeal to him. College had interested him for a while, but after his mother's death while in his third year, it no longer seemed interesting or important, and he hadn't gone back after the funeral.

His father seemed to shrivel a bit each day after his wife's death, and just lost the will to live, or so they said. He followed her in less than two years. Holger was surprised to discover that there was a substantial estate, grown even fatter when he sold the family's house and his father's office. It was not enough for champagne and the Grand Tour, but as long as he was quite modest in his lifestyle, it was sufficient to support him.

He'd gotten to Bonn, Cologne, Berlin, even Paris, although he found the French intolerable and his inability to learn their language impossible. At the moment he was, in fact, back home for one of his annual conferences with the bank that managed his money. He was living in Cologne, so it wasn't much of a trip, taking odd jobs here and there as the spirit and his needs above the annuity dictated, but he was now trying to decide where to move on to. He required a major city, but one in which he could keep a certain amount of anonymity. He was tempted by Austria, and particularly by Vienna, which had an open atmosphere like Paris but also spoke the correct tongue.

He was a pure blond with large, soft blue eyes and a complexion so fair that he appeared far younger than his years. If, in fact, things had been different, he might well have gone far in any profession he chose, but he did not have that freedom. Position meant being a public person, and he could not afford that luxury.

He had simply never been able to get close to, or feel anything for, any woman except his mother. All other women had seemed rather boring and shallow, and certainly unappealing sexually. From his earliest sexual awakenings, Neumann had been attracted to young men.

In a town like Trier that meant total suppression, but in the open atmosphere of Heidelberg things had been different. Within a year he'd discovered that there were others like himself, and that revelation hit him with tremendous force. It had, in fact, been a graduate assistant assigned to help him with the exams who had spotted in him what he thought he had so completely concealed. Through him, he'd discovered a secret society, a brotherhood of sorts, that had made life turn on its head. Still, there was fear, constant fear, of being exposed.

It was that constant level of near-panic among the brotherhood, all of whom were looking to successful careers, that convinced him that he was wasting his time with that sort of academic pursuit. He simply could not live with the fear that he would lose a professorship or judgeship or some other high post in one moment of loose guard. Still, all of the German states were to one degree or another police states, which tolerated this sort of behavior only on the lowest of levels. That, in fact, was why he was now thinking of moving on. Austria was no Paris, but it was far looser and more tolerant—perhaps because, as it was often said, it was less competently run—than anywhere else he'd been.

He awakened in the small hotel room, dressed, and went

down first to the communal toilet in the rear, then across the street for breakfast. It was a beautiful, warm, sunny day.

Time is a creative bastard, he thought while eating a pastry and drinking some strong Turkish coffee. *First a thirteen-year-old dying orphan, now a gay man forced by his time and place to be a wastrel.*

Ron Moosic wondered who and what Roberto Sandoval was now.

On a hunch, he spent the morning doing some surreptitious checking, and found the name of Marx with ease. In fact, he remembered the family now, although only vaguely. He'd never had much use for Jews, even if the family were all converts. Jews might fake conversions to make life easier for them, but they were still born with the blood.

Moosic was shocked to find "himself" thinking those thoughts, but he understood that this was common thinking at the time. *If only they knew where it would finally lead,* he reflected sourly.

Still, it was rather easy then to find the Marx household, and just as easy, through casual conversation with locals he knew from his youth, to discover that their son Karl, now Herr *Doktor* Marx, was home for a while. There was gossip that he and his mother did not get along, though, and he was thinking of moving to either Bonn or Cologne, depending on how easily he could establish himself in either city. He was hoping to obtain some sort of position before marrying his fiancée, a local girl, Jenny Westphalen.

Things worked out so well he almost swore it was planned that way. At least, he couldn't have planned it better himself. In the town bookstore, where he was drawn partly out of curiosity and partly out of boredom, he met a man looking through the magazines and papers. He was originally attracted to him because he was a young, somewhat handsome fellow with a short-cropped brown beard. Moosic thought he looked the very image of the young, thin Orson Welles of *Citizen Kane*. But when the man looked up and he saw those eyes, he knew who this man had to be.

Karl Marx was not the Moses-like patriarch of 1875, but he had those penetrating, electrifying eyes. They introduced themselves, and soon Marx and Neumann, not Moosic, were talking away about socialism, Hegelism, communism, and revolutionary movements in Europe. Marx seemed even more oppressed by the small town of his birth than was Neumann, and was delighted to find a kindred outsider, a native who hated the place but had more than a bit of education. Neumann's ingrained distaste for Jews in general and the Marxes in particular faded under the direct contact, particularly when Marx unexpectedly cracked a very anti-Semitic joke.

Karl Marx was absolutely fascinating, a riveting speaker who seemed to know very much about almost every subject imaginable. His brilliance was enhanced, rather than tempered, by his unsuppressed emotionalism. Neither his Neumann nor Moosic self could resist the energy and intellect; both were in fast agreement that this was indeed the most brilliant and electrifying intellect they had ever met. It was for Moosic to additionally understand that the old man he'd seen so very briefly still had much of this power. It made him feel a great deal of regret he couldn't have known him longer, and it added to his guilt as to having shortened that man's life.

Neumann, quite naturally, was instantly madly infatuated with Marx, but frustratingly so. He knew, even without Moosic, that Marx was solidly conservative in his sex life and totally in love with and devoted to a single woman. It didn't matter in the end; Neumann could fantasize and not act or reveal himself because he feared that if Marx knew, he would never see the younger man again. Just to be talking to him, around him, near him, was enough for now.

Moosic watched the flow of Neumann-thoughts and saw where it would lead. This sort of futile passion could easily end in suicide—which might well be time's easy out all along.

In the course of the afternoon, Marx also talked a bit about himself and some of his plans. He was writing for an anti-government newspaper in Cologne, as well as other essays and critical articles for a variety of places. He was thinking of a university career and was shortly going to Bonn to see his closest friend and contact, a professor at the university there. In the meantime, he was staying not with his family but with the Westphalens, the family of the woman he intended to marry.

Moosic wondered if Sandoval knew that. The mysterious woman had said that the radical had landed far from Trier and had to make his way here. The setting for a quick panic jump would not be easy to do without a computer. He remembered his own problem in reading any sense into location on the time suit's readout.

Over the next few days he contrived to meet with Marx here and there, and also was introduced to Jenny, a really pretty young woman. It was very hard to repress the cold, sheer hatred Neumann felt for her. Although he was cautious enough not to be a leech, this shortened considerably his stakeout time, divided as it had to be between various key points in the city. The most important of those, however, was the hotel itself. If Sandoval was to be a stranger, he would need a place to stay while here.

Late on the second night, he retrieved the time suit from its hiding place near the ancient Roman gate to the city and managed, with the aid of a very large laundry bag he'd purchased earlier, to get it up to his hotel room. There he sat down with it, opened the pouch, and was surprised to see some more material in it. Then he remembered that his mysterious savior had told him that things of interest would be there.

What there was was a very modern-looking pistol with one full clip and a note saying, "Peter's Fountain, 2

A.M., the 22nd,'' and nothing more. The note was written in a terse and unfamiliar female hand.

It was now Saturday the nineteenth. He replaced the pistol in the pouch and put the whole thing back in the suit, which would at least give it the energy protection from time's ravages. He would not like to need it and find it turned into a flintlock.

He'd prefer to stick Sandoval with one of those and take his chances. With this gun, he couldn't miss.

MORE PLAYERS IN THE GAME

He didn't see Marx during the weekend; this was a time for personal matters, although he knew, too, that Marx had fallen behind in his writings and wanted a little bit of time alone to catch up.

He was most interested in the Monday morning coach from Cologne, which brought three newcomers to town. One was a middle-aged man who apparently sold barber and surgical equipment. Moosic tentatively dismissed him, although one could never be sure. If Sandoval had undergone assimilation a hundred miles or more from Trier, he was not likely to have a profession that would normally take him here. The other two, however, were equally improbable—a man in his early twenties in Prussian military uniform accompanied by a pleasant-looking young woman who could not have been out of her teens and was introduced at the desk as the military man's wife. It didn't seem to fit the pattern—both young and attractive-looking, and newly married. He began to wonder if Sandoval had yet to arrive.

He had a quick lunch with Marx, who was effusive about finally being exempted from the obligatory year of compulsory military duty. He'd been fighting the battle for some time with the bureaucracy, and he'd finally won. "The first and only time these sickly lungs of mine ever did me any service," he told Neumann.

To avoid problems, Marx had most of his mail sent to the post office for pickup, and they walked over to it,

Marx hopeful that a couple of articles he'd submitted long ago to two journals had finally seen publication. He was disappointed, though; there was, in fact, only a single letter, with no return address. Marx opened it, still talking cheerily, and glanced at it, then stopped talking and just stared at the pages.

"Something wrong?" Neumann asked him, concerned. "Bad news?"

"No, no. But someone, somewhere, is playing tricks with my privacy and I will have to get to the bottom of this." He frowned and handed a page of the letter's contents to Neumann. "What do you make of this? It appears to be handwritten, yet it has something of the appearance of a photograph of some kind."

He looked at the page, which seemed to be a fragment of a letter. Moosic realized with a sudden thrill what had disconcerted Marx so much.

It was unquestionably a photocopy. And the copier would not be invented for almost a hundred and twenty years.

He handed the sheet back to Marx. "Very odd. I see what you mean about the photographic quality, but I can't imagine how such a thing is possible to do. Is the text of any importance?"

"It is a personal letter of mine to my father from some years back," Marx responded angrily. "A letter I am certain I personally destroyed."

"Even given the means as possible, which it must be, for there it is, who could have gotten their hands on such a thing, and why? The police?"

That was the obvious first thought, since Prussia was in most senses of the word a well-controlled police state.

"It is possible, for some of my writings have already made me less than popular with the authorities. But, somehow, I think not." He seemed to be mulling over whether to go further, and finally made his decision. "What do you think of this?"

Neumann took it and glanced at it, and the effect was to

heighten his already overbearing sense of excitement still further. It was a small, handwritten note which said, "I have the power but not the mind to change the history of the world. If you would be that mind, come to Peter's Fountain, alone, at 2 A.M. on the 22nd." It was unsigned.

He handed it back to Marx. "This sounds like the rantings of a maniac. You are not going, of course?"

"I am thinking about it. Otherwise, I shall never know how this letter was acquired, and I shall spend my life wondering if my most private moments are someone's public business."

Neumann frowned. "Let me go instead. If this person is truly insane, he will betray it to me, not you, and we will know. If he is not insane, then a subsequent meeting could be arranged."

"I have never put much faith in dueling, my new friend, but if I were to have a duel, I would never permit my second to stand in my place. No, I must think on this some more, but whatever I do, I must do alone. I thank you for your counsel and your kind offer, but if you value our friendship, you must forget that you ever saw or heard this."

"I will come with you, then. . . ."

"No! You will get a good night's sleep, and tomorrow I promise you I shall describe the results in glorious detail. But you must swear to me that you will forget it now, on your honor."

"I . . . value this friendship above all things," Neumann waffled, hoping Marx would not press further.

The younger man considered it sufficient, and they parted soon after.

A Xerox copy had lasted at least a day, perhaps more, out of this time frame. That, at least, was to the good. It meant his pistol would probably work as advertised.

The central square of Trier looked eerie and threatening in the early morning hours, lit only by a few huge candles in the street lights, their flickering casting ever-changing and monstrous shadows on the cobblestones and the sides of the now-dark buildings.

Moosic gave the square a professional going-over between midnight and one, noting the rounds of the local policeman. He wanted no repetition of the debacle in London. This time there would be one target and one target only, and that target would be taken out as soon as positively identified. That should not be too difficult, he thought, if he could shoot straight. He already knew the policeman, and he knew Marx, so anyone else likely to be here at two almost had to be his quarry.

It was an eerie wait, back in the shadows of an alleyway looking on the square. All was silence, and there was no movement except for those shadows and the noise of the multiple fountains pouring into the catch basin. In the stillness they sounded like huge waterfalls, the noise caught by the buildings and echoed back again and again.

It was a short wait compared to London, but it seemed forever in the stillness. When the church clock struck the three-quarter hour, he tensed, checked his pistol for the hundredth time, and began to look for signs of another, either Sandoval or Marx. At approximately 1:50 the policeman patrolling the area walked into the square, panicking him for a moment. The cop checked all the doors facing the square, looked around, and finally made his way from the square and down a side street, but not before the clock chimed two. The minutes now crept back as the patrolman's footsteps receded and finally died away in the distance, but there was still no sign of anyone else in the square.

Then, quite suddenly, he heard the clicking of shoes on cobblestone. Someone was coming down the same street the policeman had used to leave, coming towards the square. He tensed, praying that Marx had decided not to come after all, and waited until the oncoming figure strode into the square. He strained to catch a glimpse of the newcomer, and saw him at last, in the glow of a street lamp.

It was certainly no one he'd ever seen before. He was tall, thin, and at least in middle age, with a long and unkempt black beard and a broad-brimmed hat that concealed much of the rest of his features. He was dressed in the seedy clothes of one who was used to sleeping in his only suit. He didn't seem armed, and he certainly didn't have the time suit with him, if indeed he were Sandoval and not just some bum avoiding the policeman.

Moosic stood up and was about ready to go out and confront the man, when there was a sudden noise behind him. He felt a pistol at the back of his head, and quietly a man's voice whispered, "I think you better remain where you are and not make a sound. Put the gun down, nice and quiet, on the ground. No false moves, my friend! At this range I could hardly miss."

He did as instructed, then slowly got up as the pistol was pulled away. He turned, and saw his captor. The man was dressed entirely in black, in a uniform rather similar to the one his mysterious woman in London had been wearing. But this was no ordinary-looking chubby woman; this man was tall, lean, and extremely muscular, with a strong face like a Nordic god's, his pure blond hair neatly cut in a military trim. Behind him lurked two large black shapes that looked somehow inhuman, but whose features were impossible to determine in the near total darkness of the alley. One thing was clear, though—from the blinking little lights—all three wore belts similar to the one the woman had worn. This, then, was the true enemy.

Knowing it was hopeless, he turned again to watch the scene in the square. More footsteps now, and the seedy-looking man leaning on the lamppost stiffened, then stepped back into a doorway for a moment. In another minute, Moosic saw Marx walk nervously into the square from his right and look around. He appeared alone and unarmed.

The twin personalities inside the Neumann body con-

verged in an emotional rage. He glanced back briefly at
the mysterious blond man, and noted with the professional's
eye that his captor was looking less at him than at the
scene in the square. The time agent was larger and more
powerful than Neumann, but if he could just idly get one
step back, just one step, that might not mean a thing.
Pretending to watch what was going on in the square, he
measured the distance and moves out of the corner of
his eye.

Quickly he lunged around, his knee coming up and
hitting the blond man squarely in the balls. The man in
black cursed in pain and doubled over, dropping his strange-
looking pistol. Quickly Moosic rolled, picked up his own
pistol, and was out of the alley and to his right.

"Herr Marx! It's a trap! Drop to the ground!" he shouted.

Marx was about ten feet from Sandoval, and at the noise
and yell he froze and turned to look back in utter confusion.
Sandoval reached into his pants and pulled out a gun,
while behind Moosic, in the alley, two strange figures ran
out into the light. Two figures out of nightmare.

They seemed to be almost like living statues, black all
over, although they seemed to wear nothing except the
time belts, their skin or whatever it was that was glistening
like polished black metal. Their features were gargoyle-
like, the stuff of nightmares in any age. Both had automatic rifles in their hands.

They had, however, overrun Moosic, who unhesitatingly
brought up the pistol and fired at them. The strange pistol
seemed to *chirp* rather than explode, but a tiny ball of light
leaped from it and struck one of the creatures in the back.
There was a scream, and the thing collapsed in pain.

Sandoval panicked, raising his own pistol and firing
continuously at Moosic, the bullets or whatever they were
coming out like tracers. But Moosic was no longer there.
He'd rolled back towards the alley and found cover. There
was no sign of the blond man, but in the square there were

two bodies sprawled out, one of them bleeding into the cobblestones.

With a shock, Moosic realized that Sandoval's panicked fire at him had hit Marx instead. There was no way to really aim such rapid fire, and he had been in the way.

The other creature roared, and Sandoval, nervous, nevertheless approached it, seeming to know just who or what it was. With a snarl, the creature's rifle came up; there was a quick burst, and Roberto Sandoval was pushed back several feet by the force of whatever was striking him.

The creature then turned and started back towards the alley. Moosic fired a few shots that caused the thing to drop, then fled down the alley as fast as he could run. Sandoval was dead. He hoped Marx was not, but it hadn't been *his* doing. Let these black-clad maniacs and monsters sort it all out—he was heading back for the hotel, and fast.

The ancient city became suddenly a nightmarish place, a surreal horror whose shadows reached out and threatened him at every turn. Behind, and possibly from above him, he thought he heard the sounds of pursuit.

The hotel door was locked, of course, at this time of night, but he'd made certain he had a key, telling the proprietor earlier that he had a very late party. He fumbled in panic with the key, finally got it in and shut the door behind him. He almost ran up the stairs until he realized that he hadn't his room key, went back quickly and got it from behind the desk, then bounded up the stairs not caring whom he awakened. He unlocked the door and went immediately to the steamer trunk, where he'd locked the suit. Fumbling for yet another key in the darkness, he dropped it twice and had to calm himself down before he could find it again and fit it in the large brass lock.

A scratching sound caused him to turn towards the window, and in a split second he saw the horrible face of the second gargoyle framed in it, gun coming up. He picked up his own and fired, and the thing was gone. He didn't know if he'd hit it or not.

He kicked off his shoes and got into the suit, which fit his new frame rather well. Placing the gun so he could easily pick it up again, he put on the helmet as he heard noises and shouting both in the hall and outside. The noise had apparently roused half the town.

He got the helmet on and sealed it, then adjusted the small pentometers for across-the-board zeroes, then pressed "Activate."

Inside the helmet, a little message flashed saying, "Insufficient power."

He cursed. The dials still said ninety-five percent power reserve. That should be more than enough to get back home! He tried again, and again the little words flashed inside the suit.

He reached up to adjust them again, and at that moment another, perhaps the same, grinning black monstrosity showed in the window. He spun the damned controls and activated.

The creature got off a shot, but where its target had been, there was suddenly nothing at all but an empty room. Behind, there were loud yells and curses and somebody shouted, "Break the door down!"

The creature, looking very disgusted, vanished from the window just as the door came crashing in.

FLYING BLIND

The sensations of time traveling were becoming almost routine to him now, and even the process of merging and integrating yet another real person into him seemed almost beside the point. What seemed far more pressing was the problem that something more than the goals of the job had gone wrong at this point.

The suit should have brought him home with even ten percent power, possibly even less. Releasing the settings acted, or so they'd told him, almost like a rubber band released from its hold. The suit power was needed only to keep him alive and breathing until he reached the leading edge, or zero point. Why had the microprocessor refused to take him there? How could there be insufficient power with a fully charged suit?

And where could he find a mechanic?

After the dizzing effects of the merge had passed and he had calmed down enough to think clearly, he checked out the suit's instrumentation. Both Sandoval and Austin-Venneman were dead; their suits would no longer have anyone to guide on and would automatically return to their own source of power. Cline had destroyed the third suit, so he was the only one now traveling in time from the Calvert installation. That probably meant that he had a hundred percent of their generating energy, which supposedly could take somebody back as far as Columbus' time.

He checked his settings. He hadn't changed the setting on location, but it was more than probable that it had been knocked around, at least slightly. There would be some drift, but not a great deal. Certainly he should still be in Europe when he emerged—but when?

The central LEDs read 603.2 The very size of the number was a shock. How far had he turned the dials? And did he have enough power and air to reach that point? There was no turning back now—he had to ride it out. Once locked in, they were fixed until you arrived.

He had settled down now, resigned to a very long "trip," and was surprised to arrive in whenever it was within little more than two hours by the suit's relative time clock. He checked the air supply and saw that it was still at rather high levels—seventy-four percent full—while the power read eighty-two percent. It was not the drain he expected from such a journey, and he began to wonder if perhaps he had not gone back as far as the setting indicated. Both the set clock and the check clock agreed, though, reading 603.2. Nothing was making sense any more, or working out as they'd told him. That would make him now in the fourteenth century!

It was night—he was beginning to suspect that it always landed you in the middle of the night—and there was little that could be seen, no lights anywhere at all, nothing to get a bearing on. He remained in the suit for a bit and again carefully reset the dials, all of them, to zero, and attempted activation.

The suit said there was insufficient power for it.

What could have happened? Clearly, he could travel back and forth in time with it, until the air and power wore out, but there seemed no way to go home and he was flying blind, unable to determine a correct destination. *Was* there a correct destination anymore? he wondered.

Certainly, he needed some time to think things out, and this seemed as good or bad a place as any. He switched the suit to maintenance level, released the seals, and removed the helmet.

The air seemed fresh and clean, although a little cool for

what he had expected. The decimal in the readout, if that readout could be trusted, indicated two months from when he'd left Maryland—July. He got out of the suit, but found himself still in near total darkness. He walked around a bit to keep an air supply coming in, but did not want to wander far. He was afraid that if he got too far from the suit, he'd never find it again.

Once freed of the helmet, he found visibility much better, thanks to the light of a nearly full moon. He seemed to be in a mountain meadow of sorts, a bit high for trees but covered with grass and shrubs. Down in the valley far below, he *thought* he could make out a small village, although it might be a trick of the moonlight. The other way, a bit further up in the mountains, he thought he could make out a single large stone building with what looked like a steeple inside. At first he thought it was a castle, but then he decided that it looked more like a monastery. That suited him, to a degree. Being a friar in such a remote place might well give him the chance to sort things out.

The area didn't give him many places for concealment of the suit, but he managed to find a small crack in the rock wall that would fit it, then covered it with brush. It wasn't perfect, but the spot was so remote it was better odds than the rock pile in Trier that it would remain unspotted. The one thing that unsettled him was the fear that *he* might not be able to find the spot again. Using the moonlight to best advantage, he tried to memorize all of the reference points he could, particularly some uniquely formed peaks that seemed in the darkness to be the top of a giant cat's head.

Then he wandered a bit, both to breathe well and to protect himself against the chill of the altitude. Already he was thinking of the events in Trier, and the cool, blond man who'd intervened to stop him. Him and his monsters.

Clearly there were two sides from the future, two sides going back in time to try to change things to their advantage. But why had the blond fellow chosen to act through radicals of his, Moosic's, time? Perhaps, he thought, because it might lead the other side to believe that their enemy was not the cause of the change. Or perhaps it was because each side had some way of tracing the energy sustaining their own time equipment to the other's source of power. Surrogates would be less risky.

But why, when they'd failed, had they risked coming after him?

He was still pondering that question when the nausea hit, and he passed out.

It was a time of terror and schism for the Church. Much of the Catholic world was in revolt against the Pope throughout much of the century, particularly after the Papacy had moved to Avignon and become, in effect, an ally totally under the control of France and highly corrupt. Much of Italy was in revolt against the Papacy, and now the ultimate horror had happened, with Clement VII, backed by the College of Cardinals, pope in Avignon and Urban VI, elected earlier by that same College of Cardinals, pope in Rome. Each had excommunicated the other and the other's followers; each had a legitimate claim to the Papacy, since Urban had been elected under death threats by the Italians to any of the cardinals who did not choose a Rome-committed Italian, while Clement had been elected more or less freely.

Kings and mercenaries clashed over which was the true pope and true church; philosophers tied themselves in knots trying to sort it out. The increasingly fat and corrupt church—both of them—backed one side or the other that best preserved its own money, power, and prestige. In the midst of this, a devoted and disgusted nun lived in the little finger of Milan above Venice, a forgotten and ignored little area near the boundary with the Holy Roman Empire. Dismayed by the corruption and lack of leadership, and frustrated at being unable to either do anything about it or sort it out, she gathered like-minded nuns from throughout the region and led them to a monastery, one abandoned in the theological strife, that was high in the Alps. Convinced that one of the popes was the Antichrist, but unable to determine which one, she resolved to remain there, with her flock, praying and anticipating the Second Coming, which looked very likely.

More than a hundred and fifty women from several orders had followed her, and there were occasionally others drifting in as they heard about it and made their way there. There they established a convent that soon was quite heretical to both churches, but so minor and so understandable it was ignored. For their part, the scared and confused nuns, many of whom were run out of places like Florence by anti-clerical governments and mobs, became convinced that they were in the presence of a delivering saint. For her part, the new Mother Superior, who had been Sister Magdelana, more or less became convinced of that, too.

The theology of Holy Mount was simple, basic, and heretical in the extreme. No man, not even a priest, was permitted entry, for one could not be certain if the priest were of the true pope or the Antichrist. Magdelana convinced them that she had visions from the Virgin Mary herself establishing the place, and none who had come this far with her doubted her in the slightest. As they were all Brides of Christ, Christ Himself would say the Mass and administer the sacraments, through the body of the Mother Superior. All reaffirmed their vows of poverty, chastity, and absolute obedience. An additional vow of silence was imposed if not in the performance of religious duty or dire emergency. To cement them to the new order, they were also to renounce all worldly ties, including their names and their nationalities. They were a unit, a sisterhood; henceforth, there would be no individuals or individualism.

Thanks to some good salesmanship on the part of the Mother Superior with the nearest town, almost ten miles away—mostly down—they acquired a few cows and goats and a rather large number of sheep. The wool from the latter the sisters made into fine wool garments, and traded their products with the town on a seasonal basis. The town's lone parish priest, disgusted himself with the situation but allied in the heart with the Italian Urban, went along with them and helped them to a degree, thanks to the sponsorship of a local nobleman who had been caught up in the political and religious turmoil and who liked to think of his help as a thumbing of his nose at what had become of the Church. With his sponsorship, however slight, the nuns on Holy Mount were allowed their pious heresy and enough food and materials to get by.

The townsfolk, of course, were not told of the heresy, just the fact of the convent and the extreme otherworldliness of its occupants. When a local peasant gave the sisters some fruit as a gesture, and then his wife who'd borne him two daughters presented him with a son, word got around that these were holy folk indeed, ones that would bring God's blessing if helped.

It seemed as if she had always been on Holy Mount. Certainly she'd had a life before it, but it was a total blank in her mind. Only a scar, the remains of an old but serious burn, indicated that her past had at least terminated in violence which had driven it from her grasp. She had been brought to Holy Mount by those who knew of it and thought it the best place for her, but even that was just a hazy memory. Certainly, she had been a nun, for she retained that much as her identity and knew the prayers and rituals.

It was strange for Ron Moosic to recognize brainwashing and understand the nature of a cult even as he was a part of it. Far stranger than being a woman. He had wondered how Sandoval had adjusted back in London, but now he understood that it was just like the gay Neumann in Trier. One was what one was, and had the knowledge and intimacy that being raised female brought. Even with the amnesia, the result possibly of some war or being caught in some terrible fire, it was *natural* and *normal* to feel your body this way, and to know and accept and cope with the periodic cycles of the body.

The routine was simple and automatic. Up before dawn from your straw bed in the tiny monastic cell, don the simple woolen habit, then make your way up to the chapel for morning services, which were always the same. Then down to the kitchen, for her, to knead the dough and bake the simple bread that would be part of the breakfast meal. The kitchen was a horror by twentieth-century standards, but familiar and normal to her. She felt a familiarity as close as to any family member with the others helping her in the kitchen, each doing her own tasks. She felt no boredom at the tasks, for prayer was joy, and she was mentally reciting prayers constantly, over and over, in her mind, while her hands did the work automatically. All except the sounds of the crackling fire and the clatter of pots and pans was silence.

So unvarying was the routine and the work that there was an almost telepathic bond between them, and even when more than one pair of hands was required the other always knew and was there to do it right.

She looked into those smiling faces and knew that she loved them as much as humans could love other humans, that they were one in total love and harmony. Their minds and hearts were with each other and with God; the rest of the world simply did not exist.

The power of this total and absolute emotional commitment was beyond Moosic's power to fight, for even if he exerted his will, he would stand out and call attention to himself. The more the sister sensed his worry, fear, and confusion, the greater and more powerful was the assault on his own psyche. Unlike the first two times, he found himself quickly swallowed up and dominated by the pure fanatical power of this host personality.

After breakfast there was cleanup, and then several hours of intensive communal, repetitious prayer. Others then served a communal midday meal that was more of a snack, a hot porridge of lumpy consistency and the taste of bad library paste.

The afternoons were her favorite time, spent looking after the sheep that grazed all over the meadow. This, of course, was also a time for prayer and glorifying God, but at least it was outside the walls and the view was tremendous.

He realized that the woman, all the women, had effectively ceased to think at all, but were, rather, some gloriously happy automatons full of tremendous, overpowering emotion. Although he might want to do something different or think of something different, the social pressure from those around her prevented him from any sort of deviation. Deep inside her mind, he found that deviation was the one thing to be feared—and the one thing not to be tolerated. The punishment was so painful that one eventually no longer even wished to deviate.

The Mother Superior was clearly centuries ahead of her time.

Evenings for her were spent cleaning the interior of the place. Although a pigsty by modern standards, they kept it as clean and as neat as was possible under the circumstances.

There were even prescribed times to use the pit-type toilets that emptied into a small stream below. Bladder control was considered a part of the test of faith and endurance.

Finally, after fourteen hours of prayer and hard work, there was an evening meal that was hardly much but was elaborate by the standards of the others, another service, and then, finally, to bed, where she was so dead-tired there was no time to think or reflect before sleep.

The more pressure Ron Moosic put on her to get some control, the more counterpressure was applied on him. At the end of a mere five days, he, too, found it difficult to think at all, and he knew intellectually that the longer this went on, the less he'd be able to fight it.

But Thursday was to be a feast day, and that meant someone had to be sent down to the village to fetch back from the town the makings for the feast. This was known from the morning service. Volunteers were requested, and no one really wanted to volunteer, to leave this cocoon even for a day.

No one except Ron Moosic, that is.

When she went forward to the Mother Superior, another sister, a thin, mousy little woman with strong Italian features, went with her. Two would be enough.

They knew what was expected of them, of course. They would hitch the two mules to the cart and drive it down the steep mountain slope to the village. There, at the small market, they would get what the villagers were willing to donate, and be gone. It would be an all-day journey, and they would not return before dark.

The road was long, winding, and narrow, and Moosic strained to spot the meadow in which he'd hidden the time suit, but things looked different in the light of day and nothing looked really familiar. Still, finally out of the automatics and the prison of the convent, he managed to get some time to think on his own.

He had to get away, get to the suit and away from this time, place, and existence, he knew—and quickly. Still, there was little chance to do much on the way down.

Her companion kept the silence admirably, but it wasn't until they stopped for a while to give the mules a rest and snack on the bread loaf they'd brought along that she saw why. The other nun, it appeared at least, had little or no tongue. It seemed that way, anyway.

It was sobering to Moosic. That's what you get for breaking *that* vow.

The village itself was a tiny, ramshackle affair that showed its poverty and its primitiveness in every glance. Chickens ran down the lone street, and there was the smell of human and animal excrement everywhere.

The man who seemed to be in charge of the tiny outdoor market in front of the church looked more German than Italian, which was to be expected in this area. The language was harsh and barely understandable at all to her ears, but the people were emotional, seemed genuinely pleased to see them, and extended them every courtesy. They responded with smiles and signed blessings, which seemed to be payment enough.

The sister who came with her began acting a bit strange, though, as they went through the assigned tasks. Although the village was tiny and quite poor, even by the standards of the day, it seemed to awaken in the other long-suppressed memories. The sight of fruit, and even some wines, seemed to draw her, but it was the simple *normalcy* of the place that was the real kicker. It was certainly a far cry from the gloom-and-doom, end-of-the-world scenarios painted in the services. The implications of the simple village were strong indeed, and questioned the dogma upon which the convent was based.

Surely, Moosic thought, the Mother Superior must have suspected that this was a potential rebel before sending her down. Why do it? As a test of faith and loyalty? It was possible, of course, but more likely the girl was expected to run away. The only thing standing between the other and some measure of freedom was—her companion. Did the Mother Superior suspect two rebels, and decide to try and get rid of them? But that, too, hardly made sense, since she in whose body Moosic was trapped was totally committed and, with her amnesia, truly had no place else to go. She expected that one was to run away, the other to bring back the food.

Thus, it was with some surprise that, with the cart fully loaded, the tongueless one climbed meekly back aboard and they set out again for the distant mountain lair. They had spent more time than they should have in the village, but it was impossible to fend off the townspeople and not give them their blessings, particularly so with a vow of silence.

They were only a bit more than halfway back at dusk, and they soon had to stop on the steep and winding trail to wait for the rising of the moon. They had no flintstone to make a torch to lead the way, so they just had to wait.

They unhitched the mules to let them graze, and Moosic, at least, took the opportunity to lie down in the tall grass. She was tired, and grateful to God for the opportunity to have some extra rest. Tomorrow, back at Holy Mount, it would start all over again.

She was startled first by a strange noise that grew increasingly close and which Moosic's mind identified as electronic. She sat bolt upright. *Electronic? In this day and age?*

Suddenly one of the mules brayed a protest, and she heard the noise like someone was over there. The moon was not yet up, but her eyes were accustomed enough to the darkness to see a shape trying to mount one of the animals. Her first thought was thieves, but suddenly two larger, hulking shapes rose up out of the darkness on either side. The rider saw them and screamed a horrible, deep scream and kicked the mule fiercely.

Moosic knew those shapes now, particularly as one adjusted something on what seemed to be a belt and then soared into the air after the fugitive nun. The other stood and watched for a while, then went over to the cart and started examining the contents. Moosic crept slowly towards the figure, getting as close as she dared. Her time-frame personality identified the creature as a demon from Hell, and it was entirely possible that it wasn't too far off the mark. Whatever future had spawned these creatures was certainly no earthly paradise.

The gargoyle found food in the cart, and after a quick glance in the direction his companion had gone, it put down its rifle and picked up an apple.

Now the sister understood for the first time why God

had placed the unhappy soul in her head to accompany her. Some soul had been plucked from the tortures of Purgatory to give her the knowledge and strength to meet the demonic threat.

There was no time to get the best angle, for the creature's companion could return any moment now. With a silent and fervent prayer to God from the both of them, she ran, rolled, came up with the rifle, and as the thing dropped its apple and roared, she fired, holding down the trigger.

Tiny little tracer balls leaped out and struck the thing in the chest. It fell backwards against the cart, screaming in agony, twitched for a moment, then died.

Moosic wasted no time. The noise, if nothing else, would certainly bring the companion back, and this time they wouldn't be so lucky. The creature had come to rest on its side, and she saw the belt and clasp securing the time mechanism and undid it.

It was tough for the slight girl to roll the thing over, particularly with it oozing blood and body parts, but Moosic saw his chance and, through sheer will to survive, beat back his saintly host.

It was far too large for her, of course, but the straps bracing it allowed it to be worn by almost anyone. She saw with panic that one shot had struck off the top of the mechanism, burning a deep groove in it, but the rest of the lights and symbols were still on. She twisted the dials at random, just wanting to be anywhere and anywhen from here. Nothing happened, and, off to one side, she heard a *whooshing* noise nearby and the sound of a heavy object landing. That was enough. She just started pushing everything on the belt.

There was the sensation of falling a great distance very fast through near-total darkness. It was quite different than the sensations of the time suit, but Moosic was only dimly aware of the comparison. He seemed frozen, immobile, not even breathing.

Suddenly she suffered a drop of several inches and came down hard on rocky ground. It was still night, but the scene had changed dramatically. There was a paved stone road off to one side, and off in the immediate distance was the unmistakable glow and skyline of a low city.

Moosic relaxed a bit and was surprised to find that he was still in the body of Sister Nobody, and that she was still very much with him, although too scared and in awe of anything to give even a peep of protest.

The refined time mechanism, then, was far more versatile than the suit. No air supply was needed, and it apparently wrapped the body in some sort of energy shell to protect it. Arrival, too, had been different. This was not any frozen tableau, but a moving city. Time was progressing at its normal rate, yet the time traveler was unchanged.

Again Moosic remembered the woman in London. It took a great deal of energy, she said, to maintain someone without assimilation. So it was not only possible; it was done all the time—the woman had done it, as Blondie had done it in Trier, and those creatures, whatever they were, also did it.

Those creatures. . . . How had they found him back in that randomly selected time and place? And, more important, *why?*

He remembered the noise, the electronic noise, earlier. They had been using some sort of device to sort him out among all the others. It wasn't perfect—when the other one had run off, they'd naturally assumed *she* was he—but it was close enough.

Energy bands. One led from the suit to the power source, but another had to lead from the suit to the traveler who came with it. Power was needed not only for travel, they'd said, but to maintain yourself against assimilation. Somehow, the body of Sister Nobody was not quite like all the others of her time. Some little part of it was . . . out of phase? As good a term as any. But what good was Ron

Moosic to them? Certainly, he hadn't mattered much in the square at Trier until. . . .

Until everything had gotten so fouled up.

"*I recharged your suit*," she'd said. But how? Not with the folks back at Calvert, that was for sure. She'd done more than recharge it—she'd changed its power source from Silverberg's crew to her own!

That explained a lot. His assumption since Trier had been that two groups were fighting a war against each other in time. If they both had devices to scan the time stream and find anomalies—unassimilated people—they would be targets for the other once they took off their belts. Hence, all this business with contacting Sandoval and his people and getting *them* in position to do the dirty work. Early time-travel experiments would tend to be ignored or discounted by the monitors even when discovered.

Why hadn't concealed time suits, belts, whatever, ever been discovered? It had to be because they *couldn't* be discovered. Perhaps they were only real, only tangible, to people out of phase with the time frame. Maybe *that* was why you got assimilated after a certain point! After that point, you were in phase with your time frame, and so no longer could access the suit.

Not being in phase, the time suits couldn't be adequately tracked or pinpointed by their sensors—but slightly out-of-phase people could. That would mean that they weren't really after *him* at all—they were after his time suit! A suit which now was linked to their enemy's power supply. With it, perhaps, they could track down that power supply, send an army of these gargoyles to it, and destroy it. Time would be left at the mercy of the other side.

He was sure he had it right, as far as it could be taken, but that didn't help; it only raised more unpleasant possibilities. He had on one of the enemy's time belts. They could turn it off or bring him back involuntarily, as soon as they knew it—and if they didn't know it already, they soon would. The longer he wore it, the greater the possibility that they would do so—or worse, since with their devices they would know exactly when and where he was. Even Silverberg could do that.

There was no question in his mind that he had to get rid of it, to take his chances in this new time and place no matter what. He would then appear on the sensors of both sides, and they might well come after him—but at least it would be even odds.

Unhesitatingly, he unloosed the straps and let the belt fall to the ground, then stepped over it.

He was hit almost instantly by the nausea and dizziness, and passed out in less than a minute.

Time continued to play its sick sense of humor upon him, and his luck continued to be really bad. Now, at last, he knew he was trapped for good. After several tries, time at last had killed him in its sardonic way.

At least, this time, he had no worries about assimilation. He would not last that long.

Even without the elaborate and sad past of Marcus Josephus, he would have known that this was the end.

They were roused once more by the Roman soldiers and lined up. They were not fed, as usual, and the lack of both food and water was taking its own toll on the prisoners. It made for some will power, some extra strength on the part of those for whom hope never fled, for the ones that collapsed or could not go on in the chains they wore were the first.

It had been but two weeks since the final battle, the one they had so decisively lost, and now they walked, thousands of them in a line six across, down the Appian Way, guarded by two combined Roman legions. The men who had defeated them this last time were curiously merciful, even sympathetic. They did not goad or harm, and some even occasionally would offer a marcher a sip of water or a crust of bread in defiance of orders. It wasn't just that they respected their fallen foe for a battle well fought or that they felt the merciless punishment for rebellion was too terrible, although clearly many did. Six thousand prisoners, although starving men, women, and children, could still be formidable death-dealers, should they be goaded into a last suicidal attempt.

The crosses had begun at Capua, at the start of the Appian Way. They now stretched out behind them as far as the eye could see, but there was no hurry. It was still quite a ways to Rome, and the column of the condemned was still huge. He was a young and strong man, and near the end of the line of marchers. He might have three or four days yet, before it was his turn.

Like his host, Ron Moosic felt now a totally defeated man, one who no longer had anything left to fight for or live for. He had precipitated the death of a great man, possibly altering history far more drastically than if he had not gone back at all. For that, he had been cast adrift, flying blindly backwards in time, pursued not because he was of any value, but because he alone knew the location of a time suit that held a possible key to victory in a war being fought by two groups he did not know over things he could not know.

He considered ending it quickly, but knew he could not. Where life remained in him, he had to cling to it, no matter how terrible the end might be.

It was sickening to march slowly past that endless line of crosses. He almost had to wonder where the Romans had found enough wood for them. Wood and nails. For these were not routine crucifixions, where one was strapped on and left to slowly starve or die of shock and exposure. The army could not afford to tie up so many men to guard such a line. If the nails, and wood, held out, all, even the women and children among them, were to be nailed on, their cries and screams of pain and pleas for mercy so commonplace now that his senses were dulled to them.

Had they known this would be the result, they would have fought to the last, every one of them, but who could ever have imagined that a civilized society would order this terrible death for *six thousand people?*

But the Spartican Rebellion was more than a simple revolt or war; it was, in fact, a threat to the slave basis of that very system. Six thousand who could never again be trusted, who had Roman blood on their hands, would be sacrificed in order to set an example, to reassure the citizenry and to so terrify the slaves that it would not happen again.

In fact, it took four days before they got to him, and even then he had a feeling of unreality about it. They grabbed him, and when he fought, they knocked him half unconscious with clubs. Then they strapped him to the cross on the ground, and in rapid fashion drove the nails in his wrists, waist, and legs. They were fast and professional; they had been getting a lot of practice.

The terrible pain of the nails was nothing to the pain felt when the cross was raised and gravity tugged on his body. Shock quickly set in, not ending the pain but somehow making it bearable. He still passed out, and came to only intermittently. He was no longer rational or wholly able to see or concentrate, and he knew he was slipping fast. Some of them lingered on for days, but he knew he would not be one of them.

Lord God, I will be with you tonight, if the time maniacs have not killed you as well, he thought. *It would take a squad of Marines to get me out of this now.*

THE TIME HAS COME, THE WALRUS SAID, TO SPEAK OF MANY THINGS

The squad of Marines landed just off the Appian Way, and quickly they took up positions. There were eleven of them, clad in boots and camouflage uniforms, but they were not the Marines Ron Moosic was used to, nor were their weapons and belts standard issue.

The Romans had posted guards every twenty crosses, mostly in order to make sure that none were freed before death overtook them, for all the good rescue would do. The shock, loss of blood, and crushed bones would make them useless, and perhaps hopeless, in any case.

The squad spread out, each taking the five guards closest to either side of Moosic, while the eleventh stood poised, waiting for a clear path. On a signal transmitted to each member of the squad, they fired as one, their rifles issuing brief bursts of light. As they struck the guards, those guards went down; then each advanced to the guard's previous position and assumed it. There were few torches along the Appian way at this point, and it was hoped that the Romans nearest to the fallen guards would simply see a figure there in the dusk. It wouldn't have to be for long.

Waiting a couple of minutes to make certain they had not been discovered, and prepared for a display of firepower if they were, they relaxed and all but the outermost guard replacements moved in to aid the leader, who was already at Moosic's cross. Quickly they lifted it up, then gently lowered it to the ground. Moosic had passed out by that time and had seen none of this.

The leader, a huge, fat man with Oriental features who resembled a Sumo wrestler, whispered, "Doc—check on him. Are we in time?"

Another figure approached and ran a few checks with some portable instruments, then nodded. "Barely," she told him. "No way we're going to risk taking him down, though. Get this spare belt around him and I'll program it. He hasn't reached a trip point yet, so I think we can get him back to the base as his original self."

Quickly they strapped the belt around him, and around the cross as well. He groaned lightly, but otherwise remained unaware of the activity.

"Hurry!" somebody else whispered. "Those guards will be coming to in a couple of minutes!"

Doc nodded. "All set. Chung, you sound recall. I'll set his and mine for the same point. Let's move! He can die on us at any moment!"

Chung, the huge leader, unhooked a small wireless microphone from his time belt. "Recall to Base. Ten seconds, everybody. Acknowledge!"

As the acknowledgments were still coming in, Doc reached over and with one hand tripped Moosic's belt, and with the other her own.

Both vanished into time.

Ron Moosic awoke slowly, as if from a very bad dream. He lay there for a while, confused and disoriented, as strange sounds around him began to resolve themselves into voices.

"Shock is as much mental as physical," Doc told a couple of worried-looking young men in the small base hospital. "He'll be O.K., as we know, but don't expect an immediate recovery. We were very lucky with him, I can tell you."

Moosic understood none of the words, not because of

his condition but because they were spoken in a language he did not understand. Still, he recognized the language as real, opened his eyes, and groaned.

Standing near him was a white-clad woman who was rather tall and dark-complected, sort of Polynesian in appearance, with dark brown eyes and jet black hair cut very short. The two others with her were both men: one was dressed in a camouflage uniform and appeared almost too large to fit through any known door; the other, a light-skinned black man with strong Negroid features, was dressed in a one-piece outfit of black leather-like material. Even so, he looked like everybody's vision of a military drill instructor.

The white-clad woman saw that he was awake, turned to him, and smiled down at him. She had a very nice smile. "Glad to have you back among the living. I am Kahwalini, generally known to everyone as Doc. That way they don't have to remember how the name is pronounced." She had excellent command of English, but her accent was strange, like no other he had ever heard before.

"Ron Moosic," he croaked. "I take it I'm not dead?"

She laughed. "No, you're not dead, although it was a very close thing. Minutes, perhaps."

He realized with a start that he *was* Ron Moosic—real and in the flesh. But, somewhere in his mind, he also knew that he was a little bit of Alfie Jenkins, and Holger Neumann, and Sister Nobody, and, yes, Marcus Josephus as well. He could still feel the pain of the nails and the agony of the cross, and a little part of him, certainly the Sister, seemed to take some perverse satisfaction in that.

"Where—when—am I?" he managed, and tried to sit up. He felt instantly weak and dizzy and settled back down.

"Don't try to move for a little bit yet," the doctor warned him. "You have had a great shock, and it will take some small time to convince your body that it is not the one which suffered. As to where you are, we call it simply

Home Base, although it has many names. As to when—well, that is something even *we* aren't certain about. Some period after the age of dinosaurs but before the domination of mammals, although mammals there are around this place."

In the prehistoric past, even before the appearance of apelike beings, he thought wonderingly.

"The very large gentleman over there is Commander Chung Lind," Doc told him. "The other just calls himself Herb."

"Herbert Axton Wethers," Herb added, "for all the good that does now. Me and a hundred other folks." His accent was as strange as Kahwalini's, but totally different.

"You don't have a tall, rough-looking blond fellow with you, do you?" Moosic asked hesitantly.

Chung Lind laughed. "Hardly. That'd be Eric. Him and we don't get along very well." A third accent, equally odd, equally unique. Now that he thought of it, the woman in London and Blondie had both had such accents as well.

"What about a short, chubby woman with short black hair?"

Kahwalini's eyebrows rose slightly. "Yes, she's here. You'll meet her and the others soon. Right now you need sleep most of all. You two—get out of here! I'm going to let him rest."

"But I don't want—" Moosic started, but he saw he'd been too slow to win this battle. It wasn't exactly a needle, but it hissed slightly against his arm and stung for just a second, and he began feeling very groggy in a matter of seconds.

It was a deep and apparently dreamless sleep, and when he awoke, he felt much, much better. He looked to see if he was attached to anything—IV tubes or the like—and, finding nothing, he sat up. He was still a little dizzy, but otherwise he felt pretty good.

The door slid aside with a hissing sound and Kahwalini entered, this time dressed in the basic black outfit that seemed the standard around here—wherever "here" really was.

"Glad to see you're looking good," she said cheerily. "How do you feel?"

"A little dizzy, and hungry enough to eat a horse."

"Excellent! The dizziness, I think, will pass, and will be helped by a meal." She opened a small cabinet and took out a package, then unwrapped something and offered it to him. "Here—eat this. It's a sort of candy-and-cake roll, lots of sugar and not much else, but it should help until I've finished my examination and we can get you some real food."

The examination seemed like a normal general exam—stethoscope on the chest, a look at the throat, eyes, ears, and such—but it also included placing two small instruments on him, one on his forehead, then another on his back. She checked both and nodded to herself. "Looking good," she told him. "I think you're fit enough to join the rest of the human race, such as it is in this day and time."

The confection had helped a lot, although he was still thirsty and starved for more food. She got him a black suit of their standard issue, and he was surprised to find how well it fit when he put it on. It was, in fact, a two-piece affair, top and bottom, but he discovered that when he ran his index finger along the seam, it essentially vanished. "Good trick," he told her.

"There's a fly like that in yours, too," she told him. "To open, simply press where you want the slit to start and continue down, keeping your finger on the material until it is open enough. Reverse the process to close."

"This is not exactly one-million-B.C. technology," he noted.

The boots were less impressive, being almost exactly the same as the pairs he'd worn in the Air Force. They were, however, without laces, and he found that you sealed them like you did the suit. Finally, she gave him a black belt with a small, and empty, leather-like pouch on it. The buckle, of flat black metal, was disappointing—it was a simple clasp type with no special features.

"You'll find the pouch useful, since you have no pockets," she told him.

"No underwear, either," he noted, seeing every shapely part of her anatomy. He looked down and found that it worked both ways.

"We wear whatever is needed, no more. Most of so-called Western civilization overdressed to death, even in the tropics."

He couldn't argue with that.

They assigned him a small, comfortable apartment in the complex and got him a good meal—the meat was apparently synthetic, but tasted very good, while all the rest was organically grown on the base—and then took him down to meet the others, answer questions, and show off the base.

There were a total of twelve members in the squad, which was all they ever called themselves. They were, in fact, the only humans on the base or, as far as they knew, in the time frame, except for himself, although the place could accommodate about a hundred people, if pressed.

"The whole place is automated," Doc told him. "In fact, much of the complex is a large, totally sealed computer. It's the computer that keeps watch on the time stream, charting its phases and changes, and dispatches some or all of us."

He nodded. "But why back this far in time? I would have thought that you would put this in your present."

"*Our*—oh. I should explain. None of us are from the time of the builders. We're all just like you—nightsiders originally from the other times. You *are* the earliest, I think, but we recruit from those who go nightside. The amount of power required for time travel is enormous. To do it the way we do, the power complex here could power your world for a year all by itself."

He was shocked. "You mean you have never seen who you work for?"

She shook her head negatively. "None of us. Oh, as nightsiders, we could travel all the way to the leading edge, but that wouldn't do us any good." Several others joined in the conversation, and at last he was given a picture of just what was going on.

The leading edge was a little well over two hundred years in the future of his time. On the main line, atomic war was averted in a most terrible way, when two small countries went at each other with nuclear weapons. The results were a glaring case study of what a nuclear war would really be like, and the climatic changes caused by even the limited exchange were dramatic for many years. The larger nations did not rush to disarm, but they were clearly frightened. Together, they took steps to stamp out nuclear weapons and control such materials, no matter what the cost to smaller countries.

Seeing the results but still not convinced an all-out holocaust could be avoided, both East and West turned their energies to space, both as a diversion and because, both sides felt, the establishment of a true human permanence in space would guarantee the survival of humanity in the future. This, in fact, was the case, but the results were not at all what they expected.

Terraforming Mars, for example, was very possible, but also very lengthy—the time involved being at least several centuries. Other places in space that would be self-sufficient and require no Earth support were even less hospitable. So, instead of risking the time that it would take to radically change those places, they changed the people themselves. There was no shortage of volunteers, which surprised them, but between those who felt it was the only salvation of the human race and the romantics, the dreamers, the scientists, and, indeed, the down-and-out looking for a new start, it was irresistible.

By the time of the leading edge, colonies had been

established not only on Mars but also on some of the distant moons of the gas giants and on asteroids. Expensive terraforming was done, but it was bargain-basement by comparison and short- rather than long-term oriented. The people, by a process they didn't know, were altered to fit what the engineers could create.

The dividends were enormous beyond the salvation of humanity. New ways to find and use energy, and new sources of it, were discovered and even created by those who became known collectively as the Outworlders. They also bred new generations true to their mutated forms, and those new generations made new discoveries. But there was a great push on Earth now for large masses of people who wanted to undergo the processes and live as Outworlders. Many who were sent were political dissidents or criminals; other places used the new colonies, which had fragile ecosystems able to support only limited numbers, as population control valves.

Ultimately, the Outworlders faced the historic choice that all colonies eventually face. They could continue to supply the rapidly resource-depleted Earth with all it needed, while getting little in return, and continue to absorb new groups of people, many of them undesirables, until finally their ecosystems would collapse, unable to support the vast bulk of people and Earth's requirements—or they could quit.

Soviet, Chinese, Japanese, European, and American the Outworlders had been, and culturally they continued for a while as these groups. But transport interdependence and their alienness from Earth's race which had spawned them drove them ever closer together, no longer as echoes of Earth nations but as Outworlders. Political control was difficult anyway, since even the controllers had to become Outworlders.

Eventually there was a revolt. The Confederation of Outworlders was proclaimed, an association of free and independent races with a common military force. They took many of the spaceships of Earth, and revealed that they had many more of their own.

Earth did not take it easily, for they'd come to depend on the Outworlds for much of their resources and technology. For the first time, countries always hostile to one another put aside their differences and pooled their resources to mount a fleet to wrest control from the still weak Outworlders while they still could.

The Outworlders struck quickly, destroying the vulnerable orbital power stations and spaceship relays, where transfers were made from Earth to Orbit shuttles to deep space vessels. The installations on the moon were overrun or destroyed.

In the political backwash of this action, and as the standard of living for Earth's vast population dropped like a stone from this cutoff, governments fell and the semi-combined military forces stepped in. The Earth came quickly under a ruthless worldwide military dictatorship formed from the officers of the multinational force. There was no nuclear war, for the very people on both sides who would have to ultimately fire the warheads refused to act—except against those who refused their rule.

The military men may not have liked each other, but they understood that the future of Earth depended on retaking the Outworlds at all costs. National and even ideological disputes could wait, for they were of no consquence.

If humanity in the twentieth century had suddenly lost all use of electrical devices, all civilizations would have fallen and much of the world would have died as surely as it would by nuclear bomb. Their ancestors had gotten along without it, but they had grown up without it and in an economy and culture that had never had it. The knowledge of how to survive in a society without such power had essentially been lost.

In the twenty-third century, this had been taken a step further. The economics and very survival of human civilization depended on what the Outworlds produced and managed. Without the orbital power satellites, without the minerals and miracles of space production, the basis of civilization could not stand. There could be merely a holding action.

The Outworlds, too, understood this, but had expected to come to terms after presenting Earth with a *fait accompli*. They had not expected, however, to be dealing with a massive multinational military complex, but with the old political leaders they were accustomed to. They had struck too hard and too well.

The military ruthlessly stamped out all opposition, killing millions in the process. Their technological base was dwindling, but hardly exhausted, and they used all they had in the single effort to get back out there at all costs. The Earth became effectively a slave labor camp dedicated to the one goal of retaking space.

The Outworlds, stunned by this, realized that only a massive military defeat would insure their future. Ironically, they also found themselves fighting to free Earth from a form of oppression no past dictator had ever dreamed possible. They had the high ground, and could bombard the Earth almost at will, although the Earth had formidable defenses and took her toll. Still, Earth's position was hopeless until some formerly Soviet generals happened on the American time-machine project.

The project, in fact, had been shut down for years for lack of funds, but the great store of knowledge was intact, and many of the laws and limitations of time had been worked out. A theoretical plan for the defense of Earth from a possible time war was uncovered.

It had been discovered through instrumentation and unmanned probes that beyond the dawn of human civilization time was far more tolerant. With sufficient power, a computer could be placed far back in time, perhaps to its origins, with no true link to the leading edge at all. With a supporting self-generating power supply, it could monitor time forward, with all its changes, and power at least a small force of time-traveling agents. If need be, much of its output could be diverted in the event of a complete collapse or nuclear war to take the leadership and selected others all the way back to the complex. A few hundred, no more, but it was another way to perhaps preserve humanity, which could then wait it out until enough relative time had elapsed, the leading edge advancing a few centuries, to return to a future Earth in the process of righting itself or finding a new balance.

Such a computer *had* been sent back, in the golden days of limitless Outworlder power. It could be accessed.

"Then this is that station," Moosic said wonderingly. "And those things I called gargoyles—Outworlders?"

They looked shocked. "Oh, no," Lind responded. "This is the base the Outworlders built to counter the time threat. The gargoyles, as you call them, are the products of the same process that created the Outworlders, but changed to produce the perfect soldier—dumb, totally obedient, very tough and strong. This is the Outworlder base, and we're the enemies of Earth."

A bit later in the afternoon, he met the woman again. She'd not been there for the initial bull session, and he'd been too curious to inquire, but now that she'd come in from wherever she'd been, he had the feeling she was avoiding direct contact. He dismissed that as crazy and went over to her.

"Hi! I finally get the chance to say thanks for saving my life," he said cheerfully, sitting down in a chair opposite hers. "How's that for a good opening line?"

She smiled, but there seemed to be a lot of thinking going on behind those dark eyes. She seemed much younger than he'd remembered her, but, then, he'd been drugged and the light had been poor, and Alfie had a different perspective of what old meant. She sighed, and seemed to decide whatever it was that was troubling her, or at least she put it off for a time. "I'm sorry for not being a little more hospitable," she responded. "I'm afraid I've got a load on my mind and a lot of hard decisions to make. I've just had a nasty personal shock."

"Try being crucified," he suggested, surprised he could make light of it so soon.

"I have. It's not very nice. Not much *has* been nice lately."

He shrugged, a bit disconcerted by the answer, and made as if to leave. "I don't want to intrude on what's none of my business."

"No, no. Stay, please. I'm still a little new at this myself, and it's pretty hard to get used to. As soon as you think you've found out everything, you find you don't understand anything at all. This whole business of time is the craziest thing you can think of. Just think of this, for starters—neither of us is a real person."

"Huh? We both look pretty solid to me."

"Maybe. But we're nightsiders. We have no existence outside of this base, outside of the Safe Zone—the time before people. Neither of us has a home to go to anymore."

He considered that a moment. "I imagine I still do—if I could ever get back to my own time."

She shook her head. "They haven't told you yet. Go ask Doc or Herb. I think I understand it, but they'll explain it better than me."

He excused himself and found Herb, who told him. Karl Marx had now been killed in 1841, at twenty-three years of age, before he'd even formed any of his ideas, let alone committed them to paper. Thus, the potential theoretician of the Communist movement had also been killed. Without him, competing theories dominated, particularly Bakunism, which is essentially anarchy. The theories of the left remained classical rather than radical. Because there was no Marx, there was no Marxism to inspire Lenin and Trotsky. Instead, they drifted into the more radical anarchy of Bakunin, and went nowhere. Because there was no Lenin and Trotsky there to take firm control, the Russians, when they overthrew the Czar, remained a weak social democracy.

"Because it was a weak democracy dominated by liberal nobles, it did little to really better or modernize the Russian nation," Herb continued. "Stalin did not rise to power and ruthlessly modernize, mobilize, and arm the nation, building it into a twentieth-century country. There was also an independent Ukraine, so Russia did not have control of its breadbasket or a firm buffer. But Germany still lost World War I, and Hitler still rose to power, only this time there was no strong Soviet state under a firm leader to hold on." Moosic was reminded that on his own time line Russia nearly lost the war to Germany again: Now it *had* lost, allowing Germany to put its full might into North Africa and against England. "With the collapse of England," Herb informed him, "America turned its full attention to the Japanese."

He blanched. "You mean—because Joseph Stalin *didn't* come to power, the U.S. lost World War II?"

"Oh, no. It finally won, the same way it had won the original one—at least, I *think* it was the original one. I'll have to ask the computer sometime. But an untouched German Empire, stretching from all of Europe into all of the Saharan regions and across to the Urals, was able to do what America did. *They* had the bomb, too. Fortunately, Hitler died, they tell me, in 1947, before delivery systems were perfected. The hierarchy that followed him wanted to consolidate its empire, and so an informal peace was struck, dividing the world in much the same way as the pope had back in Columbus' time. They have Europe, the Middle East, much of Africa, and Russia. The U.S. has a Chinese ally—no Mao, remember—that is weak but which it supports, as well as southern Asia and the Pacific, and most of Latin America is under its thumb."

He left Herb, his mind reeling from the magnitude of the deed. And yet, somehow, the world had come out pretty much the same, only more messed up than ever. He rejoined the mystery woman. "I see what you mean about complicated. And your original present isn't there, either?"

She shrugged. "No, not really. It doesn't mean anything to me anymore, anyway. I can't even remember it too well, and I don't think I want to. What's the difference? I mean, you feel bad about that guy Marx, right?"

"Yes, I do."

"Well, forget it. Eric and his things were out to kill Marx all the time. They don't know why, since the end came out pretty much the same in any case. Time jokes abound even with the big things."

He was thunderstruck. "What do you mean, 'they were out to kill Marx all the time'?"

"Not at the start. At least, they don't think so. The first trip was more of a test. I doubt if that fellow—" she halted, as if trying to remember something.

"Sandoval?"

She nodded. "Yeah, Sandoval. They don't think *he* knew this. But, you see, if they just went back and did it, *we* could go back and undo it. We would be able to spot just where and when they showed up, like they did with you, then go back to a point just before that. But that time is pretty crowded for the Outworlders. Almost all of the team has been somewhere in that time period, and not anywhere in Germany."

"I see. So, if Lind, say, went back, he'd be in America someplace, taking up the life he'd lived when he was there before."

She nodded. "That's where they have it all over us. They can take their creatures and come into a time for just an hour or so, staying who they are. That's about the limit before you become somebody else regardless. Since they can use their creatures for this, they don't have to worry about becoming somebody else the way we do. They *make* the damned things, any of which can be sent back for an hour or so. They breed them in tanks somewhere back here in the Safe Zone, or so it's said."

"Blondie was real."

"Eric, they call him. He has a lot of names, but that's the one they use the most. Somebody has to direct those things. But we don't know if he has ever stayed more than an hour in any time frame. We know nothing about him, except that he is the leader of the enemy's time project."

"So they put Sandoval and Marx together in the square, materialize just before the fateful meeting, and if I hadn't acted, *they* would have shot him, having him in the right time and place so they could go to the very spot."

She nodded. "It was the only way to be sure, since so much of Marx's early life isn't really known."

A funny thought struck him. "They said Soviet generals rediscovered the time project. The idea of Soviet officers ordering the death of Marx and a German victory over Russia just doesn't ring true."

"No, it doesn't," Herb put in, coming over and joining the conversation. "They would never allow such a thing. That's what makes Eric so fascinating. He's the wild card in the game. *They* trusted him, and he double-crossed them as well, although there are no consequences, of course, because there now never were any Soviet generals. We don't know what kind of game he's playing, but it's one to win, that's for sure. Win for Earth and win for him, too. I suspect, at the expense of his bosses." He paused a moment. "Um, I see you two have met."

He looked over at the woman. "I still don't know your name," he pointed out.

"When you've nightsided past your trip point, you may as well pick any name," she told him. "I call myself Dawn, because it's a new start and I kind of like the sound of it. I have lots of other names, but they don't mean nothing to me anymore."

He liked her, felt a strange attraction for her, although he couldn't really say why. She reminded him of a lot of people, but he couldn't really put his finger on even one. Certainly she was no looker, but there was a lot inside there, including much that was probably never revealed to anyone, yet that spark showed through. And she had raised an interesting question. "What's this trip point business?"

"You can reach a trip point in several ways," Herb told him. "One way is to become so damn many people you're more *them* than *you*. It's an occupational hazard. Another way is to stay in a time period too long, so that your self-identity is changed. Despite the folks you've been, you're still Ron Moosic, because at the core of your mind that's who you are. But if another personality became dominant, got into that core, then you wouldn't *be* Moosic anymore; rather, you'd be somebody else."

He thought of Sister Nobody, who was still very much a part of him, and grew nervous. "I had one that I couldn't really fight," he told them. "If I hadn't been attacked by those creatures, I might never have gotten control. So, you mean that if I stayed as her too long, then *she'd* be the dominant personality?"

Herb nodded. "Yes, indeed. And Ron Moosic would become one of the subordinate elements—but he could never rise again. The only reason we were able to get you here with your old body intact was that you still are Ron Moosic. You see, that's what makes you different than any of us. We—none of us—are the folks we started out as being. And the more you're somebody else, the less real that original fellow becomes."

He began to understand Dawn's problem now. She was still new at this herself, she'd said, so she wasn't long, perhaps, past her trip point. Somewhere, deep down, there was an identity crisis that she was only just starting to be able to handle. He sympathized, and realized with a nervous start that it was probably his fate, too. He frowned, a sudden thought striking him as he realized the extent of Dawn's comment on the insanity of time. "Uh—is there, or was there, a Ron Moosic in my own time—now?"

Herb shrugged. "Beats the hell out of me. If there is, you could go home—but to a nastier America than you left, and a dirtier world. You'd just merge with him and fade out the old you. Certainly, the time project still exists, but it sure wasn't invaded by any Marxist fanatics. There aren't any anymore. I heard her explain that to you.''

"Wait a minute! If Sandoval and I never went back, nobody was there to kill Marx! This is crazy!''

"Oh, there's a logic to it; it's just not the kind you're used to. No, time rippled from the event and flattened out at the edge. The main line now has Marx killed by whoever the hell Sandoval was in that time. He died there, too; so it's complete. *You* didn't kill him—that fellow born in that time did, for whatever purpose. It doesn't matter a bit. Marx and his murder ain't even a footnote in the history books anymore. Only the computer and us nightsiders and Eric and *his* computer know the real truth. That leaves you hanging in a paradox time can easily resolve. It just removes the paradox, meaning you. Either you go back and merge with yourself and that's the end of it, or you assimilate elsewhere, or you stay nightsided. Any way, you're no problem to the fabric of time now. See?''

The trouble was, he *did* see—sort of. Time took the best shortcut to keep its integrity. He was not a problem. "Uh—but what if *I* had shot Marx in Trier, instead of Sandoval? What would time have done then?''

"You would have been instantly assimilated. The same way you'd go if you shot your father before he met your mother. Another Ron Moosic might exist up front, but it wouldn't mean anything to you.''

So that was it. The basic law seemed to be that time resolved paradox in the most direct manner it could. And Holger Neumann, distraught at the death of Marx, would most certainly have killed himself. End of problem. Time is changed, but the equations balanced out.

And that left him, here, with an unpalatable problem. Remain, and therefore be the newest recruit in the squad, eventually reaching a trip point and becoming someone elsc entirely, someone not of his own choosing. Or pick a time and assimilate there. No, that was out. Time had shown him no favors at all, and there'd be nobody to rescue him the next time. Or have them return him to his own time, but a time far changed from the one he'd left, to become a Ron Moosic who might have come out very differently than he. If he existed at all. If not, there was assimilation again.

He was beginning to feel as worried and confused as Dawn.

AFTER THE FALL WAS OVER

Over the next few weeks, Ron Moosic was able to explore much of the complex and the surrounding area. Dawn still seemed somewhat uncomfortable around him, but also drawn to him, and she became his guide. He kept having the feeling that she wanted to get something off her chest, but he didn't push it. She would tell it, if she had to, when she was ready for it.

The area was perfect as a hidden base. The complex itself, viewed from outside, looked like nothing so much as two huge, shiny metallic cubes, one on top of the other, the whole complex rising several hundred feet into the air. Around it were the gardens abundant with fruit-bearing bushes and trees, vegetables, and more. Some of the plants were unfamiliar and native to the time; most, however, had been brought back after being altered to fit the existing conditions. The Outworlders were master biologists, that was for sure. The place could feed a population of hundreds if it had to, and it required very little maintenance.

One day Dawn said, "Come on. I'd like to show you my favorite spot around here," and led him outside the base perimeter.

Beyond the base itself was a dense, jungle-like forest which showed what it all must have looked like before the area was cleared and the complex built. Here there were insects and even small mammals, although nothing large or particularly threatening. A small, clear stream flowed through the dark jungle, until, a bit over a mile from the complex, it suddenly plunged a hundred feet or more in a spectacular, if small-volume waterfall. Here was the sea, looking much as it did during anyone's time, clear and blue and untouched.

They sat there, letting the wind carry some of the spray from the falls to them, and just enjoyed it. It was, Moosic had to agree, a truly pretty place, a place to come and sit and think.

His indecision, and unwillingness to really commit himself, made him more of a hanger-on than a member of the squad. Dawn, for example, always carried a time belt when outside the base—just in case something happened, for, back here, there was no way to wait for rescue. He had not been issued one, and wouldn't be until and unless he told them he was freely joining and undertook some training.

Dawn, however, was willing to show him the basics of the belt. "It personalizes itself to the wearer," she told him. "No one can touch it or see it except the person it brought to a particular time and place. Still, it's a good idea to hide it, since you never know when the enemy will show up. If they traced anyone to a time frame and got them to retrieve and deactivate the belt, they'd have a homing device leading straight here."

There were four master controls, noted by squiggly little symbols that meant nothing to him. He soon learned, however, that they were "Activate," "Standby," "Home," and "Off." The last two were the most interesting. "Home" would immediately bring the wearer to the frame and location of the power supply—in this case, to where they were. "Off" was used only at the base or in Safe Zones, since it made the belt phase into a frame and thus would not only allow anyone to see or find it but also subject it to the assimilation process. The Safe Zone was safe not only because no one could affect the course of time to any great degree there, but also because it was impossible for a human being to be tracked in it. Time simply disregarded human beings this far back; it had so much room to correct whatever they might do that they simply were no threat to the orderly time stream. Even a nuclear explosion could be adjusted for in the space of a million years.

"They say they picked this spot because it's a volcanic island," she told him. "Inactive now and for the foreseeable future—they checked—but still an island, and a transitory one. It will disappear in the ages, and so will any trace we make on it. That's why it's so safe."

To set the belt, you merely picked a reference point and set it with the dials. All of them being from near his time, the basic Julian calendar was used. Place basically used a grid of latitude and longitude in degrees, minutes, and seconds, but in a pinch the microprocessor could come up with the coordinates if you used the little microphone attached to tell it—and if it had the place you wanted in its files.

It was almost three weeks before he made his decision. He and Dawn walked out to the falls on the coast and he told her there. "I'm staying," he said simply. "After all is said and done, I suddenly realized that I didn't have anything to go back to, even if it were back to my own time. I kept fighting against it, I don't know why, but then I remembered why they asked me to go back in the first place. I really did have the least to lose of the available qualified personnel."

"I know why you hesitated," she told him. "It's this whole time business. It makes everything unreal. There's nothing left solid to stand on. Nothing is fixed—it's all variables. I think that's why I like it here so much. This place is fixed, unchanging, permanent. And so are we— here."

He was about to reply when, off in the distance, there came the sound of tremendous explosions. Both jumped up in a minute and, without looking at each other, rushed off back into the jungle for the base.

The explosions continued, together with the sounds of shouting people. The acrid stench of explosives was in the air. They reached the edge of the jungle clearing, and Moosic was shocked to see a small horde of the gargoyles attacking the great structure. The base itself offered little resistance, but while they were making a mess of the gardens, the metallic building itself seemed untouched.

That was clearly changing, however. A small knot of gargoyles under the direction of a human leader were busily assembling some sort of imposing weapon aimed right for the heart of the complex. The attacks were clearly designed to keep the Outworlders inside and unable to prevent the completion of the assembly.

He looked at Dawn. "We have to do something!"

She looked back at him resignedly. "What do you suggest? We can't get through that mob—they'll kill us. We can't get to that weapon, whatever it is. It'd be suicide. And neither of us is armed."

The sheer irrefutability of her logic both maddened and quieted him. All he could do was crouch there at the edge of the jungle and watch and wait. "Why don't they defend themselves?" he muttered. "Surely they must have been prepared for this." He had a sudden thought. "Your time belt! We could use it to go back just a little and warn them!"

She shook her head. "Won't work. Just like any other time, you can't be in two places at once. Besides—they *were* warned. The computer refused to let them take any action."

"Huh? *Why*?"

"It's part of a nightside time loop. In time, causes can precede events, but the events must be allowed to come about or much worse will happen. God knows, I don't pretend to understand it. I—I just accept what must be now."

He looked at her strangely, then back at the scene, which was getting worse. The device was completed now and powered up, and what was clearly a barrel or projector was aimed directly at the base. The sound of an air horn caused the attack from the gargoyles to be broken off, and they retreated a respectful distance. Then the weapon was brought into play, shooting a continuous beam of what seemed almost liquid blue energy at the complex. The energy struck and seemed to flow over the entirety of the building.

There was a crackling sound near them, and Moosic looked over to see tiny fields of electricity dancing around Dawn's time belt. The small red displays blinked on and off erratically. "The time belt!" he almost shouted, in no danger with the din of the attack masking them. "It's shorting out!"

Dawn seemed to be in almost a hypnotized state, but she suddenly snapped out of it. She picked up the microphone and dialed the base frequency. "Dawn to Base—we are caught outside and unarmed. Advise!"

There was a crackling sound, and then a tiny voice responded, "Use the belt and get out now! It's your only chance. . . ." And then it went dead. She turned and looked at him and seemed almost ready to cry, but she did not.

"Here! Let's open the belt wide so it goes around both of us. It'll be tight, but I think we can manage," she said.

"You mean use it now?"

"While we still can. The base may fall or short out any minute!"

He felt guilty about running, but it was clear that once the base fell, the occupying force would scour the island for any survivors. There was literally nothing they could do but take the chance.

The belt was never intended for two people and was an extremely tight fit, but they seemed to make it as she'd predicted. More electricity danced, and she had trouble making the adjustments on the belt.

Everything blacked out and they were falling, but ever

so briefly. Then all exploded again into reality, but this time into darkness.

The belt continued to sputter. They got it off as quickly as possible and it fell to the ground, then lit up the area with a display of dancing sparks.

"Where'd we go?" he asked her.

"Nowhere. There wasn't time. I just tapped the advance for a decade. We're still on the island, ten years in the future of the attack. That should be safe enough. I didn't dare try any long jump. What if the power failed? And if we did make it, we'd be assimilated."

He nodded, crediting her with some swift thinking. The belt continued to crackle, then made a single electronic whine which slowly faded and died. They were again in darkness. There were no dancing sparks, no red readouts on the belt.

"Oh, Jesus!" he breathed, half cursing and half praying. "The power's gone out!"

She stared down at the blackness. "Or the belt's O.K., but no longer connected to a power source. I—I think they shorted out the base."

And then she cried, long and hard, and he did his best to comfort her, although, truth to tell, he felt like crying, too.

In some ways, the island had not changed at all. In others, the change was dramatic.

Where the base had been, there was now simply a large depression of impressive size and squared-off dimensions, but with growth already creeping into it in profusion. Around the area, much of the gardens had gone wild, yet there were still fruit trees and bushes and even vegetables growing.

Surveying the place, Ron Moosic sighed and sat on a rock. "Well, in one way it's not so bad. Almost the Garden of Eden, you might say. We won't starve, that's for sure, and the stream is a secure water supply. From the looks of the sun and the jungle I'd say this place has two climates, hot and hotter. Of course, there are no doctors, no dentists, no nails or hammers or saws. Nothing but the clothes on our backs, such as they are.''

"These flimsy things aren't going to last long out here,'' she noted. She kicked off her boots and started to remove her clothes.

"Going natural, huh?''

"You should, too,'' she told him. "We won't have these forever, so we better get our skin and feet toughened up. We might eventually figure out how to rig lean-tos and maybe even huts, but there's nothing I've seen on this island that can be used to make clothes or shoes. I'll use these, as long as they last, when we explore the island, but not otherwise. There's no use.''

"You've got a point,'' he admitted, and stripped as well. They stood up and looked at each other. "You know,'' he said, "we really *are* Adam and Eve.'' He went over to her and hugged her.

"You're turning on,'' she noted softly.

"Oh? I hadn't noticed.'' He grew suddenly serious. "You know we may be here for the rest of our lives.''

"However long they may be,'' she replied. "I'm making a personal decision right here and now. I'm not going to think about time at all. Not now, not unless I have to. There's nothing else except now. There's nobody else but us. There's no place else but here.''

"That's fair enough,'' he agreed. "Maybe it all worked out for the best. Maybe this is the place for nightsiders. Let's make the most of it.'' And, with that, they kissed.

It was in many ways a new beginning. After a while, they set out to explore the island and found it relatively large. In the end, Moosic estimated it at being more than forty miles across and perhaps fifty long, the product of two undersea volcanic peaks breaking the surface of the deep ocean. One peak, on whose slopes the base had been built, was extremely old and worn, a low mound now, with even its ancient crater partly caved in and difficult to distinguish. From there the land ran down to a flat, though not level plain that made up the bulk of the island. The product of old lava flows, it had long been overgrown into jungle. There were, however, unspoiled black sand beaches where plain met sea.

The other end of the island's peak was by no means a grand mountain, although it surely was if one could have rolled back the ocean to see the whole of it, but it was certainly newer, with a clear cone shape caved in on one side and evidence through its growth of clearly less than ancient flows.

Although they could roam some distance, and did, they realized that their permanent home had to be in the remains of the old base, for it was only there that a continuous and guaranteed supply of edible vegetation was found. One day, Moosic decided, he would try and transplant some of the more valuable edible plants to the beach areas and perhaps the far slopes, but for now the first item of business was setting up a permanent home.

There was something about the passage of time that dimmed their memories and calmed their demons. Dawn had said that there was no assimilation possible in the Safe Zone, but, whether for psychological or physiological reasons, they did not, after a while, think back on or dwell upon the past. It was not that the information wasn't still there, simply that it was filed away as irrelevant. Conversation turned to the practical thoughts that seemed directed at nature and solving the practical problems.

As Dawn had predicted, the garments didn't last long, particularly after they began to explore the jungle. Mildew and mold seemed to crumble the boots and the rest, until, within a year, there was nothing left from the past at all, save only the seemingly indestructible but inactive time belt.

It took considerable trial and error to turn some of the jungle leaves and vines into crude and primitive shelters, but they finally did so, giving them some shelter against the occasional strong tropical rainstorms that blew across the island. With that problem solved, and with no worries at all about food supplies, other ambitions seemed to fade. They became as children once again, playing games, swimming, making love and just lying around. Moosic developed a substantial beard, which Dawn seemed to like, and their skins toughened and their bodies browned dark.

They had some minor injuries and suffered some occasional aches, pains, and bruises, but nothing very serious. It began to seem as if they would never get sick, but Dawn finally developed what at first seemed to be a persistent case of nausea.

Both had put on weight, both from the lazy life and from some of the less familiar fruits which seemed particularly sugar-laden, but now she began to eat far more heavily.

"Ronnie?"

"Yes, Dawn?"

"I haven't had a period in months. You know that?"

"I guess so, now that you mention it."

"Ronnie—I'm pretty sure I'm pregnant."

Even though he should have expected it, the news stunned and somewhat unnerved him. He realized sheepishly that he'd been shutting the obvious out of his mind. Now all the worries began.

"But how can you have a baby? Here, I mean. Hell, Dawn, I don't know how to deliver a baby."

"Well, you're going to have to learn. I sure can't do it myself."

Within another month, there was no doubt of the fact, and since there was no way to date conception, they began to prepare early. There really wasn't a whole lot, though, that could be done. Rocks were worked and sharpened to fine cutting edges, and, for the first time, he worked to find a way of making and maintaining a fire. Some coconut-like shells from jungle trees seemed able to resist being heated, and more stone was broken up and used to form a fire pit of sorts. Shells and shell fragments, some of them huge, had always washed up on the beaches after storms, and they proved to be decent water containers.

Still, he was scared to death of actually having to deliver the baby. She was not much help at that. "I've never had one before," she told him.

She was in tremendous pain the night the baby came. The labor took all day and went into the night, and he feared that he was going to lose both the baby and her. But, finally, she managed to push it out to where he could get hold of it and pull it all the way. He was prepared to cut the cord and wash the baby off, but not so prepared for it to be all purple at the start and even less prepared for the subsequent delivery of the placenta. Having a baby was a painful and messy business under the best of circumstances, and this was hardly that. But now they had a child, and it quickly gained color and showed a fine set of lungs.

They named the boy Joseph, after Moosic's father.

It was both the same and not the same after that, for now they had a purpose in their lives and it restored some of the lost ambition. He began to look for a more permanent sort of dwelling, and he found it in the mouth of an old lava tube. Dried straw and leaves formed the floor, while huge jungle leaves, held together with the bracing of small tree limbs tied with vines, created a wall that protected them from the elements while affording good ventilation. They made a primitive rope from some of the vines and, using sharpened stones and sticks, managed to create tools to do a utilitarian job. They had progressed from the Garden into the Stone Age.

From that point, Dawn seemed to enter into a state of perpetual pregnancy. After Joseph came Ginny, Sarah, Cathy, and Mark. He wound up having to build a vine and stick fence for a play area, and they found parenting, particularly on this level, a full-time occupation. Then, to their relief, there was a long period with no childen at all. It gave the others time to grow up.

There was no real way to tell time now, since they'd not started a calendar until Joseph had been born, but they knew he was ten and that they had been there a very long time now. Dawn remained fat and didn't much care about losing it. Her focus was strictly on the home and on the children now, to the exclusion of all else. Ginny broke her leg once, and while they painfully set it, it never did heal quite right, causing her a bad limp. All of the children had visible scars, and Sarah had almost died from a deep puncture, but, all in all, they had been very lucky.

Moosic found his black beard and hair turning gray, then white, which bothered him a great deal. Despite the fact that he'd always kept himself in reasonable shape and was relatively thin now from all the work, in one sense the Outworlder squad had done him no favors restoring his body. Dawn was perhaps in her early to mid-thirties now— she herself wasn't sure—but he knew he was in his middle fifties, and feeling it. His eyesight was getting poor, although, ironically, it was far better than Dawn's, which had deteriorated into such nearsightedness that anything more than a couple of feet away was a blur.

They taught the children as best they could, explaining their origins as much as the parents were able—how do you explain machines to someone who has never worn clothes or even seen anyone wearing them?—and taught them the skills they knew or had learned, and told them stories both real and fanciful.

It was on a day perhaps twelve years after they had arrived that it happened. A storm was brewing; Joseph was still out somewhere in the countryside, and Dawn, after all this time pregnant again, was worried about him. Although Moosic calmed her and tried reassuring her that he was a man now and well able to take care of himself, he finally got a little concerned when the wind picked up and the other kids battened down for a blow. He went out to see if Joseph could be found.

Near the edge of the jungle, up by the fruit trees, he heard an answering hail to his call. He ran to the boy, intending to give him a scolding, but stopped when he saw what the boy had.

It was dirty, and mud-caked, and long forgotten, but it was unmistakable. The time belt, lost for some years.

"What is it, Dad? I found it over there, in the pit. I guess the last storm unburied it."

He nodded and took it, then looked at it and shook his head. "It was the way your Mom and I got here, son."

Joseph stared at it in wonder. "How'd it work?"

He laughed, and found to his surprise that the clasp still functioned. There wasn't a real sign of wear or even rust on the thing after all these years.

"Ha! Maybe I should shock your mother." He put it on around his waist. "You just put it on like this, press one of the buttons, and away you went."

"Wow!" The boy looked closely at the belt. "Hey! That's neat! The funny red things, I mean."

"The what?" He looked down and froze in shock.

Although he was certain they had not been so a moment before, suddenly the small red indicators were glowing.

He started to take it off, to run with it up to Dawn, when Joseph reached out. "You mean you just punched something like this?"

He pressed the home key, then let out a sudden, terrified scream that was cut off midway.

The wind stopped. The noise stopped. Everything blanked out, and Ron Moosic felt himself falling helplessly.

The sensation, however, did not last long. He expected to arrive somewhere at night, but he suddenly stood in the middle of a brightly lit room that his memory knew well.

It was the lounge of the very same Outworlder base he had seen—or thought he'd seen—destroyed.

Chung Lind was thumbing through some book or other on one of the couches. He looked up, nodded, and said, "You know something? You look like hell."

TRIP POINT

"Moosic, you're a mess," Doc told him. "How long were you downtime, anyway?"

"Hard to say," he replied. "Eleven, maybe twelve years."

She nodded. "And you aged twenty-five. The only way I can explain the results of these tests is that everything came along gradually and you became inured to it all. You've got kidney problems, four kinds of internal parasites, several ill-healed breaks too far gone for much correction, and that's only for starters. You had eye problems?"

"Some," he admitted. "Not as much as Dawn has."

"Well, you probably had slightly better eyes to begin with. The radiation levels are different back here than in the period when humans evolved. It's so minor for a day or so that we don't bother about it, and your body can self-correct to a degree, but you had a dozen years of straight exposure."

"The kids—they were born in that environment!"

"I wouldn't worry so much about them. They're probably better protected than you, and they're young. Whatever their problems are, we can certainly correct them. I can't say about Dawn, but she's a lot younger than you. I can say, with some certainty, that your vision will continue to deteriorate and you would have been stone-cold blind in another year back there. Here you maybe have three or four years, but I wouldn't worry about it. The cancer will get you first."

He swallowed hard. "You mean—that's it? I'm going to die?" She seemed mighty unconcerned about the news.

"Not necessarily. Or, rather, yes and no. It's usually accidental, but, if it's carefully planned and timed, I think we can work it out. It'll take some guts, though, on your part."

"What are you talking about?"

"Going past a trip point, of course. Be someone else. Someone younger and healthier."

That idea disturbed him almost as much as the medical news. "Be . . . someone else. That's like committing suicide, isn't it?"

She stared at him. "Do I look dead?"

"No, no, of course not, but—O.K., you've all gone through it, but you said yourself it was mostly accidental. It's something else to talk about it cold-bloodedly instead of just letting it happen."

"Nevertheless, it's what you'll have to do. It's not so bad. Everyone I ever was is still in here," she told him, pointing to her head. "You don't really lose anything, unless you make the mistake of getting assimilated. That's a close thing with trip points. We're constantly monitored by our computers to make sure we don't make an unintentional jump into someplace that could get us." She sighed. "Look, it would have happened to you anyway, you know, if you'd joined us. It was inevitable."

"But Dawn and the children . . ."

"Are no problem at all. This is time, remember? Safe Zone time. No assimilation, no trip points. We'll go get them, and before they have had time enough to realize you're gone. There's no rush. None of us have been to the time frame you were in before, so there's no relative time problem. Don't think of them stranded there while you're here. We could do it tomorrow, or next week, or next year, and we'd still get there ten seconds after you left."

He sighed. "You're right, of course. That's not what I'm really worried about, although I admit it's tough not to think of time passing there as it is here. It's really—well, me. No matter what, I might see *them* again, but they'll never see me.''

She had no answer for that.

"Look," he said, "why not go get them now—before? I mean, one last time?"

She shook her head sadly. "I understand, but it's not possible. First of all, it'd be sort of cruel, like facing them one last time so *they* know you're dying. Swift and clean is best. It hurts, but it's not as prolonged. But even if you *did* want it anyway . . ."

"I do. Very much."

". . . It wouldn't matter," she continued. "Ron, this is hard to say and even harder to explain, but you're caught up in and committed to a loop."

"A what?"

"A loop. It's not your fault—you had no say in it—and it's unfair, but it's the due bill the Outworlders are rendering."

"What do you mean? Due bill for what?"

"Saving your life. Time always takes the shortest method to resolve people like us. If we'd left you as Alfie Jenkins, you would have died, either in prison or at the hands of a fanatic or a mob. I'm afraid you would have been left there if Sandoval hadn't been able to jump back. But he was, and our computer monitored it and monitored the consequences of the actions, particularly the early death of Marx. It ordered us to save you. In so doing, it initiated a loop—a string of effects stemming from that cause. A loop is initiated backwards. The last action comes first. This causes a backwash, as it were. Everything leading to that action is assumed by time to have already occurred. Saving you was the last action of the loop. You are now living the events leading up to that, under our management."

"Wait a minute! Slow down! I've been away a long time, and this gets dizzier and dizzier!"

"It's easiest to put it this way. Dawn appeared to Alfie

and allowed him the means to escape. He did—and so you did, and continued to live.` But, you see, Ron—*Dawn hasn't gone forward in time and saved Alfie yet*. Didn't she tell you?''

He shook his head wonderingly. ''No, no. And I think I can see why. No wonder she was so upset that first time we met here. Time is insanity, she said.''

''No, it's not insanity, it's good mathematics. What it is is extremely complex. As complex as elementary particle physics or the biochemistry of viruses or any other complex science. What we're doing was discovered by trial and error. It's all been recorded in the ultimate mathematician, the computer here that is so complex and so advanced it is, in fact, an artificial intelligence of a high order. It's capable of viewing the time stream, seeing any disruption, and postulating the results from that disruption. It's equally capable of looking at those results and seeing how it would be best to minimize or even erase those disruptions. Time is on the Outworlders' side in the conventional sense. If things just go the way they naturally would, they will win. So we are the guardians of time. A major disruption has taken place. You were not the cause of that disruption, but you are the key to minimizing or erasing it.''

''Me? How? And why me?''

''I don't know. I don't want to know. Sometimes it does things, or tells us to do things, that we don't understand at all. Later on, we're able to see how a result was obtained. Sometimes it seems insane that we did it our way, or far chancier to do it our way, than some other, but it always has its reasons and it generally works. It seems easier if a couple of us were just sent forward to that square to neutralize dear Eric and take Sandoval out, but that's not the way this one is being played out. Why you? Because you are a direct participant in the original action. The fewer outside elements introduced, the better the result. Why? Again, I don't know. It just *is*. And until this is played out and you're a free person again, you must play the hand it deals you.''

He considered that. "Why? What if I don't?"

"You forget, there *are* alternatives at our disposal, just not alternatives as good as the one it's using, in its opinion. I told you that Dawn has not yet gone forward to save Alfie Jenkins. If she does not do so, and the computer has real control over that, the loop will be broken. You will die as Alfie Jenkins. None of the rest of this will ever have happened. The children will not exist. *You* will not exist.''

He opened his mouth to say something, but nothing came out. So there was no real chance at all. None. Because they had control of just one not-yet-taken action, all depended on him being a good boy and doing whatever they ordered. He and his other selves, except Alfie, and his children, his whole experience in the Safe Zone—everything wiped out, like it had never been. And they could leave Dawn in the Safe Zone, as she'd said, for weeks, months, or years. And all they had to do to wipe it all out was not to rescue her at all. Just shut down this complex and move to a better one. That's all.

Round and round went time, looping and whirling and doubling back into itself. And yet, in the end, there were no paradoxes, only alternatives. All time, up to the leading edge, was the sum of what had gone before. But it didn't matter *what* that sum added up to—as long as it all added up. The mathematics gave order to chaos, but in that mathematics was the master mathematician who gave the orders. Human beings, given their orders, might be driven insane by the complexity of it all, but they had to obey or die.

The exterior of the base looked quite different, because it was. When the attack had come, they'd been ready for it, but the computer had made the decision not to defend but rather to leave. Maintaining the loop had taken precedence over the inconvenience of moving the complex. And moving the complex had taken every single ounce of power the computer and its mysterious power source could command, hence the cessation of function in the belt. That was why the impression in the ground ten years after the attack had been so regular. Rubble, or even disintegration, would not have been so neat as to leave that enormous rectangle. The thing had simply moved itself through time and space, to a secondary preselected time and place in the Safe Zone. It was a demonstration of the amount of power that the Outworlders had at their command—and that they were denying Earth.

All the belts had, in fact, been repowered within a year of relative time, but by that time he and Dawn had lost theirs, having pretty well tossed it away as a useless reminder of a no longer relevant past.

How had the computer been so certain that Joseph or somebody would find it? Or was he thinking too linearly while the computer thought only of wholes? If one event, his salvation in London, had already preceeded its cause, a cause that had not yet occurred; then, perhaps *all* events in the loop did the same. Was he, then, only acting out a preordained future that had already occurred and could actually be changed only by his failure to follow orders?

And, if so, did the mathematics require much else, or did, in fact, everything done have to be undone? He wasn't sure, but it didn't really matter. Not only was he at the mercy of this crazy computer, but so were a lot of other folks he cared about.

They gave him a couple of weeks with physical therapy and some medical treatment—and lots of rest—just to let him sort it out. It didn't matter to them how long he took; the sequence was as good if initiated late as it was if inititated early. No matter how ill he was, though, he couldn't help but be terribly depressed by what he was being forced to do. For the first time in his life, he had people he loved, and with all the pain and all the problems, the years on the island had been among the happiest in his whole life. That, and they, were now denied him, but still dependent on him.

He spent what time he had trying to learn all he could about the Outworlders, their squad, and the war they had fought. He was not sure he liked what he found, and he certainly was less sure of the motivation.

Their entire picture of the Earthsiders, as the Outworlders called the masses who remained on the planet, was tremendously skewed in the negative, a portrait of a suffering and miserable planet of horror under a regime that made Hitler look like the head of the Boy Scouts. Outworlders, on the other hand, were romantic, democratic, and all things wonderful, the true future of the human race. He doubted if it was that simple, and he found that many of the squad agreed with him about that. The difference between them and himself was that he wanted to know the truth; they considered the truth irrelevant, which, in a way, it was.

It wasn't, as Herb explained, that they felt that they were on the side of the good guys against the bad, but rather that they were on one of two bad sides. One of them had to win, and all they could do was their jobs and be thankful that *they* neither had to live with or pay the consequences of the win.

The evidence that the time war was more elaborate was also clear, and it was plain that the Outworlders played the game better. The computer that ran the war was not so much the guardian of "natural" reality as public relations liked it to be, either. The end result of history to the leading edge was littered with improbabilities in the extreme. Clearly, some of those had been tipped in the Outworlders' favor. The best evidence of this was his discovery that, unlike the primitive time suit he'd started out with, the computer could understand enough variables to place a time traveler in a specific place at a specific time and often in a specific role. That meant that members of the squad were not at the mercies of time, but truly its masters.

Downtiming the night side was truly a science, not an art, and the mathematics was unthinkably precise.

That did, however, give him a little encouragement when he met with Doc for another treatment for his ills.

"If I decided now to go through with this trip-point business, it seems to me that this thing is precise enough to practically make me who I want."

"It's not that exact, and there are lots of limitations, but what did you have in mind?" she asked him.

"Tell me—can it know if I exist in the present as it's currently constituted?"

"We thought of that already. You *did* exist, even in the revised future, but you didn't live long. You were premature, you know, and it was touch-and-go for a while even on the main line. Conditions are changed just slightly enough on that level in the new main line that you didn't make it. That's pretty common for a wave. Of course, it works out. Some others who originally didn't make it are alive because of the wave."

He nodded. "But it might be easiest if I made it again, wouldn't it? Is that possible?"

She considered it. "It would be very tricky. I don't know if you can ever manipulate things to the degree to be a specific individual, particularly one that was real. Short of our intervening to save the baby, I would say no. And if the baby were saved, you would exist there and so it wouldn't be possible. I'd say forget it. Now, if you wanted to be a security man from Pennsylvania, *that* we might work out."

In other words, they could be exact enough to put him in the time project at the right time and place—but as someone else, and not under the same conditions. He might be any of the security staff.

"That's close enough," he told her. "Let's do it and get this show moving. The sooner it's over, the sooner everyone can take up their lives and the sooner I can be out of this madhouse."

"I'll get a belt now if you like."

He nodded, but was surprised. "You can do it just like that?"

"Well, either the computer knows it already or it's overheard us and is now doing the work. Something as tough as what you want might take it all of half a second to completely predetermine—it's that difficult."

She wasn't being funny.

The time belt was pretty much the same as all the others he'd worn, but it had no settings. "This is designed for projects like this," she told him. "The computer simply reads in the requirements directly to the belt, and when you activate, you'll go forward to the spot. Then just take note of your surroundings, find a good spot to stick the belt that you'll remember and will be likely to get to in a pinch, and take it off. The rest is automatic as far as the identity is concerned."

"Yeah, but how do I know when I reach this trip point or whatever it is?"

"We've done the figuring. You're overage for this, and the process of assimilation really accelerates as you get older. We're going to put you in a year before you first arrived on the main line, to avoid any problems with a potential takeover again. That would be too confusing. May the ninth will be the day you'll wake up, and that's the key. You would be assimilated now in just twelve days. This is the tricky part, which we'll try and help you with. You *must* use your belt again on May fifteenth. Any time on that day during daylight hours. By nightfall, it'll be too late and we'd have to come and get you. We will if we must, of course."

He nodded. "I see. So I come back to the belt and activate it again and wind up back here?"

She nodded. "Try and keep enough presence of mind to do it yourself. Keep thinking of Dawn and the children. Hate Eric, or us, if you must. But if we have to come and get you, all sorts of things might go wrong."

"O.K. I'm ready," he told her.

"Farewell, Ron Moosic," she responded.

He pressed activate.

Michael O'Brien awoke in his own quarters at precisely six A.M. He always had, ever since he'd been in the Marine Corps.

O'Brien had been in the corps all his life, since graduating from high school in Shamokin, Pennsylvania, many years before. He loved it, even though the only time he'd ever been in a combat situation, he'd had the shit blown out of him within three hours.

He grabbed the bars atop the bed, pulled himself up and around, and eased effortlessly out into his wheelchair. He was proud to be self-sufficient, and if you wanted to make him mad, you simply had to show pity or try and help him do something he was perfectly capable of doing himself.

He was also proud that they didn't just discard good men with good brains and skills anymore, just because they were handicapped in the service of their country. No, with a massive perimeter stretching around half the world, anybody who could do a desk job to free some other for the hot areas was retained. It was only fair, of course, particularly for the ones like himself who'd paid the price for being where he was ordered to be.

Sure, he felt depressed sometimes. Here he was, thirty-three years old and pretty good looking, if he did say so himself, with no feeling below the waist. None. And no movement or control, either. It was bad enough to be in diapers again, but much worse to know he'd never again make love to a woman or ever father a child. But he was tough, Irish-tough, and full of life and the will to live. If nothing else, his deeply felt Roman Catholic religion made suicide the immoral way out, but his Marine religion, just as strong, made it the coward's way out. Nope, let the little Reich boys cry in their beer and either end it all or be finished off by their own as useless. He was living proof of the real difference between Americans of all types and the enemy.

He shaved and gave himself a change and a sponge bath, then pulled on his uniform and got back into the chair. Staff Sergeant O'Brien, ready for duty, *sir!*

Ron Moosic expected the disability joker or something similar. He knew how much time hated these things, and him in particular, it seemed. Still, he liked O'Brien, whose general background and religion matched his own, and he liked the man's spirit and outlook.

He didn't as much care for the world that O'Brien inhabited, a world with two great empires, one run from Berlin and the other from Washington, both bristling with nuclear missiles, both higher tech than his own time had been, thanks to a longer war and nearly unremitting tension since, and both less than democratic.

Of course, he still preferred America, which stretched by force from what used to be Canada to Tierra del Fuego. The country itself was heavily rationed and on a permanent wartime footing; the standard of living of the average citizen was well below what he expected, but far better than the lot of the Latin Commonwealths, which were essentially run by American military decree. Still, Presidents ran for election, and so did Congress, and there was still a Constitution worded much the way he remembered it. In fact, there were a couple of amendments there that hadn't been there in his time, including a sexual equality one—and, in fact, women as well as men had to serve, and at all levels, including combat. And, of course, the seventy-two states took some getting used to.

And yet, oddly, there was still a Wicomico Group, by that name, and it was still run as a cooperative venture between the War Department and the State Security Bureau, the latter having far more sweeping powers, including many inside the country, than the NSA he'd known.

It was, in fact, a bit unsettling that his old bosses had

become what the NSA's old critics once feared—a sort of electronic secret police.

Private ownership of automobiles was banned, of course, but at 0715 sharp the van pulled up to take him to work a few miles to the south of his apartment complex. It was a special van, outfitted for handicapped people. No wonder those in the service were intensely loyal.

The day was pretty much routine. The place looked as secret and as disguised as ever; the entrance was just as tough to get through, and the interior central hall, which he'd last seen in shambles, was remarkably intact. About the only really strong change was that it was a bit drabber, with everybody in some sort of service uniform and everything a dull military gray, including his central admissions desk, from which he monitored the entry areas and also dispensed information and clearances through his computer keyboard.

The security chief was a cold fish named Sorban, and all of the SSB men and women seemed like the kind of folks who enjoyed robbing widows and kicking little children, but that was routine to O'Brien and he mostly ignored them or even cracked jokes about them as only somebody on the inside would dare.

At 1630 he was relieved and rolled back out through what they all called The Gauntlet to the lot where the vans and buses were waiting. All in all, a very routine day, but for Moosic something of a surprise, not that so much was different but that so much was the same. Indeed, Dr. Aaron Silverberg headed the project, although even on O'Brien's level they knew only the general details of what went on below.

He wondered if Silverberg was the same sort of fellow as the one he'd known. Certainly he was in the same position, so much would have been the same. It would be interesting, he thought, to see the subtle differences in the familiar.

Back at his apartment complex, he considered his options.

He could go over to the club, but he tended to eat too little and drink too much when he did that. Besides, tonight was a dance night.

Not that he was inactive. There was a wheelchair basket-ball team he was on that was pretty good, and a local Handicapped Service Organization social club that was nice, but he decided he just wanted to relax this night. He went inside, wheeled into the elevator, and went up to his floor, then down the hall to his door. He put the key in the lock, turned it, and pushed himself in, the door sliding out of the way to accommodate him and his chair. He stopped just inside the door and cursed. He always left a light on so he wouldn't have to fumble—whoever had built this place had done a lot for the handicapped, but hadn't done much for light switches near the door—and yet it was fairly dark in the room. Bulb burnt out, he thought; then he began to tense. It was *too* dark. He always left the drapes open, and they were closed. The maid, perhaps? But she never had done that before. . . .

The lights came on. Five glistening inhuman creatures stared at him, rifles aimed at his head. In the big stuffed recliner chair sat a man he'd seen before, a blond man with a strong Nordic face, dressed all in black, leaning forward so that he didn't have to sit back on his time belt.

"Come, come, Sergeant O'Brien—or should I say Mr. Moosic? Surely that is not the kind of expression used to greet old friends."

UPTIME DOWNBEAT

"Time," said the blond man, "is very, very difficult to handle. Change one major thing, you wind up with the same mess—or one much worse. Change anything else, and it just grabs hold of you and gets you. Or you find out you've shifted something very subtly and wound up causing the nuclear war they narrowly averted. I, by the way, am Eric Benoni."

He had no intention of moving with all those guns on him. "You'll pardon me if I don't get up."

Eric made a simple hand motion, and the guns went down and the creatures stepped back. "That better? I must say you're looking very . . . sympathetic."

"And you're looking much the opposite. In fact, you haven't changed a bit since the last time we met, although that was very, very long ago."

"Very long—hmmm. . . . We are in one of those cross-temporal problems. It probably *was* very long to you in relative time, but it seems only a short while ago to me—which it was. One of the hazards of this business."

"Mind telling me how you found me so quickly and so easily?"

"Oh, it wasn't difficult to anticipate. Admittedly, it takes a week or so relative time for the sensors to determine an anomaly with their random sweeps, but if one *knows* that someone else is likely to appear in a given time and place, it's child's play to set a permanent scan on it. It was still a bit of luck, but this was the one time and place that both of us knew precisely and which you'd have some likelihood of returning to. Our psychologial profile of you indicated that, if you ever received major injury or reached a critical age point, you would most likely choose this time and place for a trip point."

Moosic was not pleased at that. "Am I so easy to read?"

"In many ways we all are, Mr. Moosic. Don't take it so hard. Had you tripped in any other time or place, I might never have found you. Even if you'd shown up here after that, I'd merely know an enemy agent was here, not you. But—come. Let us be off. I'm afraid I'm overstaying my welcome in this period even now, and our power is far more limited than yours. Shall we get your belt now?"

"I don't think so. It'd lead you right back to the base, which you've already caused to jump around. Even if they could escape again, I doubt if I'd be any good in the ten years it'd take them to get the power back on. No, I think you might as well shoot me now and be done with it."

Eric Benoni's manner was such that it was impossible to determine through the cool, aristocratic tone if he was serious or sarcastic, but he at least sounded surprised. "I have no intention of shooting you, Mr. Moosic, unless you make it an imperative. I *could*, however, use rather unpleasant means to *make* you reclaim that belt and give it to me."

Moosic returned a sardonic smile. "So why haven't you? Partly because you've overstayed your welcome in this time frame, I'd say, and are in very close danger of getting assimilated here yourself. Those methods take time. And partly because you know, as I do, that this body couldn't stand very much before it gave out."

"Brave talk. You're going noble on me, and that's unbecoming. However, I will be honest enough to say that you are correct in both assumptions. I can waste no more time here, nor can you stand harsh methods." He turned to one of the gargoyles. "Strap a belt on him!"

With those guns trained on him, Moosic couldn't argue with them. He allowed the belt to be strapped to his waist because there was no alternative. "Where are we going? To make me a healthier torture victim?" he asked the blond man.

"Well, yes and no. If you think I'm going to take the risk on assimilation just to get you in better shape, you are wrong. Too chancy. Come. Activate!" he commanded. The belt must have been voice actuated, because everything blacked out and he was falling once more.

Ultimately, the world returned, a world of artificial light. It was not any place he'd been to before, but he could guess what it was. There was a delay of sorts on his belt as well, because they were all there just waiting for him to materialize.

He materialized, of course, as the prematurely aged and terminally ill Moosic of the island.

There was no mistaking Benoni's shock and surprise at seeing him like this. He sighed. "Well, now it's clear why you required a trip point."

"Failed again," Moosic almost taunted him, feeling pretty good about it despite his desperate situation. "This body's in at least as bad shape as the other one." He looked around. "Your base in the Safe Zone, I presume?"

Benoni nodded. "Yes. Exactly so. Founded, I might add, only two decades after those first experiences, as soon as they had the capability. The ultimate retreat and escape for the rich and powerful when and if the bombs are launched. The world's most luxurious, and secure, bomb shelter. Never used for what it was intended, of course, but still here." He sighed. "So what are we to do with you, Mr. Moosic? I suspect we could easily gain the location of the belt from you, but we could hardly force you to go up, retrieve it, and hand it to us. Either your body or your mind would give, and you are a trained security agent." He thought for a moment. "Perhaps a different tack is warranted."

"You're going to be my buddy now, right?"

"I wouldn't insult you like that. But—consider. Why am I doing this? Money? What use is money to a nightsider? Power? What sort of power am I wielding beyond what I could have by other means?"

"I assume you're a soldier doing your duty as you see it."

He nodded. "Exactly! But unlike you, I have had an advantage. I have been on both sides in this terrible conflict."

That piqued Ron Moosic's interest. "Both sides?"

"Indeed. In fact, I lived with the Outworlders for some time before getting directly involved. Have you ever seen the Outworlders, sir?"

"Of course not."

"Well, I have. Many of them. We went too far in our quest to colonize, Moosic. Much too far. They are monsters. I've seen creatures with glistening exoskeletons who breathe poisonous gases and glide along in a sea of methane. I've seen tentacled things that can take the oxygen out of rocks and transmute granite. The first generation was already lost, as soon as they accepted what they were. The second had no human origins. We are fighting the third."

Moosic had to admit he was shocked. "Biology went that far that fast?"

"Not so fast. Consider it was but sixty-six years between the first powered flight and the first man on the moon. Consider the genetic manipulations and the medical wonders in your own lifetime, and use the same developmental scale. In the technological era, a decade is revolutionary; a century is radical."

He had to admit he'd never thought of it that way before, but there was truth to what the blond man said. There was, however, a rather compelling counterargument standing not so far away. "Those creatures of yours—they're the humanity you want to save?"

Eric looked slightly embarrassed. "A technological

revolution, I fear, is not limited to one side. However, these are different in a hundred ways. For one thing, no one was changed into them. They are laboratory created and bred. They save lives. One can make the poor your cannon fodder, as it has always been, or one can artificially raise cannon fodder. An interesting moral choice, is it not?''

He had no answer for that.

''So,'' Eric continued, ''it becomes a matter of *us* versus *them*. When it was decided by the Outworlders that all remaining humans would be converted into their own kind, a few of us rebelled and planned. We stole a ship and got it to Earth. The story is a true adventure in and of itself, but it is not relevant. We got here and, somehow, avoided being shot down, although we were, of course, captured. They were quite surprised to find us as human as they.''

''I've heard about Earth up then. I didn't much like my own time anymore, after what we'd both done to it, but I think I like it better than what I hear of the edge.''

''Indeed, it is miserable. The Outworlders wish conquest, not elimination, so they do not extinguish life as they could easily do with their present command of space. Instead, they sit up there and hurl rocks at us, some hundreds of kilometers in size. The rocks are broken up by Earth defenses, but they still hit in large chunks. They destroy as surely as nuclear bombs destroy, but without the mess. Of course, they are mostly random, but when you get several a day for years, it tends to leave things pretty ugly.''

''If they're so inhuman, what do they want with the Earth?''

''Control. So long as Earth exists, it is a potential dagger at their throats, if not now, then in the future. They have plans for the Earth. An adaptive Earth, they call it. A population all changed into monsters, all working for extraterrestrial overlords. An enslaved Earth populated with *practical* monsters adapted to various needs. The end of humanity, Mr. Moosic. The end. I'm not going to pretend that the Earth I know is a nice place. Wars make nice places ugly. The cost in human suffering is enormous, on a scale that almost makes the annihilation of the human race by nuclear arms seem preferable. Those old warheads still exist, Moosic. Not in the numbers they used to, but they are still there. Earth has suffered too much to surrender to the monsters, to become monsters and make misery permanent.''

"You mean that they're willing to wipe out humanity if they lose?" He was aghast at the idea. "Commit racial suicide? But is there no hope for a reconciliation?"

"None. But like all things in time, it is a possibility, not a certainty. Earth is losing. It cannot win against the massive power of the Outworlders. It no longer has the power to even move more than a handful of people back into the Safe Zone, let alone the equipment and staff required here to build up this base and increase its power. It's too late. Either Earth wins by changing the equations so that it *does* win, or humanity is wiped out. Except for the very elite, of course, who will be able to sneak out the back door to here before it blows. There is no way to bring more. Oh, we'll bring a huge number of fertilized eggs and try a new race here, but, even then, if a sufficient human presence is truly established for a civilization back here, the Outworlders will be able to know it and come for it."

Moosic sat down on the cold floor, feeling weak and dizzy, not so much from his health as from what he'd been told. It was always true that there were two sides to every story, and this one was a doozy. If both sides were to be believed, there were no good guys at all in this, only tragedy for all humankind, no matter what the result.

If Benoni could be believed, and his words had the very ring of truth in them, then the fate of human civilization, of all humanity, rested with him. That was something he'd never bargained for, something he was not prepared to accept.

"Why Marx?" he asked the blond man. "Why all this stuff in the first place?"

"Because we have so little to work with. It was a way, a device, to cause the other side to act. A chance, perhaps, to catch them, to trace them back. Bait."

"I really want no part of this. A pox on both your houses."

Eric nodded. "I know how you feel. I really do. But understand, you were not originally in the desperation move. All of those antique suits of yours were supposed to be destroyed. The Outworlders were supposed to be the ones tracking our young radicals, not you. But—here you are. The loop was formed around you rather than they, and that puts you center stage. Now you see our moves, and our desperation. Tell me—what reward would you like? You have all of time, you know. Within the minimizing ripple effect, we can make you whatever you want wherever and whenever you want to be."

But you can't give me back Dawn and the kids, he thought sourly. *Neither side is willing to do that.* Aloud he answered, "What I want is not within your power, and the other side denies it to me and holds it over me like a club. I'm going to be frank, Benoni. I don't give a damn who wins or loses your dirty little war. I grew up under the nuclear threat, so I'm really only surprised to find it took so long. You ask me to make a choice, and I refuse. You have no right to ask it, and I have no right to grant or not grant it. I've never seen your Earth, but I think I'd hate it. I'll grant your Outworlder version, so I'm not too thrilled about them, either. But I've never seen or talked to them any more than I have your Earth. I'm being asked to take the facts on faith and to maybe decide the war on that. I can't and I won't. Piss on it and bring out your torture. I'd rather just die now and get it over with."

Eric stood up and walked over in front of him, looking

down, a curious expression on his face. "I'm not going to kill you. In fact, out of your own mouth you have guaranteed this. I was going to take you forward to the edge, show you what your loyalty has wrought, but I think not. Your mind-set is not prepared to make the adjustments, to see that an issue of human survival surpasses all else, including the present quality of life, or lack of it." He turned to the gargoyles. "Feed him and make him comfortable but secure. Keep him in Room 226 until I return."

Moosic found himself being lifted by powerful arms, and shook them off. He preferred to do this on his own as much as possible, and he followed the hulking creatures up a stairway and into a comfortable, motel-like room. In a few minutes, some food was delivered that appeared mostly synthetic, but it did taste something like the meat and vegetables it was supposed to be. The beer he found surprisingly good, although it had been quite a while since he'd sampled any. Then they cleared away the trays, closed and locked the door, and left him alone.

He felt very tired, almost achingly so, and suspected that the beer or food had been drugged in some manner. Well, let them. They could make him talk under the influence, but he knew full well that if they moved him up to the sergeant's time, he would once again become the sergeant and once again be awake and alert. Benoni had been very nervous in that time frame, and Moosic suspected that his captor could ill afford another trip there. Yet, with the multi-shifts of the military compound and the patrols all about, they would have to call up humans to shepherd a drugged and wheelchair-bound man, one known to almost all in the area, out to the fossil cliffs. Nothing else they could learn from him mattered.

In fact, nothing really mattered to him anymore. The other side denied him the only people he had ever loved. This side had less to offer. More, they might have to move fast—the Outworlders could easily discover him kidnapped and then cut power to the belt, bringing it back to their base and denying Eric the trace to their new headquarters indefinitely.

He did not fight sleep nor fear it; he was oddly at peace with himself, although hardly happy. He had been happy; now he was not and could never be again, but he was out of it. He was no longer the pawn in their game, and if he died, well, that was enough.

He never did really know if they'd drugged him. The drugs of the future surely were far more dependable, sophisticated, and undetectable than those of his own time. It didn't matter, although the time he spent there was certainly boring. He had no idea how long he was left there, but it seemed far too long almost from the start. At least, he thought more than once, they could have left a couple of books or something.

He had the impression that the human master of this place had gone somewhere, possibly uptime for consultations. It was both easy and difficult to understand Eric Benoni. Easy, in that he'd experienced, if he could be believed, both systems and found them both horrible, but he'd been born a human and wished to die one. Perhaps a case could be made that the Outworlders were not the end of humanity; certainly, no matter how alien they had become, they retained their cultural heritage, their history. No matter that they were monsters, they sprang from the same roots as man and might be mankind transformed, mankind changed, but certainly they were a continuation of the race. Perhaps the Neanderthal, looking at Cro-Magnon, had thought much the same as Eric Benoni.

Yet he was also difficult to know. His polyglot accent was the individually unique signature of the veteran time traveler; his manner bespoke the power and egotism that one with such a profession acquired. Yet he did not ring true, as kin as he might be to the Outworlder agents. He was a true believer with a cause, but he was no fanatic like Sandoval. He simply didn't seem the type to be on the losing end of things, gambling with the past because he had not the resources to be decisive. Comparing the two sides he'd now known, the conclusion was obvious. Eric could do an awful lot of harm and damage, but he was still on the losing side even in this battle. Not being a fanatic, he was miscast in this role.

His thoughts returned most often to Dawn and the children. He loved them all so very much, and he missed them terribly. He realized with more sorrow than surprise that he would willingly go back to the island and to that primitive existence, even if it was killing them. They were the happiest years of his life, and he'd trade almost anything for them again.

And that, of course, was the one reason why, if he ever got the chance, he'd return to the Outworlders. The chance was highly unlikely, but if it came, he knew he'd go. The Earthsiders held his body hostage; the Outworlders held his heart.

Seven meals and two sleeps of indeterminate lengths and Eric was finally back from wherever he'd been. He seemed less confident and some of that aristocratic impassiveness was missing, yet it was clear that he was a man with instructions.

"How have you been? Did they treat you well?" the blond man asked.

Moosic shrugged. "It's a comfortable prison, but a dull one."

"Well, that is all over now. You see, the time stream keeps moving forward. Events keep happening at the standard pace. It is not that they are running out of patience with me, but that the masters of time are running out of it. Ironic, is it not?"

"From what I can see, it's just inevitable, not ironic. You work for pigs, Benoni. They're going to destroy humanity, not the Outworlders. All but them. They'll come back here and live fat and comfortable while the billions fry."

"I have accepted the fact that it is fruitless to argue

philosophy with you. Still, I must have that belt, and quickly. I think maybe we should try a bit of persuasion. You believe you are impervious because I cannot use the primitive methods and I cannot use blackmail. I understand that the other side has the ammunition, but you get used to it in this war. I think perhaps we have a weakness." He snapped his fingers, and one of the creatures brought in a time belt. "Put it on," Eric ordered his captive.

Moosic shrugged and complied. "You seem pretty sure I won't kill myself," he noted calmly.

Eric smiled. "I think you will not, so long as there is a chance of gaining anything personally. No, I think we will give you a choice. The belt is preprogrammed, I should warn you. Once you are uptime, you have only sixty seconds before it is recalled, so get out of it fast. The recall will not kill you, but it is very painful and the age is not one that knows how to kill pain or treat burns very well. I calculate your trip point at six days, and at seven you will be over the edge, more of that time than of this with your memories fading fast. So I will return and find you in five days. Again I will make you an offer. If you refuse, I will return again the next day, after your trip point. Perhaps the new dominant personality with the old knowledge will be more agreeable. If not, you will remain."

He didn't like this, not a bit. That old smugness was creeping back into Eric's tone and manner, and it made him uncomfortable. He decided to argue, if he could. "If I go past the trip point I won't be me anymore, right? So how can I get the belt?"

"It is in the nature of time loops, a rather bizarre mathematics. No matter how far gone you are, if you are not totally assimilated or dead, it will recognize you, even if you cannot recognize yourself."

"Unless they found me gone and cut the power."

"A remote chance. The date and place are fixed. We can return there only an eye-blink from when we left. That is hardly sufficient time for them to act, I would think."

"I could kill myself, or die, wherever you're sending me."

"You won't," Eric responded confidently. "Remember what I said—sixty seconds, or else you will endure terrible but nonfatal agony." He paused for a moment, and there was the hint of a self-satisfied smile on his face. "We have gotten to know you very well, nightsider. All of you. *Activate!*"

The speaker and the room winked out, and he was falling once more. . . .

The sensation seemed to last an abnormally long time, particularly for the modern belts, but ultimately the world exploded around him once more and was, as expected, very dark. He did not doubt Eric's threat with the belt, and moved to quickly remove and step away from it, but as the forces of time caught him up and caused him to pass out, he managed to think defiantly, *O.K., Eric, do your worst!*

When he awoke, he realized that Eric Benoni had done exactly that.

DOIN' THE TRIP POINT SHUFFLE

Eric Benoni may have made a number of mistakes in his life, but this one was going to cost him dearly. That much, at least, she understood. Benoni had calculated the Moosic trip point from the previous length of stay, based on the original calculations. He had forgotten, or overlooked, the fact that the Moosic who journeyed back now, like that professor long forgotten until this moment brought his story back, was overaged.

This knowledge and these memories were in her mind, as were all the memories of Ron Moosic—but that was all there was of Ron Moosic now. It was a marvel that she had those memories, and with it the understanding of them, yet they were not hers, but those of a stranger, someone from another time and place. The knowledge, the memories, seemed both real and unreal to her. Some things, the more subtle things, the feelings and the emotions and the sense of actually having lived them, were absent.

And yet, she knew, God had chosen her for this moment and for this purpose. She did not understand it, but one did not question miracles. It was clear only that this one had come to her and had grappled with her mind, and in her blind faith she had tamed it. So vital was her holy mission, though, that the Dark One himself had sent his agents to ambush and kill her. She had seen the demons, and with her strange knowledge and memories she had slain one through the grace of God.

She stood there, beside the cart, and stared at the slain demon, already smelling of its foulness. She remembered then the other who had been with it, and quickly slipped into the darkness of the rocks and grasses. She looked around but saw nothing, and realized that clouds must have obscured the moon, although it was starlit back towards the valley. The mountains were often covered in clouds and mist, particularly at this time of year.

And yet, after giving the cart as wide a berth as possible, she began to make her way back across the trail and towards those mountains and their darkness. She did not, however, feel fear. God had not put her through this to have her fail now.

Briefly she considered going back to the old monastery, but she realized that it would not be possible. The world was not ending any time soon, not for a very long time. The Mother Superior, the whole of the new Order, was, then, at best a terrible error, at worst a Satanic blasphemy. Sooner or later word of it would reach the hierarchy of the Holy Church, and the Inquisition would come for them. God would have mercy on their souls, for they had been pious and sincere.

She prayed to the Blessed Virgin for guidance, and as the night wore on, she seemed to sort it out, at least a bit. Her own pitiful memories stretched only to just before coming to this place, and these mountains were the only home, the order the only life, she'd ever personally known. Without the order, she had no place, no reason to exist at all.

But she had those alien memories, that alien knowledge, although it seemed almost to be growing weaker by the hour, yet she understood that God had given them to her for a reason. They were not hers, but they were real, and so were the terrible things they whispered. The blond Eric was a demon, perhaps the devil himself, surrounded by his minions. The others fought him in all times and places, and thus they surely must be God's chosen instruments.

Satan wished the time belt, for from it he might get the whereabouts of his enemies. She, then, was the anointed one who had to retrieve that belt.

How?

God would not have acted thus unless there was a way. The dead demon's belt was gone, of course. She had taken it to travel to purification on the cross in the manner of Our Lord. She understood that all now, and the knowledge that she had been chosen by Him and had been honored by trial on the Sacred Cross gave her a thrill that was beyond measure.

How?

The man whose memories she had been given had been real once. Had been here, in fact. The Lord had guided him to this spot, to her, and had then transformed him into a spiritual presence. His whole purpose, then, had been to anoint her, to leave his memories with her.

And his time suit.

She grew suddenly very excited and praised God for His revelations and His wisdom, tears of joy coming unbidden to her eyes. The knowledge from Ron Moosic's experience mixed with her own interpretation, and she knew and understood the purpose of it all.

He, this man Moosic, could not return for the belt ever. Satan would keep watch over the spot, waiting to trap him if he did. But, said the memories, if someone else came, someone not Moosic but connected to him spiritually, as she was, they might not detect, but that new person could still touch the suit, touch the belt, even use it. Use it to go to those in God's service who had passed through the trials as she had.

She was now to become one with them.

It was a high calling, and she felt doubly humble to be so chosen. She hardly felt like a saint, yet she would obey the Lord and gladly give her life in His service.

But first she had to find the time suit in the mountain wilds.

This was, she realized, one last trial, for her time was limited. The memory of where the suit had been hidden was already very dim, and it would not last much longer. Every moment she felt a little more of that strange set of knowledge and facts in her head fade away. Nothing specific, but she knew that she had little time.

She tripped over something in the darkness and came down hard, the pain shooting through her. It was a sign that she was being foolish, that nothing could be found in this darkness but injury and perhaps death. She must sit, sit and think, as hard as that was with the adrenalin pumping through her.

He had had a full moon on a clear night. She, on the other hand, had no moon at all up here, and even if the clouds parted, as they seemed they might, she'd have less than a sliver.

The monastery was above him, perhaps half a mile, she reflected, using his measurements and searching his dim memory, trying to force it forward. The valley was a bowl-shaped affair with no stream visible. Looming above it was a . . . cat's head? She searched for the pictorial, but it was dim. A rounded shape with two small peaks angled off opposite one another, that was all.

Satan had caused the clouds, she knew, but even without them she'd have a rough time. She knew the surrounding countryside, though, had chased sheep and goats at least this far. The monastery had always been her point of reference when this had happened, of course, so she understood the proper distance required for his vision. From the angle, it would have to be off in that direction, to the southwest. There were three such valleys in that general area that she knew, perhaps others. She would search them all, looking for those two telltale tiny peaks that must have been stones or mountain tops. But she could not do it tonight.

Feeling the bruises from her fall, she got up and probed around for a soft or grassy spot, and prayed herself to sleep.

* * *

She awoke aching and sore, and found that her habit had been torn in numerous places. There was blood on it, too, in several places, from scratches and small wounds. It didn't matter, and she knew it. What mattered was that there had been a definite fading in the alien memories, not so much in content but in her ability to use that content. Sleep had been the inevitable thing to do; she'd been tired and injured and could not have accomplished anything in the pitch darkness anyway. Still, time was running out on her and she knew it. Every obstacle was being placed in her way to prevent the doing of God's will.

Ignoring her hunger and pain, she paused only long enough for morning prayers and then set off.

The day was cloudy and damp, and a mist was falling that made the rocky areas slippery. It took her the better part of two hours to reach the first of the alpine meadows leading to the bowl-shaped valleys, bowls which her alien knowledge said were carved by ancient glaciers, although she rejected that as a Satanic attempt to divert her and question her faith. The world was not that old.

Reaching the meadow, she stopped to get her bearings as best she could. There were clouds above and below, but it was amazingly clear in the central part, and she could see the distant winding road. She could even see the cart, although not clearly from this distance, and she saw in that area the tiny moving shapes of many people. Some were undoubtedly nuns from the Order, but others were apparently on horseback, either people from the town or, equally possible, members of the local duke's household. It wasn't possible to tell what time it was, but she began to fear, from the sight of the mounted group, that she had passed out for a very long time.

They would find some of the bodies—perhaps the demon's, if its fellow had not carted it back to Hell, and certainly the poor sister who'd died in her place. They would see blood and mount a search for her. Time was now pressing in more ways than one.

She had received an instant education beyond measure, but she was not one to think quickly or accept or understand all that she now knew. For a long time she'd been in a situation where thinking at all was suppressed, and, oddly, this gave her a stronger will than perhaps any other would have to accomplish the task God had set for her, for she was single-mindedly devoted to this and no other thing.

All the facts, all the memories not relevant to the search were simply suppressed or ignored. She understood her relative position as regarded the monastery and the town below, but until and unless the clouds parted or the sun burnt through them and gave her a glimpse of the monastery and the peaks, she would have to proceed by chance, climbing to the level of the highest of the three valleys, searching it, then descending to the next, then the next, and doing likewise if need be.

Her bare feet were cut and bruised by the time she ascended to the upper valley, but what was such pain and discomfort to one who had been crucified in the manner of Our Lord? It certainly didn't take long to realize that the climb had been for nothing; the upper wall of the valley turned inward, blocking any possible view of the monastery from within it.

By the time she reached the entrance to the second and then climbed back up to get into it, the sun threatened an appearance. It was well in the west, though, which indicated that the hour was growing late. More than once she'd heard the distant shouts of people around her, echoing back and forth across the mountainsides, and she knew that they were searching for her even now, and she had to constantly check to see if she were in anyone's line of sight.

The second valley looked right, as far as she could tell from the point at which she surmised the position of the monastery to be, but without the mountain landmarks it was difficult to tell. She began a methodical search of the place, praying all the while for divine aid and intervention. The suit had been hidden in a cleft in the rock and concealed with brush. There was nothing to do but to make her way along the inner bowl of the valley and examine it bit by tiny bit.

The light had definitely changed for the worse by the time she had gone three-quarters of the way around, and she began to fear that she would have to spend yet another night. She was growing weak, although small springs had quenched her thirst, and she wasn't certain how much more she could take of this. She sat down, finally, on a rock to catch her breath and closed her eyes, praying intently to the Blessed Virgin for both the strength and will to continue. The strange memories, while all present, were taking on a strange quality of unreality, and she felt doubt creep into her mind about them.

Was she, in fact, now insane? Had the experience on the trail driven her mind to this strangeness, or had Satan corrupted her and caused this to happen? Were these strange memories and voices within her truly from God, or were they in fact demons inhabiting her body? Certainly what much of them whispered to her was sheer blasphemy.

Holy Mary, Mother of God, Blessed art thou among women and blessed is the fruit of thy womb, Jesus. . . .

Trip point. . . . Assimilation. . . . Outworlders. . . . Night side. . . .

Holy Mary, Mother of God, Blessed art thou. . . .

Four dirty, naked little children and a fat old woman. . . .

Holy Mary, Mother of God. . . .

There was Joseph, and Ginny, and Sarah, and Cathy, and little Mark, who had never been well. . . .

Holy Mary, Mother of God! How was she to know the truth? Tears welled up in her eyes, and she felt totally defeated, miserable, and alone. Finally, she pulled herself together enough to raise her head and look out again at the valley.

The sun was very low in the sky, but not yet beneath the mountains in the west. The clouds had moved off, although they were still off below the peaks, beautifully illuminated by the rays of the sun. Over to one side she could make out the village far below, but for only a brief period. It looked like. . . .

She turned her head and wiped away the rest of her tears. The monastery was clearly visible at the correct angle. Frowning, she wondered for a moment, *the correct angle for what?* Then memory returned, single-minded memory, and she turned and looked back and up at the peaks, now briefly revealed. She squinted and tried to block out all the detail, leaving only the dark silhouette of the peaks against the darkening sky. It didn't look quite right, but if you used a little imagination and thought of a bright, moonlit night, those two little peaks over there might almost look like ears. . . .

Cat's ears?

She stood up and studied the area again. There were bushes over there, a hundred feet or so back and to her right. She walked cautiously towards them, almost in a trance-like state, unthinking, not daring to believe.

She had passed the spot earlier in the day and had given it a good going-over, but now she dove into the brush and found behind it brush of a different sort, dead and discolored. She pulled it out anxiously, and saw it before too much longer.

So it had not been a dream. And if the suit was real, then the demons were real, and since the demons had tried to prevent her from reaching the suit, that meant. . . .

The sun had set below the mountains, although there was still a murky twilight. Clouds were again rolling over the peaks above her, and there was a dank chill in the air. She was weak and had never weighed much, but she managed with her last ounces of strength to pull the heavy suit out and stare at it.

The red readout on the display was dim, but there. Power, measured on a bar, read at less than fifty percent. Clearly it was a fight to hold the suit in this time.

The suit was huge on her. She was almost standing on its seat to get her head out of the top, and the tremendously heavy helmet threatened to slip again and again from her grasp, but she finally got it on and barely remembered to switch on internal power to the suit. Cool air came in and filled it from somewhere as she managed to close the seals.

She wiggled to get her small arm into the massive arm and glove of the suit, but she brought it up to the controls and watched the liquid crystal display change as she did so. She needed more knowledge now; she reached back for it.

She cleared the readings to zero and tried activation, but the suit would not comply. With tremendous difficulty she made out the strange characters and understood that they were telling her that there was not enough power.

Not enough to reach—where? The heavenly base, of course. But she had known that.

The dateline readouts were zero, but the location indicator was not. Again her mysterious knowledge allowed her to guess that the location shown was indeed the suit's home—where, in fact, she wanted to go.

But what should the numbers be? And would the suit, in fact, return her to the time chamber if she did get it right, the time chamber now held by a very different power? But, no—the suit was no longer linked to that early chamber or it would have ceased to exist. It was linked to the forces of heaven, so wonderfully named the Outworld.

Perhaps, she thought, even if she determined the correct setting, it might not be best to proceed there directly. The demons could tell when the Outworld moved in time, and because this suit was now Outworld-powered, they had been able to track its original occupant here. But they could not see or touch the suit, so perhaps it might be best to throw them off, to do it in small jumps here and there. The "Home" control would always give her the right setting when she needed it.

They had caught her once, in *his* maimed body, in that time. They would know it, and be waiting.

She reset, and saw the numbers for her present return. So that was how easy it was. *He* had tried, as she had, to press the "Home" key, and that could not work. But if the controls were simply set by hand to zero, they would take her back, since the suit's logic worked on the basis of that key time as zero and all else plus or minus that time.

So, no—not directly there. Lead them a merry chase first. God was on her side. Did not the forces of Hell admit they would lose Armageddon in that future? Did not the Holy Word state that Satan would rule before the Final Judgment?

Curiously, it was not Moosic's memories but those of Neumann that held some of the key, for he'd had a keen interest in geography. Cautiously, she reduced the numbers to 385.5, a good, experimental time. She knew little of history, and there was not the information she needed in anyone's memory, but she thought the Holy Land a good bet. Neumann, at least, could get her in the neighborhood. The other memories indicated that the Crusades had liberated the area, and, indeed, in her own time it was taught that this liberation was a great thing. There was nothing in anyone's memory to contradict this. It seemed safe, and a very appropriate place, should the forces of Hell follow.

Neumann, in one of his attempts to reconcile himself with his faith, had in the process memorized, without really realizing it, the basic latitude and longitude of Jerusalem.

Eagerly she punched it in, then pressed "Activate." There was the sensation of falling and the passage of much time, but she did not notice. As soon as all had winked out, she'd passed out from sheer exhaustion.

* * *

There were stronger personalities lurking inside the fragile mind of Sister Nobody, as Moosic had termed her, and in her exhaustion and freed from time's constraints, they all rushed in to fill the vacuums created. It was not a conscious thing; all of them had essentially ceased to exist in that sense. It was, rather, a mind trying to create order out of chaos and was, in fact, a natural process when the newly forward personality, after the trip point had been passed, was neither strong nor dominant.

The frail young woman who came to in answer to the buzzing alarm in the suit was not the same as the one who had activated it. In a sense, she was a new personality, a composite of all those she held. She was, in a sense, reborn. It was merely an extension of the process by which those humans created by the time-travel effect merged into the master mind, although, in this case, that mind was too weak and too shallow to contain them.

Still, she was in the weak and nearly starved body of the Sister, and hadn't much strength to do more than undo the seals and get out of the terribly large suit. It was night, as expected, and well within the ancient walled city. Few prowled this hour, except for the authorities, and none were in sight. She managed, somehow, to drag the suit back into a narrow alleyway between two huge multiple dwellings of eastern adobe, but that was about it. She spent time studying the street itself, taking particular note of the square not too far down the street. It was, to her eyes, a large and confusing city, but not one that could have this many distinguishing features.

Summoning every ounce of will and strength left in her, and feeling near death, she managed to find a half-burnt stick of charcoal from the alley and make several marks on the building's wall. This was not to say that rain or the owners would not erase them, but it was something, anyway. At least, from the way the place looked, none of the owners ever erased or otherwise cleaned anything.

She used the small breathing tube in the suit helmet to help her; she was simply beyond walking to keep a steady air intake. She knew, though, that she might well have to undergo another trip point here, if only to keep her from expiring should she use the suit again. Let's see. . . . Would it be six days, or . . . what? No, that was for Moosic, and he was no more. Just how old was she, anyway? Impossible to tell.

How do you know you've reached the trip point? *You'll know,* they'd assured Moosic, although it might take some will to get to and put on the suit after that.

It seemed forever that she sat there, sparingly using the helmet to breathe, but finally the moment came when time was ready for her. She felt the nausea almost as a welcome friend, and soon passed out.

Nowhere in her collective mind was the specific fact that the Crusades had indeed more or less liberated Jerusalem, and for quite some time, but had lost it, again and forever, in 1291. After the repeated failures of the Crusades of the fourteenth century, and in the schism in the papacy and Church that had followed, this fact tended to be glossed over to the low and the ignorant.

It was 1605 now, and Jerusalem was, as it had been for over three centuries, firmly in the hands of the Ottoman Empire.

Waking up as Ismet had shattered forever any hold Sister Nobody might have had on the new personality. For the rest, it was simply another shock to get used to in the cruel tricks time played on those who would play with it.

She had been born and raised in Egypt, had come from a good family and been married to an important Ottoman official when she was fourteen. She was his second wife, and thus had no voice in anything.

Two years after her marriage they moved to Jerusalem, where her husband became chief of tax administration. He was an important man, and already had two daughters by his first wife, but, of course, he wanted a son most of all. He had hoped that Ismet would provide that son, or many sons, for that was her purpose in life, but in the two years in Egypt and one more in Jerusalem she had borne him nothing. Finally, just after her seventeenth birthday, she had become pregnant, but joy turned to horror when the child, which was indeed a boy, was stillborn.

He blamed her for that, and beat her, but finally his rage cooled. Still, he could not bear to have her around anymore, and so divorced her. She was, in effect, thrown out into the streets of Jerusalem with nothing, including any skills or experience outside her sheltered existence.

Such women were easy prey for those who had need of them, such as Mufasta the Procurer, whose street people told him of this and who found her, weeping and alone, and had kindly taken her in. Helpless, alone, feeling abandoned and dishonored, she was perfect for what he had in mind. She proved to be easy to domesticate, and he soon moved her to his port operation in Tyre, where sailors had money and great lust.

After the first hundred men, she no longer thought of being anything but a woman of pleasure.

Now, however, she was back with him in Jerusalem, having had some difficulties with an official of the empire in Tyre over the amount of certain bribes to be paid for doing business. Business was, in fact, not nearly as good there, but he had opium to keep his ''harem'' girls happy, and as his political contacts there were far more friendly and far less greedy, it balanced out.

She had broken easily, and it did not trouble her. She called him ''Master'' and was grateful to be the property of one who provided for her needs. She was quite good-looking, and her barrenness had proven to her that this was indeed the mission in life Allah had selected for her. Mufasta was not a harsh master, for he was skilled and did not have to be.

She danced near naked for unruly, drunken crowds in

the back rooms of places where wine flowed freely and religious laws were not highly regarded, and she laid more than twenty of them in nine days, and it was acceptable to those who inhabited that body with her because it felt good and was new.

The decision, however, had to be made, for they had to decide whether to risk all on Sister Nobody's frail and broken body or to take Ismet's far preferable one—but with Ismet as the primary.

Ultimately, they decided that there was a great possibility that Ismet could not be convinced to go, so they took charge. In the very early morning she had snuck out of her dingy little room, donned a *chador* and veil as was necessary to travel unescorted, and made her way several blocks to the square. She had made certain that she knew the spot, having had to fetch water and other things at her master's bidding. The mind was very close to control, terribly frightened and confused, but she'd done it.

Compared to the last time, the suit was amazingly easy to find and only slightly worse a fit than it had been. It was, however, only Ismet's compliancy and drug-weakened will that allowed her to come this far. The trip point was reached while she was actually in the suit, but before it could be activated. For quite some time she sat there, confused and frightened, but then something inside her fought, reached out and adjusted the numbers she could not quite understand, then pushed a button.

The date and location were basically random, but with reality blanking out around her the process of assimilating all of the personalities into her went on. Again the will was not a strong one, and a synthesis occurred, although the new personality was, in fact, less decisive and more prone to fright than the first one had been.

She came out in the water. It was an eerie sensation, literally standing atop an unmoving ocean, but soon she began to sink into it. She realized immediately what "random" meant, and struggled with the controls as she sank, hoping to reactivate before the pressure crushed the suit.

The next time, thanks to a bit of luck, she struck land, and knew that this new body, while young and attractive, also would not do, for it was addicted to opium.

In 1741, in India, she was a prostitute serving the British soldiers.

In 1854 she was a prostitute, this time serving seamen of all nations in Honolulu, in the Kingdom of Hawaii. But one was a navigator who knew quite a bit about latitude and longitude.

In 1905 she was a prostitute on the Barbary Coast of San Francisco.

She had by now realized that time had found a convenient outlet for her and was not going to let her go. She realized, too, that her power in the suit was waning, and her reserve air supply was so thin there was a question of whether it would reach. By this point she was three trip points beyond the first, and someone else entirely. Someone, in fact, who did not regard the life time was imposing on her, that of a barren whore, as something to be ashamed of.

Still, she decided to go for the abandoned time belt. There was more chance at a future there than in a past time in the oldest profession, and there seemed no reason not to take a chance on it.

She didn't want to risk assimilation in Moosic's present, if only because it would signal to the inevitable watchers that someone was there. The locator on the suit was not, however, designed to go down more than seconds, so where she arrived was not precisely where she wanted to be. It was, however, only two miles north of the plant.

The air gauge said it was empty, and had said so for some time. Not that she could move in that suit, anyway, but that left her with an hour or two, no more, before assimilation would take over. She abandoned the suit with no thought of hiding it. It was useless at this stage. Two miles was two miles, and her current body was quite young—seventeen, in fact—but also not in the best condition for walking or running. The men had liked large breasts, and the penalty for them in her case was to be large in other places as well. She would probably not make the distance in time, and it was too close now to take the chance.

There was a small communal housing development nearby, however, and she checked the outside and found a number of possibilities. Cars were out, since, even if she could find one, in this regulated society it wouldn't mean anything. The machines would not run while she was out of phase.

She looked around the rear of the complex, which seemed some kind of cheap family housing, and eventually spotted a child's bicycle sitting in one of the yards. It was a bit small for her, but it would certainly do. She feared it might be locked, but found to her relief that it was not. There was, apparently, one advantage to living in a rigidly policed state.

It was kind of fun, riding a bike stark naked down a major road, but it still took her some time to reach her destination, and the ups and downs of the road in this seemingly flat country were not easy to overcome.

The Calvert Cliffs, known as one of the east's richest fossil beds, were just below the nuclear plant and its secret time project. She turned into the small parking lot for the cliffs and nearly jumped off the bike, running down the small trail a bit to where she, as Moosic, had left the belt, all the while praying it was still there.

It was, and it appeared to be functioning normally. She began to feel a bit dizzy, and worried that phasing might catch up with her before she could activate the belt. She had tripped as Ismet while actually in the suit, and only Ismet's fear of returning and being discovered as having left without permission caused her to activate at all.

It had been, in a sense, lifetimes since she'd used one of

the belts, and for a moment she was struck with confusion as to how it worked. Finally, though, she remembered the "Home" button, found it, and pressed it as nausea started to overtake her.

The feeling was replaced almost instantly by one of falling slowly, and she relaxed. The journey, which might have taken many hours in the old suit had it had the power, would not take long with this device.

Feeling a bit shaky, she appeared in the lounge area of the Outworlder base. Sitting there were Herb, looking much as he had so many lifetimes before, "Doc" Kahwalini, beautiful as ever, and a small, weasel-like man she barely recalled as Nikita.

Doc looked over at her and smiled. "Right on schedule," she said approvingly.

THE WORM OUROBOROS

"Do you ever feel rotten about being in this business?"
Kahwalini asked Chung Lind as she studied the results of
her diagnostic computer's run on the newcomer.

"Huh? What do you mean?"

"Never really knowing, I mean. Never really being sure
what's wrong and what's right, whether all this means a
great deal or nothing, and whether it's our right to do it to
the ignorant and unknowing?"

Lind shrugged. "Not particularly. Conscience getting to
you again, huh? This little operation's a bit smelly, and
we're coming up to the rough part, so you want a way
out."

"That may be it. But *I* don't want out. There's no place
to go, anyway, and certainly no place as interesting as
here. No, I just dislike doing this to other people."

"It's not the first time," he pointed out. "And when we
mount a major operation it can affect millions, not just one."

"But you don't *see* those millions, or feel them. Still, I
suppose you're right. Setting fire to the orphanage *is* worse
than setting fire to one orphan."

"You're just down in the dumps, as usual, when this
sort of thing comes up. We're soldiers, or cops, or whatever you want to call it. What's right and wrong isn't our
choice. All I know is that we've saved more lives than
we've taken, and that's all that counts with me."

She sighed and nodded. "I guess that has to be enough.
O.K., I'm ready for her. Don't worry—I'm a pro."

"I know you are and I'm not worried. Anything?"

"Some minor bugs and internal stuff, the product of 1905 or whenever it was. There's a progressive astigmatism that's going to get worse."

"She'll survive."

"I know, I know. O.K., to work."

She left Lind in the lab and proceeded back to the medical examining area. The patient was about five foot four, twenty years old, with medium-length black straight hair and large brown eyes. She had a pudgy face that was somewhat cute, but she was not really pretty in any sense of the word, a fact made worse by the forty extra pounds she carried. Her low contralto had a throaty, rasping quality that sounded either cute or sexy.

Doc sat down in front of her and looked over the chart. Finally, she asked, "How do you feel?"

"All right, I guess," the patient responded. "A little tired."

"That's mostly from relief of tension. I wouldn't worry about it. I'm going to run you through a decontamination chamber to kill off some of the bugs, but it's no big thing. Actually, I was asking how you feel inside, in your mind."

The young woman thought about it. "I—I don't know. So much has gone on in there, but I guess I never really thought much about it. Never tried to."

Doc nodded to herself. "I'd like to run a psych stat on you."

"Huh? What's that?"

"It's a medical device, like decontamination and diagnostics. It was developed for this operation, for nightsiders like us. It'll help us to know what your problems are, and it might help you as well. It doesn't hurt—it's more like getting a good night's sleep, in fact. Would it bother you?"

"Should it?"

"Good point. No, it shouldn't, but some people don't

like anybody else to know them really closely. Herb, for example, won't take one."

"Doesn't bother me, if it'll help you out. I spent all my time and effort just getting here. Now that I'm here, I don't know what I'm going to do anymore."

"Well, that's pretty well assured. O.K., just stretch out here on the examining table." Doc reached up, pressed a button overhead, and a small device that looked something like a giant neon office lamp dropped down. She took it, adjusted it to within a few inches of the patient's form, then sat back down again. "Any questions before we begin?"

"No, I guess not for now. Well, maybe one thing. How come I tripped so much and still could go forward in time? I mean, I thought if you were assimilated that couldn't happen. I never thought about it much at the time, but it just came to me."

"Fair question. It's because you weren't assimilated. The trip point is the halfway marker in assimilation, remember. After that time you become slightly more the new person than the old one. But you're still connected, still a time traveler, a voyeur, so to speak, until full assimilation takes place. Basically, if you can remember enough to ask a question like that one, you're still you as far as the devices and time are concerned, no matter what's going on in your head."

The woman nodded. "O.K."

"Any more?"

"Lots, but I guess they can wait. What's this thing gonna do?"

"Analyze all the people who make you up. Tell us, maybe, who you are in the here and now."

"Sounds fair. Will I remember it?"

"Not consciously, but if you like, you can monitor the recorded results later. Ready?"

"I guess so. You're the doctor."

Kahwalini flicked some switches on a small control

panel, and the little machine glowed a dull purple and began to move, tracing the contours of the patient's body.

"Feels good. Like a massage," the woman commented.

Its back-and-forth scan seemed to penetrate into every bit of her body, and she found herself becoming relaxed and drifting off.

The doctor became busy now, attaching a spider's nest of probes not only to the head of the sleeper but to various parts of the body as well. Satisfied, she stepped back and triggered the process.

"Who are you?"

The question confused her for a few moments, and memory channels opened to pinpoint references. At that point, each of the elements from the various human lives and personalities that made up the sum of her mind were distinct, although interactive, and revealed to the computer analyzer.

The human mind, in fact, remained the most complex and amazing organic mechanism known. The human race had existed, and survived, not so much by physical as by mental adaptability: the ability to filter out or suppress; to add, file, and retrieve what was needed; to learn to cope with radical changes. Still, there were individual physiological limits on a specific brain, and the brain of the subject was not the brain of the others.

The information from all of those people she had been was there, but each trip point had caused the information to be reconfigured and refiled. All relevant data was integrated; all irrelevant data was relegated to those dark and seldom-used areas. Intelligence really was the ability to access those areas; the speed of access and the amount of data that could be combined and retrieved and assembled by that intelligence was the measure of how high it was.

The dominant, or shell, personality, which the body matched, was that of Megan Clark, b. San Francisco, 1885, but since it was the dominant shell and not an assimilated, or totally integrated, personality it was only partly Megan's. Alfie, Neumann, and Sister Nobody were there, although only as data, not even anymore as memories. The original personality and life, that of Ron Moosic, was also there, as data of course—but, strangely, as an abstract as well. Intellectually, she understood her origins; as a practical matter, Megan could not actually remember being Moosic, or any man. He had the quality of a fantasy personality, someone she might occasionally imagine herself being, but the imagining was entirely from that perspective and rather unrealistic. In effect, he had become detached from her, an imaginary or ideal lover rather than as the person she once had been.

This process had allowed the later personalities to alter her psyche as his strong will would not have done. The three people she had become were from three different times and cultures, but they were all very traditional ones, and the attitudes instilled had been traditional as well. Add to this the fact that all had been prostitutes from poor backgrounds dominated by powerful males, and the new personality was easier to understand.

In all cases she had been treated like an object in societies that at least winked at prostitution and generally condoned it, thereby leaving no real outlet, no hope of varying the life. To adjust, to survive, all three had ultimately accepted it after fighting the idea for a little while.

Both Moosic's and Neumann's IQs had been exceptional. Megan's, however, was perhaps average if used to the full. She had, generally, a low sense of self-worth. She needed someone to be over her, to make most of her decisions, to constantly reinforce her weak ego and tell her she was worthwhile. The fact that men would pay money for what pleasures she could give gave her a concrete sense of security, the only security she had. The fact that someone else got the money was actually better for her; she only felt secure when someone else was providing things.

The key to it was Moosic's surrender, his depression when faced with Eric once more. He had lost hope and, therefore, the will to live. In the absence of any replacement values from Sister Nobody, the Ismet personality had dominated, and time had complied by providing similar situations. Time had finally killed Ron Moosic.

But, still, there was a spark there. This woman would cope with whatever was thrown at her, with no reservations as to how or why. She was insecure and submissive, but she was a survivor, and her dream was to be swept off her feet by a strong, dominant man.

Doc Kahwalini frowned. The subject, she reflected, had come out exactly as planned.

The next few days were used to get her settled in and to answer some of her questions. She also spent a little time with some learning machines they had, trying to improve her vocabulary and pronunciation. She knew and understood the word "assimilation," for example, but it never seemed to come forward when she needed it, and when it was forced, she constantly mispronounced it. It irritated her, particularly because the word was there.

More unsettling was her almost incidental discovery that she couldn't read or write. Doc was sympathetic. "It happens. It's a skill, and skills are sometimes lost in this process. You can re-learn it—it's back in there, someplace in your mind—but it'll take time. I wouldn't worry about it now, though. Come on with me now. You've forgotten a lot, and might forget more. It depends on what happens from here on out. The longer you are the way you are, the more of the past you'll lose and the more of the new 'you' will dominate."

"Where are we going?"

"Outside. I want some fresh fruit."

She stopped. "I thought—I remember, I think, that it's dangerous out there."

"Not unless you spend years out in it. You once did, and you're still here."

She shook her head. "That's kind of a dream."

When the doorway slid back and they stepped out, it was clear that the dream was less so than she'd thought.

The groves of trees, the jungle's edge, the distant pounding of the surf. . . .

Doc turned to her and nodded. "I didn't know any other way to break it to you."

"But—this is the old place, isn't it?"

"The old place—yes, I guess it *would* be."

Her mouth dropped, and she shivered slightly in the tropical sun. "Then—this isn't later, it's *earlier*. Then that belt was set to bring me back *before*. Oh, Jesus! That means. . . ."

"Yes," said Kahwalini softly. "*You* are Dawn."

She stared at herself in the full-length mirror. She should have known, known right from the first time she'd looked at herself, she thought sourly. But, then, Ron had never looked at Dawn in the same way as she looked at herself.

The idea scared her; it also made her mad. For her to be Dawn, then, the computer—the all-seeing, all-knowing damnable computer—had to know it right from the start, when it sent Ron uptime with a belt that homed to this point in time instead of a later one.

The damned thing had *planned* it, planned it all out. It knew in advance all that was going to happen, even the capture by Eric. It *knew* and did nothing, except to arrange for things to come out right.

It was, Doc explained, in the nature of time loops.

"The problem is, only the leading edge is new," she explained. "All else was new once, when *it* was the leading edge, but it's already happened. Back here, near the dawn of time, the computer, anchored both here and on the edge, can monitor what happens and evaluate any changes."

"But why is it happening *now*?" Dawn asked her. "I mean, it's already *happened*, right?"

"No, not exactly. Just remember that any loop, once initiated, is assumed by time to have been completed. The record is there. The computer can then read it, evaluate it, and then accept it, change it, or reverse it, depending on the outcome."

"And what say do *I* have in this? What if *I* decide not to go along with this whole thing?"

"Then you will still exist, cut off absolutely from the time stream, a total nightside. Ron Moosic will die in the attack, and all links to you will be severed. Dawn will exist only as her least common denominator, devoid of the knowledge, strength, and understanding she—you—still draw from him. As such, you will be no further use to us. We will shift you uptime, where assimilation will be instantaneous."

She gulped and sat down. Her fury at being so manipulated was tempered somewhat by the idea of fulfilling, living, what had been a fantasy. Still, there was something bizarre in it all, sort of the ultimate in masturbation.

"And if I . . . go through with it?"

"Then we will come for you at the proper time. We know where and when you'll be."

"But—it's not fair! All that time, all that. . . . Hey! This can't be real! I can't have children!"

"Megan can't, but Megan's a product of 1905. Dawn is a synthesis, a nightsided person."

"But it's not fair! I'll lose him forever! And come out old and sick!"

"We can fix what goes wrong, either by medicine or through tripping. You know that. As for losing him—well, that's all in the way you look at it, isn't it? You'll have a longer time together than many people have."

"But—I'll *know*."

"Time and mind have a way of dealing with that. Complete your loop, and give yourself a purpose and a future. We are in the long process of undoing what has been done. It'll save a lot of lives. Isn't that worth it?"

She shook her head in bewilderment. "I don't know. I really don't. But, tell me, how can you people be so cold? What gives you the *right* to do this?"

Doc couldn't address what she herself doubted, but she could answer the second question. "We have the machine, the knowledge, and the skill to do it. So does the enemy. That last makes the rest irrelevant."

Ron Moosic arrived the next day, but she did not see him immediately. She wasn't certain how she was going to handle this, or if she could. As long as he remained out of sight, it was a problem postponed, and she spent time out by the sea and the waterfall, just thinking and trying to sort it out.

She almost ran into him the next day in the lounge, but kept out of sight, watching him while remaining unobserved. The man she saw was a shock, the embodiment of the man she saw in her dreams and fantasies, but he neither looked nor acted quite like she expected. Her mind tried to grasp it, tried to remember this moment, but she found it impossible to bring it forward. All of her that was Ron Moosic seemed to recede into a distant haze.

That day they issued her a communicator and a time belt. "Remember," Lind warned, "we're going to be attacked."

She nodded and took it, almost without thinking.

On the third day she checked out the lounge and went down there for a few moments, hoping to catch Kahwalini in an off moment. She feared going back to Doc's lair; *he* was there.

Herb was over in a corner playing computerized backgammon. He looked up and waved to her, then went back to his game.

Almost as soon as she'd sat down, *he* came in, talking to Doc. She felt petrified, but there was nowhere to hide, so she just sat there and hoped he wouldn't notice. Of course, he did, and came over.

"Hi! I finally get the chance to say thanks for saving my

life,'' he said cheerfully, sitting down in a chair opposite hers. "How's that for a good opening line?''

She smiled, but was inwardly terrified. *This is it!* she realized, and in that moment had absolutely no ability to recall anything at all of this time. Her nervousness, and her mind, had blocked it out. What did he mean about saving his life, though? It puzzled her, but then cheered her a bit. She *had*, hadn't she? And she hadn't done that, yet. There was still time, and perhaps a future, yet to come.

She sighed. "I'm sorry for not being a little more hospitable. I'm afraid I've got a load on my mind and a lot of hard decisions to make. I've just had a nasty personal shock.''

"Try being crucified,'' he suggested.

The line seemed almost hilarious. "I have. It's not very nice. Not much *has* been nice lately.''

He shrugged. "I don't want to intrude on what's none of my business.''

She gave up. He was so nice and attractive he was turning her on. The longer the discussion, the less she could relate to him other than the same way she would with an attractive stranger. "No, no. Stay, please. I'm still a little new at this myself, and it's pretty hard to get used to. As soon as you've found out everything, you find you don't understand anything at all. This whole business of time is the craziest thing you can think of. . . .''

The conversation went on for some time, and she began to enjoy it and let it flow, concentrating on her lessons in vocabulary and diction to make him take her for a more educated woman than she was, and deferring the complicated stuff to Herb, who eventually joined the conversation. She liked Ron, but could not imagine ever *being* him. It wasn't the way she thought it would be at all.

"Um, I see you two have met,'' Herb was saying.

Moosic looked over at her. "I still don't know your name.''

A little thrill went through her, and she had an urge to say Agnes or Sarah or even Megan, just to throw something of her own into it, but she did not. She would go along, because these people owned her, and that's what they expected her to do.

"When you've nightsided past your trip point, you may as well pick any name," she told him. "I call myself Dawn, because it's a new start and I kind of like the sound of it. I have lots of other names, but they don't mean nothing to me anymore." The moment she said the name, it became hers. It felt right and sounded right. She was Dawn Moosic, destined to be so, and it did not seem bad at all.

Over the next few weeks they grew inseparable. Although the whole thing continued to trouble her, the fact was that he was simply the most wonderful man she'd ever known, and she wanted him, wanted him desperately. She could hardly wait for an opening, but he was still slightly aloof, slightly hesitant.

She took him out to the waterfall, and they talked, and she showed him the belt and how it operated. It seemed so natural, so nice.

Suddenly there came the sound of tremendous explosions, and her heart skipped a beat. He jumped up and began to run back towards the base; she followed right behind.

They stopped at the edge of the jungle, which still offered concealment, and both saw immediately that there was no way to get through the attackers to the entrance. The Earthsiders were building, and had almost completed, their weapon. Ron looked at her in alarm. "We have to do something!"

Until this moment she'd reserved the option of canceling out, of telling him the truth, but now she realized that it had gone too far. It was going to happen, and nothing whatsoever could prevent it now except their capture or deaths, and that she did not intend. "What do you suggest? We can't get through that mob—they'll kill us. We can't get to that weapon, whatever it is. It'd be suicide. And neither of us is armed."

They watched in frustration, enforced observers. "Why don't they defend themselves?" he muttered. "Surely they must have been prepared for this." He paused a moment. "Your time belt! We could use it to go back just a little and warn them!"

She shook her head. "Won't work. Just like any other time, you can't be in two places at once. Besides—they *were* warned. The computer refused to let them take any action."

"Huh? *Why*?"

"It's part of a nightside time loop. In time, causes can precede events, but the events must be allowed to come about or much worse will happen. God knows, I don't pretend to understand it. I—I just accept what must be now."

He looked at her strangely, then back at the scene, which was getting worse. The device was completed now and powered up, and what was clearly a barrel or projector was aimed directly at the base. The sound of an air horn caused the attack from the gargoyles to be broken off, and they retreated a respectful distance. Then the weapon was brought into play, shooting a continuous beam of what seemed almost liquid blue energy at the complex. The energy struck and seemed to flow over the entirety of the building.

There was a crackling sound near them, and Moosic looked over to see tiny fields of electricity dancing around Dawn's time belt. The small red displays blinked on and off erratically. "The time belt!" he almost shouted, in no danger with the din of the attack masking them. "It's shorting out!"

For a moment it flashed into her mind, all of it, and she froze, not certain just what to do. He was shouting, and suddenly she made her decision. She wanted him, wanted it, no matter what the final cost. She picked up the microphone and dialed the base frequency. "Dawn to Base—we are caught outside and unarmed. Advise!"

There was a crackling sound, and then a tinny voice responded. "Use the belt and get out now! It's your only chance. . . ." And then it went dead. She turned and looked at him and tears welled up inside her, but refused to come out.

"Here! Let's open the belt wide so it goes around both of us. It'll be tight, but I think we can manage," she said.

"You mean use it now?"

"While we still can. The base may fall or short out any minute!"

The belt was never intended for two people and was an extremely tight fit, but they seemed to make it as she'd predicted. More electricity danced, and she had trouble making the adjustments on the belt.

Everything blacked out and they were falling, but ever so briefly. Then all exploded again into reality, but this time into darkness.

The belt continued to sputter. They got it off as quickly as possible and it fell to the ground, then lit up the area with a display of dancing sparks.

"Where'd we go?" he asked her.

"Nowhere. There wasn't time. I just tapped the advance for a decade. We're still on the island, ten years in the future of the attack. That should be safe enough. I didn't dare try any long jump. What if the power failed? And if we did make it, we'd be assimilated."

He nodded. The belt continued to crackle, then made a single electronic whine which slowly faded and died. They were again in darkness. There were no dancing sparks, no red readouts on the belt.

"Oh, Jesus!" he breathed, half cursing and half praying. "The power's gone out!"

She stared down at the blackness. "Or the belt's O.K., but no longer connected to a power source. I—I think they shorted out the base."

It was done! Now, suddenly, she felt completely drained, and things seemed to snap inside her mind. She found herself crying uncontrollably, and he tried to comfort her as best he could, misunderstanding the cause.

Finally, she had cried herself out, and drifted into a strange and very deep sleep. When she awoke, she felt amazingly good, with no sense of trouble and only a sense of adventure. She watched him poking at the remains of the base foundation and checking the growths, and all she could think was, *I am his and he is mine.*

He saw her lying there, staring at him, then came over. "Well, in one way it's not so bad. Almost the Garden of Eden, you might say. We won't starve, that's for sure, and the stream is a secure water supply. From the looks of the sun and the jungle I'd say this place has two climates, hot and hotter. Of course, there are no doctors, no dentists, no nails or hammers or saws. Nothing but the clothes on our backs, such as they are."

He's right, she decided. *He is Adam and I am Eve.*

"These flimsy things aren't going to last long out here," she noted. She kicked off her boots and started to remove her clothes.

"Going natural, huh?"

"You should, too," she told him. "We won't have these forever, so we better get our skin and feet toughened up. We might figure out how to rig lean-tos and maybe even huts, eventually, but there's nothing I've seen on this island that can be used to make clothes or shoes. I'll use these, as long as they last, when we explore the island, but not otherwise. There's no use."

"You've got a point," he admitted and stripped as well. They stood up and looked at each other. "You know," he said, "we really *are* Adam and Eve." He went over to her and hugged her.

"You're turning on," she noted softly.

"Oh? I hadn't noticed." He grew suddenly serious. "You know we may be here for the rest of our lives."

"However long they may be," she replied. "I'm making a personal decision right here and now. I'm not going to think about time at all. Not now, not unless I have to. There's nothing else except now. There's nobody else but us. There's no place else but here." And she meant it.

"That's fair enough," he agreed. "Maybe it all worked out for the best. Maybe this is the place for nightsiders. Let's make the most of it." And, with that, they kissed, and the kiss turned into what she had wanted from the start.

He was very, very good. And so was she.

At first, during their explorations of the island, he referred to the past and tried to get her to tell a little about her own, but that soon stopped. She had literally blocked the past from her mind and allowed her emotions full rule. He certainly was falling in love with her, and she worshipped him. Her whole life, the center of her universe, was him.

Eventually, of course, the playtime ended, and she grew pregnant. She was delighted, not fearful, of the prospect, since deep down, she knew it would come out all right.

About the only thing she hadn't figured on was just how much outright terrible pain was involved in having the kid.

They named him Joseph, after Moosic's father.

They didn't roam so much after he was born, but set up housekeeping near the groves. With the birth of Ginny she became, in fact, a prehistoric homebody. She loved him and she loved the children and she loved having his children, no matter what the discomfort. It was, she felt, what she was *meant* to do. It was a busy time, and it was enough.

As she had Sarah, then Cathy, then Mark, she changed still more, but it was not something she noticed. Ron was getting old and his hair was turning white, but it was a gradual thing and not something either really paid any attention to. For her part, the plentiful fruits, vegetables, and the fish Ron brought from ocean traps caused her to gain more weight, and made her less and less ambitious about going very far from her tiny Eden-like world.

The fat and the fact that over the years her hair had grown in scraggly fashion down past her ass didn't bother her, but her declining vision did. By the time Joseph's voice had lowered and Ginny had experienced her first period, she was effectively blind.

Of course, the children were doing much of the work now, such as it was, under their father's supervision, and the home itself was so fixed that she could navigate it and even do some cooking and cleaning without really having to see at all. She knew, though, that Joseph and Ginny were experimenting with each other, and it bothered her, although there seemed little to do or say about it. It was, after all, inevitable.

And then, finally, came the day of the storm when Joseph had not returned, and she'd nagged Ron until he'd gone out to look for the young man. And in a little more time Joseph ran back, screaming and crying, shouting that he'd killed his father.

It took much comforting as the storm blew in and washed by the island. She felt sad in one way that it was over now, for from the depths of her mind came almost instant understanding of the moment, an understanding she could not convey to the children—particularly the guilt-ridden Joseph.

"You didn't kill him," she soothed. "You just sent him away to a different place."

"Then when will he be back?"

"He—he won't be back."

" 'Cause he's dead!"

"No, because they won't let him come back—again."

"Why?"

"I guess you'll have to ask them. They'll come for us soon."

"I don't want them here! Not if they took Dad!" The other children nodded in agreement.

"That's all right. It's for the best. You'll have to grow up now, kids. I'm afraid it's time."

They came for them only two days after the storm let up. Three of them came, anyway—Doc and Chung Lind and Herb, the three who'd been closest to them. The children were hostile, and Doc, in particular, was taken aback by their accusations that the Outworlders had taken their father from them. It was particularly tough because it was true.

They used the belts to get back to the new base location. The basic medical problems could be taken care of, including her two cancerous growths. One of them, benign but still growing, was the reason why she believed herself pregnant once more. In truth, it would have prevented any such happening.

The Outworlders, it seemed, had a cure for cancer and much else.

The children, surprisingly, were in good shape, although Ginny, Sarah, and Mark were decidedly overweight. They all had, to Doc's satisfaction, a natural extra skin layer with mild pigmentation that absorbed and diluted the most harmful radiation. The mutation did not seem natural, and was not. Doc had been unable to treat the adults for such protection, but she had been able to add the genetic instructions on both sides should children develop. The computer, of course, had provided the information and done the actual work.

From a civilization whose builders could fly through sand, stand crushing pressures and horrible heat, and take oxygen from the rocks, such a minor thing was child's play.

The children never completely lost their feelings of hostility for the team, but concern for their mother and the wonders of the base soon diverted their minds. Rather quickly they were picking up a modern education, although, so far, it had been next to impossible to get them to wear any clothes at all. Ginny, however, more than appreciated the tiny absorbent material, vaginally inserted, that took away much of the problem of the monthly period. Doc had some pills that did away with the cramps and headaches.

Doc could fix almost everything that was wrong with Dawn, but the eyes defeated her. "I'm afraid you'll need a full eye transplant, which is not only tricky but requires a perfect match," she told her. "Either that, or you'll have to trip."

"I don't want to trip—not yet," Dawn responded. "The children are having a tough enough time getting over the loss of their father. And that transplant you talk about sounds like a pretty chancy thing."

"It is, unless you went to the edge and had them grow a perfect pair and implant them with their equipment and facilities. The trouble is, not much is left up there that would be tolerable to normal humans. They will have to go, though. There are growths behind them that threaten the brain itself, and it's too risky to use my ray surgery on it."

Even though she had only a sense of light and dark and vague shapes, the prospect of that frightened her. "I—I don't want to lose them."

"Don't worry. First, we can replace them with inert copies fabricated here. You'll look more normal than the current pair makes you look now. Then we'll use a little device that I looked up in the computer banks. It's being worked on now. It'll allow you some vision, particularly in dim light."

That excited her. "You mean I might be able to see the kids? Actually *see* them as they are now?"

"That's about it."

Dawn started to cry softly. "They're what I have—now."

The operation was, from Doc's point of view, a simple one, and with her futuristic medical equipment and computer-guided and computer-operated surgical kit, it was not even all that painful. In fact, Dawn had not realized how much pain she'd been living with until it was all done and the relief swept through her.

She was already used to being blind, and now, during the healing period, she memorized every inch of the place. She spent most of the time Doc would allow with the children, of course, who were learning at a rapid pace, thanks to the teaching machines and computer-guided instruction. They had the best of both worlds, the most advanced technology together with a whole new wilderness to play in and explore outside.

Members of the team came and went on various mysterious missions, but Doc remained behind, as she did on all but the most extraordinary of occasions. They did not want to risk her outstanding medical skills unless they were needed uptime.

She lost weight, too, and felt better, although she still tipped Doc's scales at better than ninety-seven kilograms—well over two hundred pounds for her five-foot four-inch frame.

It was months before the bandages could come off, but still more time before they could try Doc's gadget. The kids approved her new look; even the eyes, they assured her, were big, warm, and natural. Her hair had been cut very short for the operation, and she kept it that way, knowing it was easy to care for.

She had been gone almost fourteen years, not the ten or twelve Ron had estimated, and was physically thirty-four. Now, after a lot of skilled work with the best medical technology, she was beginning to look more her own age, and feel it, too.

Finally came the day when they tried out the seeing eye device. It resembled nothing so much as a pair of tight-fitting goggles, but there was a lot of microcircuitry and even a small computer and power pack in it. It took in the scene and transmitters broadcast it in code to the optic nerves, fooling them into believing that they were getting correct information from real eyes. It had its limitations. Because the thing was basically an infrared device, the images transmitted were mostly in black and white, or soft gray-browns and yellows, as Dawn saw it. Images were sharp and clear at night or in a room with muted lighting, but they faded as the light source was raised. In a brightly lit room it was barely adequate; in full daylight, or in the face of a searchlight beam or fire, it was useless and even a little painful. It also had an effective range of about a hundred yards, with little or no peripheral vision.

Worse, it could be worn only for a hour or so a day. The power supply was quite limited and, when run down, it caused all sorts of random impulses to be sent to the brain instead.

Still, it was sight—real sight. Wearing the goggles, she could see again, could see the kids as they were now for the first time. To Dawn, it was a miracle.

Doc seemed almost apologetic about its limitations. "It was developed late in the nineteen-eighties," she told Dawn. "This model was actually in production in a limited way, but very expensive, early in the nineties. Then they came up with the ability to organically grow matched eyes for specific patients, and all work on perfecting this was dropped. A pity. The people who would appreciate it the most were the elderly who couldn't have transplants and those who, for one reason or another, couldn't stand the surgery to begin with. It's even more frustrating because the technology to produce eyes for you better than new is available—up at the edge. But it takes time to grow them, and a lot of equipment and skill. The Earthsiders aren't likely to do it for you, and the Outworlders are more likely to redo the whole you in ways you never even thought of."

She nodded. "It's enough—for now."

"You realize," Doc added, "that the reason they never gave us the capability was because we don't need it. We can regulate a trip point and take a different cure."

Dawn sighed. "Yes, I know. And that's what you expect me to do." She paused a moment. "But—if I do, then I won't be their mother anymore. Oh, *I'll* know, but how do you explain it to *them*?"

"I think," Doc said, "that it's time to call a meeting."

Chung Lind, as squad leader, was chairman of the base general committee. Herb, as his exec, was also on it, and Doc, the most permanent of the residents, was included, too. This trio was absolute in their decisions, although, of course, those for whom they worked severely limited their options.

The huge Oriental leader was serious, as usual, but so was the usually light and airy Herb. Doc was grim. Dawn didn't have to see them to know that.

"Doc has called this committee into session, but it had to be done anyway, as we are running out of option time from the computer and its controllers on the edge," Lind began. "Doc has put this off many times, and we have gone along, but things must come to a head—and soon. Do you understand what this is all about, Dawn?"

She nodded. "I think so. You're going to decide the fate of me and my children."

"In a manner of speaking, yes, although the ultimate choice will be yours. I'm afraid it's the same sort of thing we face here all the time. Not a lack of choices, but a lack of good ones. Doc?"

"I finally called this meeting, after fighting it for months, because something happened to make me realize that I was being, in my own way, as cruel as the other choices, although I thought of it as kindness. I wanted to give the kids some adjustment time, and a leg up on joining a very strange world, and, I admit, we wanted to give you some time as well. I think we all agreed we owed it to you. Now, however, I realize we may have gone too far."

"I appreciate the gesture," Dawn responded, "but what

is the crisis? You and I both know that we can fix things uptime now or later.''

"In a sense, that's true," Doc agreed, "but relative time moves on when we are in phase, as we are here. The war goes on, and it is increasingly brutal and ugly. Have you ever wondered what most of us are doing here?''

"Many times," she admitted.

"You may have been told, or maybe not, that the Earthside leaders have a fall-back position here in the Safe Zone. When the ultimate defeat comes, they will escape to that base, sealing themselves off by detonating the other fifteen thousand nuclear weapons stockpiled from the old days. They will destroy the Earth and every living thing on it.''

"Eric told me that. He gave it as his reason for fighting on their side.''

"Dawn," Herb put in, "they're in pretty sad shape. The truth is, the Outworlders could win very quickly. They've had the ability to do it for years. The only reason they don't is that cache of nuclear weapons. They are not out to commit genocide on the people of Earth, believe me. But they have to continue the war, at a reduced level, to keep the pressure on. If they stopped, perhaps for as little as a year or two, it's possible that Earth could regroup. They have spaceships with terrible weapons hidden in nearly impregnable bunkers far underground, but they have no way to launch them without access to surface installations. They are mother ships for hordes of fighters that can be launched only from space. We can keep them down there by incessant attack, but that's it. If we let up, they can launch. They still can't win, but they might just wind up destroying *both* sides.''

She still didn't see where this was going.

"So, you see, we're fighting a bloody and terrible holding action. The more destruction and death it spreads, the more terrible it is. The only way we can take them out, though, is to neutralize those nuclear bombs. To locate and deactivate or destroy every one of them. That's our job.''

"It can be quite subtle," Lind added. "Great caverns used for this purpose can be rendered unusable in earlier centuries, with no disruptions to humans. Even such things as soil and rain balances in certain areas can be altered so that what's there is subjected to corrosion. Trace elements made in future labs can be added to areas so that communications on the firing bands are jumbled. A tiny flaw, subtly introduced in the program used to create the weapons' microprocessors, can backfire on them over time, although it will test out in the short run."

There was enough of Moosic and the Sergeant still in there that she *did* understand, although the scope of the project was fantastic.

"You see now," Herb said, "that we're in a hell of a fix. We're not cold and immoral beings, sitting back here taking blind orders from a computer which gets its orders from nonhuman things up front. We're trying to save the human race from extinction, here on Earth as well as what it's become out there in space. Time's running out, as crazy as that sounds. There is a level of battle which will cause Earthside to collapse even without the final push, and that's approaching. Because we work in absolute time when we're in phase—relative time is a misnomer, meaning that we are related to the edge—a year here for us advances the edge a year as well. Worse, the assassination of Karl Marx accelerated that critical point."

"So Eric did them far more harm than good," she commented.

"Perhaps. Perhaps not. We think their plan is simple. We think they hope to buy absolute time by tracing us back and knocking this complex out of commission," Lind told her.

"But—they already tried that, and it failed!"

"They're not so sure it did," Lind told her. "The attack was part of the loop that is still being worked out. They have yet to steal one of our belts, which is why, once the attack was known, we preset the homing key to bring anyone back to the old location. It would match with what they know of the geography around the complex, including what they got from you. We escaped for the same reason that we can't lose up front—we have far more power available to us than they do. It's more efficient, better managed, and doesn't need to be diverted to defense.''

''The trouble is,'' Herb added, ''we still have years to work on the project. The number of weapons is just plain enormous, and we must make certain we neutralize as many as possible, in all the countries that had and made them. And, even with all the power we have, we are about at the maximum number of people for unrestricted and pinpoint time travel, particularly with the gear we must occasionally move. We need the time, but we have less than we need under optimum requirements. At least we need that much, to do what we can.''

She was more practical than that. ''What's this have to do with me?''

''First, we must undo the loop that made you. Karl Marx must not die in Trier. Ideally, however, Neumann must still escape to erase any chance of things going wrong. That will be tricky. To create Neumann, Alfie must be rescued. Loops are best undone in the reverse order that they were done, and very carefully. We want to create no more loops and ripples.''

''Why not just prevent the killing of Marx in London, then?'' she wanted to know. ''I mean, *that's* a ripple.''

''But it's a ripple in our favor,'' Lind told her. ''It has no major effects, but as a martyrdom it makes Earthside's job of changing the past as Moosic knew it even harder. You'll have to trust us on that one, but that's why Eric and the rest had to go back to Trier. Their ripple had worked against them, so they had to undo it and tilt the scale the other way.''

She sighed. "I never really understood it all before, and I'm having more trouble now."

"Time is a complex science. We *still* don't completely understand all of the things that pop up from dealing with and changing it," Doc said sympathetically. "Just when even we think we have it cold, some wild card comes up and smacks us in the face, telling us that we aren't so smart after all."

She shook her head in confusion. She really didn't want to hear anything more, except what it all had to do with her and the kids—now. "So? You're telling me I'm no longer welcome? That we're in the way?"

"In a sense," Herb replied, "but don't take that unkindly. You are one of the innocents who always gets caught up in somebody else's war. We need you, of course, to help undo the loops and reconcile the facts. We expect Trier to be holy hell, because they'll expect it and have some unknown defenses set up for us. Worse, only four of us are able to make the trip at all, for reasons you probably understand."

That much she did. The rest probably would wind up in far corners of the world, or be instantly assimilated. "Go on."

"If Trier is successfully reversed, then you must go and free Alfie. That is as much for your sake as anything, but it helps the symmetry, or so the computer says."

She sighed. "And once all that is done? What then?"

"Then," said Lind, "we will attempt to prevent the very attack that got you into this. In the process, if we are lucky and it all works just right, we have a chance of trapping Eric Benoni."

That was the one prospect she found attractive in it all, but she had a nervous thought. "But—if it's prevented, then what happens to me? None of this will have happened. You once told me I'd be a little nothing if it all didn't work out, Doc. Were you lying to me?"

"No," she responded, "not really. If the loop had been

broken instead of reconciled, yes. But we are putting things back, more or less, the way they were. If the loop is completed, then it happened. There's just no sign of memory, except ours, to say it did. You will exist because it *did* happen. And so will the kids.''

She didn't know quite what to believe, or whom. She'd been used and lied to so damned often it was hard to believe anything. She was, however, always practical. There was really nothing she could do about it anyway, and they were calling the shots. "And after that? What happens to me and the kids?''

The three squad members exchanged glances. Finally, Doc spoke. "It's for the sake of the children I'm pressing this now, Dawn. You see, Ginny is pregnant—by Joseph.''

Even though she'd feared such a thing, the news shocked and stunned her.

"It's no good, Dawn, don't you see?'' Doc continued, feeling awful as she said what she had to say. "This is no place and no life for them. Any of them.''

Dawn's gut reaction was frustration that her fake eyes, so realistic in all other respects, could not cry. "But where will they go?''

"Uptime,'' Doc told her. "It's the only way for them to gain the knowledge, the culture, everything that they'll need. They're virgins to time travel, really, so it will be fairly easy to establish them as important people, maybe educated people, not the kind of random jumpers like you became.''

"It's a matter of figuring out in advance the spot time will most conveniently put you, and putting you there at exactly the right spot in space and time,'' Herb explained.

"And leave them there, with no chance to make a mark?'' She was almost hysterical at the idea.

"No!'' Doc responded firmly. "Not unless they choose it. Once they have enough lives, enough experience, to make intelligent choices for themselves, they can choose any one of the ones they've been to live as or they can go all the way forward to the leading edge as only edge and nightside people can. Considering the circumstances, there is no other choice.''

''Just drop us back at the island! Just go away and leave us alone! You *said* they were adapted!''

''But you aren't,'' Doc reminded her. ''And what kind of a life would *that* be? You said yourself that in assimilation they'd have no chance to make a mark, and that's true. But what kind of a life would you condemn them to? You're in no condition to go back, to give them any guidance. They'd become incestuous primitives, children with no future. If we did what you say, it would be better, in my opinion, if they had never lived at all!''

There. It was said, and it was hard, but there it was.

Dawn took several minutes to get hold of herself, to try to control her emotions. Finally, she managed, ''And me? Where do I fit in all this?''

''Your bond to the kids is strong. Stronger, I think, than their bond to you, as bad as that sounds,'' Doc replied. ''You have the same choices, although, in the case of the assimilation, they're more limited. You've established a pattern which time finds easiest to continue. So you can come back here and go to the edge with them, or you can pick a person and place and return there.''

She swallowed. ''What you're telling me is that I can be a whore in any time and place I want.''

Doc was grim. ''Yes. Except on the edge.''

''I wouldn't be permitted to stay—human—up there, isn't that right?''

''Most likely not,'' Lind confirmed. ''They just no longer have the facilities for it. I can't tell you whether it's good or bad becoming one of them, and that's honest. I have trouble even imagining what they're like, let alone being one, even though I've been hundreds of human beings. But I like to think that a side, *any* side, in a war that tries to save as many lives as possible has to be better than one that's going to blow up its own people in a snit at losing.''

There was silence for a while. Finally, Doc asked gently, "What do you say, Dawn? Do we close off the loop?"

"Can I . . . talk this over with the children before answering?"

Lind looked at Doc and then at Herb. No words were exchanged, but their thoughts were easy for him to read. There was no reason to put it off any longer, for the longer it was put off, the harder it would ever be to get the job done—and people were needlessly suffering. They didn't like the situation any more than Dawn did, and they didn't like the choices, either, choices that, eventually, they themselves might have to face, for the war, inevitably, would end.

"We'll give you forty-eight hours," Lind told her. "Time is running out."

RIDING THE LOOP

She had her showdown with Ginny, and it only told her that Doc had been right, as usual.

"You shouldn't have the baby."

"Why? What's wrong with what I did? You and Daddy did it all the time!"

"But that was different!"

"How!"

How, indeed, did you explain such things to one raised as Ginny had been? They went around and around with it, but got nowhere. Finally, Dawn gave up, recognizing defeat. Doc and the others would have to deal with it, by force if necessary, but probably just by giving them the uptime experience they desperately needed.

They, all the children, even young Mark, would have to make their own decisions on their futures. She could not and would not do it for them.

Finally, during a walk outside, she told them she had to leave them.

"Like Daddy?" little Sarah asked worriedly.

"No, not like Daddy. I have to work for them now. I have to pay them back for all they've done for us." *And* to *us*, she added silently.

"I don't like them," Joseph said flatly. "They took Dad away."

"No, no! You must never think like that! Your father was a fighter in their fight, just like I was. Fighters sometimes don't come back. Let them show you what uptime is like and what it's like to live in it. Then maybe you'll understand.''

"Are you not gonna come back, too, Mommie?" Cathy asked.

"I hope I am," she told them sincerely, "but I don't know. There are some very bad people on the other side and they've done some very bad things. I have to try and stop them, try to undo some of the bad they've done. I—your father and I—sort of accidentally helped the bad things happen. I have to put it right.''

"Why?" asked Mark.

"Well, if you know something bad's going to happen, and you can do something about it and don't, then you're just as bad as the ones who did it. You let it happen when it didn't have to.''

That more or less went over. At least she and Ron had taught *some* moral lessons, although she was beginning to see where they'd fallen down on the job in some respects.

It was tough to leave them, but she really had no choice. Not only did the moral lesson make sense, but, disregarding the morals of the thing, she really had no choice. In every sense of the word, they held her and the children hostage.

The plan that was worked out was both direct and clever, although they knew that there would have to be elements of improvisation. As Lind had warned, they would expect an attempt at reversal and would have some nasty surprise waiting.

She was both surprised and delighted to find that Herb could go, but the other three were team members she knew only slightly, despite the long time at the base. Nikita she knew slightly; the small, weasel-like man was not the friendly type, but he had been civil to both her and the kids. Lucia was a tough but tiny woman who looked like a born gymnast. Her dark brown skin and wooly hair bespoke a central African origin, but, of course, it was difficult to determine anyone's true origins around here.

The fourth member was Faouma, whose name sounded vaguely Arabic but who was an enormous, Nordic-looking woman, fully six-three or better. She had a hard, permanently mean and nasty expression, and was all business.

"This has been mapped out so that each of you knows your part in the plot. The important thing is to do your assignment. Only when it's over should you move to cover someone else. Dawn, Lucia, and I have specific things to do; Faouma and Nikita will assist as needed. Dawn? You understand the weapon?"

She nodded. "I've test-fired it, but with the kind of spray it gives I couldn't miss even without the goggles."

"Good. Remember your time schedules. It's critical. Jump only to save your own life before we're all out of there. Understand?"

"We're ready," responded Faouma. "Let's do it."

Just in case, all belts were set to return to an individually specified date when none of them had been in the Safe Zone in the old time and location. To return to where they were supposed to be, they would have to perform an extra setting, known only to them, on the time and location board before pressing home.

There was a certain order to it, because of relative time. Dawn and Nikita had to go first, for her initial action was crucial to the rest. Although they might miss Dawn in the scan, in the time it would take them to do their job and work down to the square, they might well be spotted by the opposition, which might then adjust its game plan.

Dawn and Nikita stood there, and on Herb's count pressed their time controllers. Both "fell" uptime.

Dawn had half expected to become Neumann when they started with this, a personality and existence she barely remembered at all, but no longer. Neumann was Ron; she was Dawn, a nightsider. The same person could not exist in the same time period at the same time, but at this stage they were two different people entirely.

As soon as she felt solid ground and the sensations of

time travel had ceased, she pulled down her goggles. At night, in this darkened position along the road, she had better vision than Nikita. She had started her watch with the others, but now could read it. It read 01:43. Nikita faded into the neighborhood, giving her backup and cover. She checked the weapon, very much like a rifle, although weighing only ounces and feeling like a child's toy. All the settings had been perfect, but everything would be for nothing if they had made one mistake and if Marx was not, in fact, taking this route to his assignation in the square. If not, they would have to jump back no later than 01:50 and a new plan would have to be improvised.

She crouched there in the darkness, watching the road and trying to avoid the occasional oil lamps and torch lighting that smudged her vision. She checked her watch. 01:46. She began to worry that he wouldn't come.

The worst part was, the place did not look or feel familiar. She was only vaguely aware of who Karl Marx was, and couldn't even remember the name of the town they were in, although she'd studied its street maps with Herb. She had, she realized, come even farther than she thought down the road to individuality, and, oddly, it pleased her.

01:48 on the watch did not.

Suddenly, far off, she heard the sound of someone walking, heels hitting the brick walk. She tensed, ready to do the job. She was going to save a man's life, she knew, even if she no longer recalled or understood who or what he'd been.

The strange footsteps grew closer, and she could clearly see now that it was a young man with a beard, dressed in a funny, old-fashioned suit. She expected, when she saw him, to know him instantly, but found that he looked no more familiar than the photo Herb had shown them. Still, if Herb's photos were right, this was indeed Karl Marx.

He was walking very slowly, almost hesitatingly, and his manner seemed to indicate a great deal of indecision.

Clearly, Marx was uncertain as to whether or not this was a smart thing to do. He stopped near her, and she froze, fearing that he'd seen her. But the stop was to suppress a yawn as best he could, rub his eyes a bit, then continue on.

She let him get about five yards beyond her position, then rose silently and, raising the rifle, pulled the trigger.

There was a feeling in the rifle like a vibrator had been turned on for a brief moment, and her vision was momentarily wiped out by a sparkling ray of light. She heard a man cry out softly, once, and then the sound of a body falling.

Nikita was by her in an instant. "Just fine," he whispered. "He's out for a half-hour, won't know what hit him, and he'll think he tripped and fell. You all right?"

She nodded. "Knocked out my glasses for a minute. It's coming back now."

"O.K. Help me roll him over into the grass here, so anybody coming by won't see him right away." They did it, although the man was quite heavy. Marx, she was relieved to see, was breathing, but in his tumble to the pavement he'd struck his head, and there was an ugly, if superficial, gash on his right forehead.

"You want to keep safety watch here instead of me?" the little man asked her. "It's O.K. if you do. I don't mind."

"No, we'll go as planned," she told him. "I'll be all right." And, with that, she left him and went on down the walk toward the town.

It was an eerie wait, back in the shadows of an alleyway looking on the square. All was silence, and there was no movement except for those shadows and the noise of the multiple fountains pouring into the catch basin. In the stillness they sounded like huge waterfalls, the noise caught by the buildings and echoed back again and again.

It was a short wait compared to London, but it seemed

forever in the stillness. When the church clock struck the three-quarter hour, Moosic tensed, checked his pistol for the hundredth time, and began to look for signs of another, either Sandoval or Marx. At approximately 1:50 the policeman patrolling the area walked into the square, panicking him for a moment. The cop checked all the doors facing the square, looked around, and finally made his way from the square and down a side street, but not before the clock chimed two. The minutes now crept back as the patrolman's footsteps receded and finally died away in the distance, but there was still no sign of anyone else in the square.

Then, quite suddenly, he heard the clicking of shoes on cobblestone. Someone was coming down the same street the policeman had used to leave, coming towards the square. He tensed, praying that Marx had decided not to come after all, and waited until the oncoming figure strode into the square. He strained to catch a glimpse of the newcomer, and saw him at last, in the glow of a street lamp.

It was certainly no one he'd ever seen before. He was tall, thin, and at least in middle age, with a long and unkempt black beard and a broad-brimmed hat that concealed much of the rest of his features. He was dressed in the seedy clothes of one who was used to sleeping in his only suit. He didn't seem armed, and he certainly didn't have the time suit with him, if indeed he were Sandoval and not just some bum avoiding the policeman.

Moosic stood up and was about ready to go out and confront the man, when there was a sudden noise behind him. He felt a pistol at the back of his head, and quietly the man's voice whispered, "I think you better remain where you are and not make a sound. Put the gun down, nice and quiet, on the ground. No false moves, my friend! At this range I could hardly miss."

He did as instructed, then slowly got up as the pistol was pulled away. He turned, and saw his captor. The man was tall, lean, and dressed entirely in black, in a uniform rather similar to the one his mysterious woman in London was wearing. But this was no ordinary-looking chubby woman; this man was extremely muscular, with a strong face like a Nordic god's, his pure blond hair neatly cut in a military trim. Behind him lurked two large black shapes that looked somehow inhuman, but whose features were impossible to determine in the near total darkness of the alley. One thing was clear, though—from the blinking little lights—all three wore belts similar to the one the woman had worn. This, then, was the true enemy.

Knowing it was hopeless, he turned again to watch the scene in the square. More footsteps now, and the seedy-looking man leaning on the lamppost stiffened, then stepped back into a doorway for a moment. In another minute, Moosic saw Marx walk nervously into the square from his right and look around. He appeared alone and unarmed.

The twin personalities inside the Neumann body converged in an emotional rage. He glanced back briefly at the mysterious blond man, and noted with the professional's eye that his captor was looking less at him than at the scene in the square. The time agent was larger and more powerful than Neumann, but if he could just idly get one step back, just one step, that might not mean a thing. Pretending to watch what was going on in the square, he measured the distance and moves out of the corner of his eye.

Quickly he lunged around, his knee coming up and hitting the blond man squarely in the balls. The man in black cursed in pain and doubled over, dropping his strange-looking pistol. Quickly Moosic rolled, picked up his own pistol, and was out of the alley and to his right.

"Herr Marx! It's a trap! Drop to the ground!" he shouted.

Marx was about ten feet from Sandoval, and at the noise and yell he froze and turned to look back in utter confusion. Sandoval reached into his pants and pulled out a gun, while behind Moosic, in the alley, two strange figures ran out into the light. Two figures out of nightmare.

They seemed to be almost like living statues, black all

over, although they seemed to wear nothing except the time belts, their skin or whatever it was that was glistening like polished black metal. Their features were gargoyle-like, the stuff of nightmares in any age. Both had automatic rifles in their hands.

They had, however, overrun Moosic, who unhesitatingly brought up the pistol and fired at them. The strange pistol seemed to *chirp* rather than explode, but a tiny ball of light leaped from it and struck one of the creatures in the back. There was a scream, and the thing collapsed in pain.

At the same moment, a dark figure came up behind Sandoval. "Don't move or you're a dead man," Dawn said, rifle trained on him, this time with the setting on lethal charge. The man froze, then slowly turned, looking for an opening.

At the same time, the remaining gargoyle turned to fire at Neumann, but the other man in the square, whom they'd all taken to be Marx, turned and fired a bright blue ray that enveloped the creature. The thing's body shimmered, and then vanished, leaving only a scorch mark on the ground and an acrid, burning odor.

Taking advantage of the confusion, Sandoval turned to look directly at his captor. *"Vas ist. . . ."* he began, confused, and she stopped him. She did not remember him consciously, but something came from deep inside her.

*"Moo*sic," she responded, and fired. He flared as had the creature, again blinding her. She smelled him, though, and dropped to the ground just in case there was any more danger.

Back in the alley, Eric Benoni started to take aim at the figure who had pretended to be Marx, but some sixth sense warned him and, instead, he quickly pressed his "Home" key and vanished.

Herb, dressed in period clothes and with a false set of whiskers, ran to the alley, but he only met Faouma there. "Missed the bastard by a hair," she grunted and cursed.

Herb gave her a sharp look. "Neumann's already on the run. Let's collect our own and get the hell out of here. This was much too easy."

Holger Neumann was in a state of panic and confusion, but he at least had seen the job done. All he wanted now was out, out and home—but would they let him?

The ancient city had become now a nightmarish place, a surreal horror whose shadows reached out and threatened him at every turn. Behind, and possibly from above him, he thought he heard the sounds of pursuit.

The central square of Trier looked eerie and threatening in the early morning hours, lit only by a few huge candles in the street lights, their flickering casting ever-changing and monstrous shadows on the cobblestones and the sides of the now dark buildings.

Moosic gave the square a professional going-over between midnight and one, noting the rounds of the local policeman. He wanted no repetition of the debacle in London. This time there would be one target and one target only, and that target would be taken out as soon as positively identified. That should not be too difficult, he thought, if he could shoot straight. He already knew the policeman, and he knew Marx, so anyone else likely to be here at two almost had to be his quarry.

The hotel door was locked, of course, at this time of night, but he'd made certain he had a key, telling the proprietor earlier that he had a very late party. He fumbled in panic with the key, finally got it in and shut the door behind him. He almost ran up the stairs until he realized that he hadn't his room key, went back quickly and got it from behind the desk, then bounded up the stairs not caring whom he awakened. He unlocked the door and went immediately to the steamer trunk, where he'd locked the suit. Fumbling for yet another key in the darkness, he dropped it twice and had to calm himself down before he could find it again and fit it in the large brass lock.

A scratching sound caused him to turn towards the window, and in a split second he saw the horrible face of the second gargoyle framed in it, gun coming up. He picked up his own and fired, and the thing was gone. He didn't know if he'd hit it or not.

He kicked off his shoes and got into the suit, which fit his new frame rather well. Placing the gun so he could easily pick it up again, he put on the helmet as he heard noises and shouting both in the hall and outside. The noise had apparently roused half the town.

He got the helmet on and sealed it, then adjusted the small pentometers for across-the-board zeroes, then pressed "Activate."

Inside the helmet, a little message flashed saying, "Insufficient power."

He cursed. The dials still said ninety-five percent power reserve. That should be more than enough to get back home! He tried again, and again the little words flashed inside the suit.

He reached up to adjust them again, and at that moment another, perhaps the same, grinning black monstrosity showed in the window. He spun the damned controls and activated.

The creature got off a shot, but where its target had been, there was suddenly nothing at all but an empty room. Behind, there were loud yells and curses and somebody shouted, "Break the door down!"

Satisfied that the proper result had been obtained, Lucia ducked back from the window and pulled off the grotesque mask she had been wearing, then moved swiftly along the ledge and around a corner, out of sight of those breaking into the room. There, before this had even started, she'd anchored her line, and now she slid down it to the street level, gave a yank, and it fell out, then neatly reeled itself into a device in her hands which she had clipped to the belt.

"All in, all in," she heard Herb's tinny voice on the belt communicator, which should have been the signal for her to jump back to home, but she did not. Like Herb, she felt it had been too easy.

Back in the square, Herb and Faouma ran to assist Dawn, who got up unsteadily. She could see again, although it was still somewhat dim. In the distance, they could hear footsteps running towards the square, and in a few of the upper floors of buildings facing it, lights were burning now.

Herb gestured to a dark street nearby. "Back in there, quick! We'll jump as soon as we're able!" The two women followed him without another word.

They got about a block from the square when a woman's voice they had not heard before said, in the accented manner of time travelers and in English, "Freeze! Just where you are!"

They stopped, and all three fingered their guns nervously, looking for a chance.

"There are *savants* on all sides of you," the woman warned. "You will drop your weapons and raise your hands—*now*!"

"She's right," Dawn whispered. "I can see two of them just ahead on either side."

They dropped their weapons.

It was too dark for normal sight in the tiny street, but Dawn's special vision made her out. Medium build, dark hair; good build, but an ugly face. It was one she'd never seen before. The mystery woman did, however, wear a time belt.

"Now, just unhitch your belts and let them drop; then kick them away from you," the woman instructed. "Remember—the *savants* will shoot at the first sign of trouble."

"Let 'em shoot, then," Herb told her. "That way you

don't get the belts.'' Faouma seemed in agreement. All Dawn could think of was that she would never see the kids again.

"Groak! Stun beam!" the woman ordered, and there was a loud flash of rays. Dawn, like the other two, braced for it, but when it didn't come, she just dropped to the street anyway. The ray, of course, had blinded her again. Shots crackled in the air, and she felt half her body burn and then go numb.

Herb practically fell over her, but both he and Faouma had wasted no time in dropping, rolling, and coming up with their weapons. Rays crackled all over the tiny street, and there were sounds of stirring from inside the buildings. Suddenly, it was over, and Lucia from one side and Nikita from the other ran to them.

"You all right?" Lucia asked Herb, but he was lying on his side, fumbling with his belt.

"Everybody—jump now! Home! Don't wait! Lucia—punch out anybody who can't do it themselves, dead or alive!"

Somebody ran to Dawn, punched in a set of numbers, and pressed the "Home" key.

She was falling downtime.

"The plot all along," Chung Lind commented, "was the capture of the squad's belts, that's clear. And in spite of knowing we were set up, we almost fell into that trap."

"My fault," Herb said flatly. "I just got overconfident, that's all. They must have been on the rooftops around the square all the time. As soon as we picked an exit route, they moved to seal off the far end of that street. It was a clever setup, I got to admit. If Nicky and Lucia had obeyed orders and jumped, we'd all be happy little citizens of Prussia right now."

"Or dead," Faouma added. "It was doubly lucky that they were all set to stun instead of kill."

"Not so much luck there," Lind responded. "They

could have their cake and eat it, too. Get the belts, keep
the scan on tight, then come back and pick you all up in
your Trier identities and take you forward on *their* belts.
In any case, they couldn't risk a killing beam for fear of
destroying those belts. It was close.''

"You'll never know how close," Nicky told them.
"There were two of us and four of them. When the
woman gave the orders to stun, I told Lucia on the personal band we'd better move in. We just figured that
they'd stun the squad, so they couldn't bring their own
weapons back up on us. We just did a wide spray and
prayed for the best.''

Chung Lind sighed. "Well, enough recriminations. History is composed of a series of lucky breaks, and this one
was ours. The point is, they have the capacity to stage this
again and again. The next time might be different. The
only way to be secure is to turn the tables on them.''

"You got a line on who that woman was?" Herb asked
them all.

Everybody shrugged or shook their heads. "Never seen
or heard of her before. They've let Benoni run a one-man
show up to now," Nicky said.

"I don't like it," Lind told them. "Up to now, we've
been pretty secure, believing that they didn't have sufficient power to mount two simultaneous teams or the exper-
tise to handle them. Well, now we know we were wrong.
Makes me worry what else we don't know.''

Lind's attention turned now to Dawn. "Are you O.K.?"

She nodded. "I think so. I thought we were gone for
sure there, though. Half of me couldn't move. It was like I
had nothing below my stomach at all.''

"Partial stun effect," Herb told her. "We all got it.
Faouma was out cold. It wears off, though—like it did
with our friend Marx.''

She looked at Lind. "It's O.K., then?"

He nodded. "The loop's closed. Marx will live and do
his major work. I admit the irony that we just accom-

plished something which, in the long run, will strengthen the enemy and prolong the war, but it was necessary. We've bought several years of absolute time to continue our work, and time is pretty much back on its original mainline track. Everybody relax and get some rest. We've got a lot of work to do yet, and I want you all fresh and ready to go.''

Dawn sought out Doc and asked about the children, whom she didn't see.

''They're uptime, under guidance,'' the physician told her. ''Don't worry about them. They're safe and secure.''

''I—I may not even know them when they're through this. It worries me.''

''You and I know it's the only way. Get some rest now, and we'll close that second loop tomorrow.''

''Uh—Doc?''

''Yes?''

''I'm worried. I—I don't know, I just am. Killing that man back there—I *wanted* to do it, and I don't really understand why.''

Kahwalini sighed and sat down beside her. ''Long ago I told you that none of the people I've been are dead. They're all still here, locked in my mind, a part of me in some way or another. We forget it, because we no longer feel it. They're not separate anymore, and maybe it's only small parts of them, but they're there. *You* didn't know him, but a little bit of Ron did, a little bit of hate born of what he'd seen that man do. Now it's over. Mission accomplished. Now you can sleep.''

But she *couldn't* sleep. It wasn't the killing anymore, not really. She could understand at least the basics of what Doc told her, and accepted it. No, it was lying there in the permanent darkness, feeling very alone. Ron was gone, and would never be back. Any last remnants of him had been purged by the killing of Sandoval. She didn't have to have it proved to her—she *felt* it. He, through her, had finally done his job, and there was no more reason for him to exist except as a memory in her mind.

Doc, however, for all her wisdom and genius, couldn't really understand the basic problem now. Maybe Kahwalini *had* been somebody like her once upon a time, but, if so, it was a long time ago. Doc was strong, and smart—somebody who made things happen. She, Dawn, was not, and could never be.

The world was made up of survivors and victims, she thought glumly. She wasn't a victim—at least, she didn't think she was, in the sense of personality—but survivors survived in different ways. Doc, Herb, Lind, Nicky, Lucia, Faouma—they survived by being tough, by being leaders. Ron had been a leader-type, and that's what had made him strong.

She wasn't really strong, she knew, no matter what she'd just gone through. She'd done it because she had to, but she did have to have it forced on her. She survived through others, and that wasn't all that bad. She survived to be a companion, a lover, to Ron. She survived for the sake of the children. She wanted to keep surviving.

Now Ron was gone, and the children were being lost to her. She couldn't do anything more for them. When Alfie escaped, then they would try to prevent it from happening at all. Supposedly, they had a better chance of doing that because of what they were doing now, but she really didn't try to understand it anymore.

Win or lose, the next few days would be the end of what purpose she still had, what need she could fill. No matter what happened, she would be alone then, and she couldn't stand to be alone. . . .

Rescuing Alfie was not as simple as it had first appeared. To start with, she had to get down to that bridge where the time suit was anchored and haul it up, and she had to do it all herself. Not one of the squad could afford to travel in this particular time frame, which was one reason why Eric had chosen it for his test.

The suit was incredibly heavy, and large even for her. Still, she remembered all the instructions, first removing the huge, bulky power pack from the rear backpack and carrying it back and letting it drop into the Thames. Time was crucial now, for once the suit's residual power was exhausted, a matter of only a few minutes, it would cease to exist.

Quickly she snapped in the new power pack, a small and light plant similar to the ones used on the belts with framing and contacts made so that it would fit into the power pack bracket in the suit and provide the necessary juice.

It worked fine, and, as a side effect, it made the suit far lighter, although no less bulky. She wondered how she could both be somebody entirely different yet recognized as the same person by the suit, but while she'd had many explanations, she knew she'd never get it straight.

Because she was not in phase, she was not subject to assimilation and its limitations. First she reset the suit controls the way they'd instructed her, then carefully drew it to her, using an extender device to wrap around the suit, connected on both sides to her time belt. In a sense, it was an extra belt just for the suit, but controlled and managed by her belt's microprocessor.

She activated the belt, and almost instantaneously was inside a grim and drab little room. There were bars on the windows and on the heavy oak door, which was locked from the outside. A single gas lamp, turned down to dim, lit the room, which smelled of death and dying. In a corner was a small bed, and in it a very battered and bruised figure, so tiny and helpless.

Alfie was asleep.

Quietly she detached the suit, fearful of alerting the hall wardens not far away, and brought it over to the still figure. Although feeling pressed for time, her heart went out to the kid, and she laid everything out, ready to go, before awakening him. Almost as an afterthought, she pushed the goggles up, so that he wouldn't be faced with some strange-looking monster. She'd been blind so long it didn't really matter, and it was simple from here on out.

"Wake up," she said in a hushed tone, shaking him gently. He stirred, moaned a little, then said, " 'Ho're you? Some kind of prison nurse?"

"No," she whispered, "and keep your voice down. Time is very short, and the amount of power required to allow me to be here without assimilation is enormous."

He was in great pain, but much of the morphia had worn off, allowing the Moosic personality a little latitude. He mustered all his will to force himself forward, reminding himself that Sandoval had done it. "You—you are from the future." It was a statement, not a question.

"In a way, yes. I've brought you something you need desperately, but you'll have to move fast. Can you make it out of bed?"

"Oi . . . think so." He tried and, with her help, got to a shaky standing position. It was then that he saw it, there on the floor. "The toime suit!" he breathed.

He sat back on the bed and she helped him into it. It was enormous for the body of Alfie Jenkins, far too large to be practical, and he said so.

"Don't worry. Once you punch out, it'll be O.K., and both Alfie and Ron will live. Understand?"

He nodded dully.

"The power pack is on full-charge now—I did it before coming here. And I've set it for the correct time and place. There is still a chance of catching Sandoval."

"But 'istory—it's already changed."

"Very little. Marx would have died in a few years anyway, and all his important work was done. He was killed by a boy in the pay of anti-Communists, a boy who then escaped from gaol. That's all the change. Now—helmet on. Check the pouch when you arrive. And remember—

Sandoval's power is nearly gone. He's landed a hundred miles from his goal. You can beat him there. Now—seal and go!''

"But wait! Just 'ho *are* you?''

But the seal snapped in place and he was in silence, although nearly swimming in the suit. If he stood up, he knew he'd sink below and out of the helmet, so he didn't try. The mysterious woman reached out and touched the suit activation switches.

Tiny Alfie, almost smothered in the enormous suit, faded out. Almost immediately her hands went to her own belt, and she pressed the "Home" key.

Now there was only one thing left to do.

THE TWISTED CIRCLE

"In many ways, this is the most important operation of this team," said Chung Lind, looking over maps and diagrams on a huge table. "It may also be nothing at all. Still, a chance at Eric, perhaps at their whole operation, is worth the risk."

A number of them had studied all the material and made suggestions one way or the other, but the truth was, they were severely handicapped, as they were in almost any operation directly against the other side.

That was why it was so surprising that Earthside had been able to commit everything to the Trier operation. True, they had the *savants*, which Ron had called gargoyles, but they needed a smart human boss to do almost anything. Those humans suffered from the same limitations as the ones on the team. When you spent too much time in any period, you gave up some of your freedom of action forever.

In point of fact, only three Outworlders had any margin of safety in the time frame, and one of those was Dawn.

When such a situation developed, there was nothing to do but actually hire people in the frame to do most of the work. A cover, some sort of excuse, could always be manufactured, and, of course, the date of the actual action they were trying to prevent, and the specifics of it, were a matter of record.

And so a team of excellent American detectives had been hired and extremely well financed. Some were tracking down one or another members of the radical party, but the main focus was on the one on the inside, Dr. Karen Cline. At some point she had to make contact either with the radicals or with the Earthsiders directly. If not, they would have to stop it in the parking lot, and that would be pretty damned bloody.

Cline's activities had been perfectly normal and almost robotically regular and precise until just six days before the operation. Since then, regular purchases had nearly stopped, and her routine was varied occasionally by trips to a travel agency, a car rental company in Washington, and other such odd behavior. The agents shadowing her had problems keeping out of sight of the government agents regularly assigned to follow and check on her, but those agents didn't seem unduly alarmed. Apparently, she had a vacation coming in late May, and had indicated she was going to take it.

Outworlder agents, who already knew something was going on, had the advantage here, and one slick operative noted that Cline's only charge card was an infrequently used American Express card, but she had not used it either at the rental agency or the travel agency, paying by check instead. Why not?

She had arranged to rent a small van, but for later pickup. That van, it was realized, could carry the radical team and its equipment. Agents were put on the car rental agency to see just who picked up that van and where it went.

Chung Lind was particularly irritated that he had to go through all this the hard way, but there really was no other way to do it. A monitor by the master computer specifically on Cline, however, had picked up one thing of vital importance.

Cline, as of six days before the incident, was not totally in phase with the time frame.

"That explains the last of it," Doc noted. "The only

reason we didn't see it before was that she was a highly
educated woman, a Ph.D., in a very important project."

Dawn frowned. "You mean she's one of *them*?"

"Most likely the woman heading the second team in
Trier," Doc replied. "If you get rid of the surface, it fits.
She's a loner, both parents dead, no romantic entangle-
ments and, as far as can be seen, no interest in them. She's
a competent technician, but has no imagination or genius.
They managed to fit her into the most perfect slot
imaginable."

Lind sighed. "So we're dealing with a smart, extra-
competent Earthside agent. She won't have to get into
direct contact with them, though. She's done all she can to
set things up; now all she has to do is settle back and wait
for it to happen. Eric probably arranged for the team to be
recruited and he'll bring the elements together, probably in
a period identity of his own."

The date for the attack was Monday, May 14. On
Saturday, May 12, John Bettancourt picked up the van and
drove it south to the county seat of Prince Frederick,
Maryland, not much of a drive from the plant, and checked
into a motel under the name of Donald Hartman. He did
not leave it again until the next morning, so tapping his
calls was impossible, but, after eating breakfast, he drove
a few miles north and turned off onto a road leading to a
small summer cottage right on Chesapeake Bay. The cottage, rented by a young couple named Freeman, clearly had
other visitors as well.

"That's it, then," Lind sighed. "There is no sign anyone left before dark, so that's when and where we'll hit
them. It was an ideal location for them, and it makes an
ideal location for us. Almost no locals in the area, few
cops—quiet. Doc, I hate to ask it of you, but it's all yours
now. Be careful."

Kahwalini nodded and turned to Dawn. "Come. Let's
go back and talk this over." They went back to her office.

"Dawn," Doc said carefully, "now is the time to think

a little about not only this but what comes next. Louis is already uptime with the agents, as Jerry Brune, a laid-off steelworker. I'll be going up just before the raid, to handle the stakeout on Cline's apartment. If she gets spooked, we hope she'll make for her belt, and that will turn the tables."

"You think Eric is in that house, as somebody else?"

She nodded. "We think so. We've accounted for all four radicals, and there is a fifth person in the house, a middle-aged man with one leg who walks on crutches but never comes outside. We think that's Eric."

"So I'm not really needed."

"Except as an observer, somebody there at the start who should be there at the end, no. I was thinking, though, that for better or worse this would be an ideal place for you to go trip. No use putting it off, and you're more use to everyone, including yourself, in one whole piece."

There was really no reason not to, but she resisted the idea. "You know what I'll become there."

Doc nodded. "It's too set a pattern to really change. Why does it bother you now?"

"Because I was out of it for so long. I've been a person now for a long time, and now you want me to go back to being . . . merchandise."

"I don't *want* it. But it's that, over which we have at least *some* control, or one of the others, or the edge. That's it. What can it do except give you a new and better body?"

And a new mind, she thought sourly. "You said you could control it. What do you mean?"

"I mean we can at least select as optimal a situation as events allow. You can be young and attractive. There will be tradeoffs, but it won't be Hell."

"I guess the Almighty computer has already run it through."

She nodded. "It isn't possible to get specifics, because you've had too many wild card jumps, but we do our best.

That'll mean putting you away from the action, to start; so we'll insert you early. Once you're inserted, we'll know who and where you are. One of us, either Louis or I, will get you before it all blows open and bring you down, so keep your belt where you can grab it in a hurry. If we catch anybody, we'll bring them back here. Even if we don't, I'll have to stay around a couple of days to cover up the situation and pay off the agents. You trip at approximately seventeen days, four hours. We're going to insert to trip you on the fourteenth, so it'll be over by then. Then we can come back here and talk about what happens next."

"I wish I could see the children one last time."

"I wish so, too, but it's not working out. At least, after, you'll have two good eyes to see them."

Yeah, she thought—*but will they still be my children?*

Probably not, she knew, even if they were now. She felt suddenly very old, very used up. There was no more use fighting, because the decisions really had already been made. "O.K.," she said, "let's get the belt and do it."

"Now?" Even Doc was surprised by that.

"Now —or never. If I have to think about it, I'll go nuts, and if I start dwelling on it, I might commit suicide. Let's go. Let's get it over and done with."

"All right," Doc said, went out for a moment and then came back with a belt. She handed it to Dawn, who put it on. "Now, a few things you should know in advance and remember. First, the 'Home' key is keyed to the old location, as before. Use plus eighteen hundred for the period, use one hundred eighty for the latitude and three hundred sixty for the longitude. If you forget, I'll remind you."

"I won't forget. I don't think so, anyway. Anything else?"

"You'll come out in Washington, so don't panic. As I say, we'll make sure you're picked up in time. There are more choices in D.C. than in the southern Maryland sticks.

Also, it's less likely for the enemy to pick you up if you're outside the area. They'll be concentrating there, and so we all are coming out elsewhere and getting down the hard way. And don't worry so much. You have my personal promise—you haven't run out of choices yet.''

"O.K., Doc. Here goes." She pressed the activation button and fell uptime. The circle was becoming completed.

Her name was Holly Feathers, and she was seventeen years old, but while most girls her age were preparing to graduate from high school and going on heavy dates, Holly was a very experienced seventeen.

She'd been born last in a three-child family, the first two of which were boys. Her dad used to be a steelworker in Pittsburgh, but he'd lost his job both to the cuts in the industry and to heavy drinking, and after that they just sort of drifted around, with him going from one part of the country to another in search of work, hauling them along because he'd long ago lost the house and run the bank account dry.

All this was while she was very small, so she had no memory of the better times in the past. All she knew was that they seemed to be constantly moving around, almost living in an antique Chevy, her old man grabbing a job here, a job there, but never the kind you could hold for a while. Her mother just seemed to tune out the world, doing a lot of Bible reading and pretending like nothing else was wrong.

Often, after she'd grown into womanhood, her father would get drunk and take her off somewhere and undress her and, well, do things. When she didn't want to, he would often beat her or slap her around. Her brothers were wild, and no protection at all. One of them wound up doing five to twenty in Kansas or somewhere for robbery.

She had some schooling, but because of the situation and the constant moving around, it hadn't done much good. Oh, she could write her name in a childish block-print way, and get through a basic menu or maybe Dr. Seuss, but that was about all. She had no real skills, either, and except for helping out on some picking jobs in harvest seasons, she'd never really done much of anything.

What she was was pretty, almost classically so, even dressed in worn-out sandals, dirty tee shirt, and over-patched jeans. At five foot two with big green eyes and long reddish-brown hair, a nearly perfect figure with an almost impossibly narrow waist, olive skin, and a big, wide, but sensuous mouth, she was, as her father said, "something else."

When she was fifteen, she got pregnant—and got a bad whipping from her father, as if it was her fault instead of his. Panicky, he'd taken her to a back alley abortionist who almost killed her. When she wound up hemorrhaging and got rushed to an emergency room, they determined that the fetus was gone all right, but it was no longer possible after they repaired the damage for her to have children ever again.

To her surprise, her mother visited her in the hospital, looking ancient and terrible. She gave her some money, more money than she thought they had. "Take it and go," her mother told her. "He's already scarred you, child. Don't make me bury you."

So she found her shirt and jeans and dirty, worn sandals, the first two cleaned by the hospital, and she sneaked out of the place, got down to the bus station, and bought a ticket to Washington, not because it was anyplace she knew but because it was the nearest big city to West Virginia she knew on the destination list.

Once in the dirty, midtown bus terminal, though, she found she had no place to go and nothing more to do, and money that wouldn't last long.

She found no end of young men in and around the bus station willing to help her out, but soft-spoken Johnny Wenzel seemed the nicest and the least frightening. He bought her meals, took her to his very nice apartment, got her some clothes, and never tried to take advantage of her—not then.

But, eventually, he got around to the subject of her future plans. She had always wanted to be a dancer—not some cheap dancer, but one like on the television specials—but she had no training and no way to get it. That's when he told her how she could get the money for her future.

She didn't really like the idea, but he was pretty blunt, if nice. She had no education in a town where a high school diploma was needed to collect garbage. It was quickly clear that her reading and writing skills were on the level of a first or second grader at best, and unemployment was high and demand even for the most menial of jobs was low. She really had nothing marketable except her body, he pointed out, and she knew he was right.

He introduced her to some of his other "girls," many of whom had stories similar to hers. They weren't living high on the hog, but they had nice clothes and shared a small block of apartments that weren't in the slums. All of them, of course, had plans to be something more someday—singers, dancers, actresses, all that. For now, they had a decent place to live, decent clothes, steady good food, and a percentage of their income in a savings account which Johnny managed for them. They assured her that it was easy, that Johnny wasn't like those other pimps who beat and brutalized their girls, and that as long as she made her quota, she would never have to worry about the basics.

Slowly, she was broken into the business, and she picked it up really fast—the makeup, jewelry, the "uniform," usually very skimpy and very revealing, and the techniques of the bed itself. Once she started in earnest, she became insatiable, something psychiatrists might explain from her background but something she barely understood at all. She worked the streets, mostly, getting a whole range of men, and was soon turning two tricks a night, three or four on the weekends. By seventeen she had the look and the moves down so pat that she never even thought of them anymore, and she seemed to be always turned on. To the other girls it was just a job, just a routine, but to her it was life itself. Even Wenzel was impressed, and started lining her up with high-powered clients.

The merging of Holly and Dawn was dramatic. How much of Holly's near nymphomania was Holly's own psyche and how much was Dawn's desperate need to cure her depression and loneliness, it was impossible to say; but the more Dawn stopped thinking and let the Holly part of her take over, the easier it was for her. Holly was not very bright, but she was supercharged with emotion and a desperate need to be loved. If self-worth had to be measured in dollars, well, so be it. It was better than many girls ever had, and it was concrete.

It was getting dark on Saturday, May 12, and she was almost ready for work. It was a warm night, so she had on very short shorts over pantyhose, an overly small halter top, some nice perfume, and some little gold earrings and a matching bracelet and necklace. She was just putting on the sandals whose extra high heels gave exaggeration to her walk when Johnny came in, kissed her, and told her how beautiful she was. Then he added, "Easy work this time, but I'd grab jeans and a blouse and your toothbrush."

She looked puzzled. "Why? 'Specially, why the toothbrush?" She had a pleasing high soprano, although with a trace of a lisp, but she'd gotten so used to using her lower sexy voice that she did it automatically now.

"Big bucks client, but he wants you for the weekend, back Monday morning."

That was unusual. "Must be really big bucks. Should I pack a case?" She did not hesitate to go along with the assignment, even though she'd never had a long-term gig before.

"Yeah, maybe a little one. He's a lonely lawyer with a summer cottage who wants to get away for the weekend."

A little alarm went off in her mind, and for the first time she realized what date it was. "Be a minute, O.K.? I think I know the guy."

She didn't, at least not when she got into the big black car. He was middle-aged and flabby, with graying hair and a small gray-white beard. She slid in beside him with her usual "Hi!" and threw the case in the back seat, and only when she scooted over close to him did she see from the key ring that the car was obviously rented, as she suspected it might be. She had the belt in the case.

He nodded and pulled away, leaving Johnny to count his money. As they headed through traffic towards the D.C. beltway, he said, "You know who I am." His voice was thin, reedy, and not very pleasant.

She had backed off from him by now. "I guess so. Louis?"

"No. Doc."

It was a shock. Even though both Ron and Sandoval had gone female, she just never thought of it working both ways. *"Doc?"*

"Don't get funny. I needed some money and a good cover, and this is the best. I've been here before, for a few days, so I knew what it was going to be like."

She couldn't get over the change. There was no trace of the gentleness and femininity of the Kahwalini she had known. He was a little wimp of a guy and he stayed that way.

"So this is it, huh?"

"Tomorrow is it, anyway. I must say you don't seem to be suffering."

She chuckled. "I had enough sufferin' in my lives. This is dif'rent. I ain't got no worries, and I don't got to think much. Seems like every time I had to think lately, it's been b'tween drownin' or hangin'."

Doc said nothing to that.

She'd changed into a tight white tee shirt that left nothing to the imagination and jeans so tight they seemed painted on and were held up provocatively only by her hips, but that was her only change. The immediate excitement had given way quickly to boredom—her attention span was no longer very great and the complexity of her thoughts was very low—and she felt horny, even for Doc. All she could do was drown herself in the radio and go along for the ride.

Finally, she asked, "Doc? How much did you pay for the weekend?"

"A grand. That guy is a stickup artist."

A grand, she thought. Now *that* was moving up. . . .

Thirty armed men staked out and surrounded the tiny beach cottage, all armed to the teeth, some with futuristic weapons imported at the last moment for the occasion. They were facing such weapons, they knew, and the game was capture if possible, kill if necessary.

All of them thought they were working for an international anti-terrorist organization founded and financed by a right-wing billionaire. They didn't question the weapons or the information on who and what they were facing.

There was an uneasy moment when Stillman drove out in the van earlier in the day on Sunday, but he'd merely been tracing the route. He did, however, stop and make one telephone call at a booth. By no coincidence, Karen Cline picked up a phone in a Texaco station about the same time. The conversation was brief.

Stillman and Bettancourt had timed and retimed their route in different vehicles until they almost had clocks in their heads. They knew, though, that there was no margin for error. Their special weaponry and gadgets, along with the passwords they had just received from Cline, would be needed to get through a security system that was among the toughest in the world.

Louis, now a big, beefy black man with a thick, white moustache and balding head, listened to those shadowing Stillman. It was nearly dark, and he made his decision.

''As soon as you get a stretch with no cars or people, take the man out. I repeat, take the man out. Cancel him if you have to. Without him they can't get past the front door, but Cline'll go to work tomorrow as usual.''

More than two miles south of the plant, Clarence Stillman swerved to miss a car that suddenly pulled out from a side road. The car kept coming, ramming into the side of the van. Before Stillman could recover, two men popped up on both sides of the truck and one grabbed him. He roared and rolled, breaking loose, but the door wouldn't open and the other man pointed a strange-looking device like a rifle at him and fired. There was a bluish glow, and he slumped down.

Gasoline was poured inside, and the van was set afire. The two men jumped into the other car, which had backed off, and it roared away before the gas tank exploded on the van. Their own car was in lousy shape, but they were able to dump it in the lot of an auto repair company before it gave up the ghost.

Holly/Dawn heard this over the communications system, and knew that these men were getting ready to go in. Doc was supervising the Cline stakeout, but if all went well, Cline would not know of this. Whoever she was, she would go to work and wait for the attack that never came.

The men moved in. All vehicles were covered, and then they moved silently up to the house itself. On Louis' signal, and with no warning to the occupants, they tossed in concussion grenades in every window and then black-clad shapes crashed through doors and windows.

To say that the occupants were surprised was an understatement. Rays and conventional weapons went off all through the house. She could only sit back in Doc's car, parked well out on the road, and imagine what was going on in there.

The house was secured in less than forty seconds. Louis was immediately inside with a small device, checking each and every one of the limp forms. Bettancourt was dead, having begun firing blindly. Sandoval had tried to jump out the second story window in the back, and he made it. His neck was broken. The mysterious man with one leg had been stunned to unconsciousness, while the terrified Austin-Venneman was in so much shock that she couldn't even surrender. Louis went first to the mysterious one-legged man and took a reading; then he frowned. "Nothin'!" he snarled. "This ain't Eric, it's just their set-up man!"

Back along the road, the passenger's door opened in her car and a dark figure got in. She turned, expecting to see one of the others or maybe Louis, and gasped.

"Don't panic," said Eric Benoni calmly. "Can you drive?"

She shook her head, suddenly too fearful to speak.

"All right, then I will. Don't yell or make any foolish moves, please. I really don't intend any harm, but such beauty can be so easily . . . marked." He slid back out the door and walked around in back of the car to the driver's side. She was frozen in panic, unable to do a thing.

He got in, looked down and saw that the keys were in the ignition, then started the car and drove off a little ways before turning on the headlights. "Damned uncomfortable, driving with the belt. One cannot lean back and relax."

"W-what do you want with me?" she asked him, edging as far away from him as she could. She wished she had the nerve to open the door and jump, but she knew she didn't. She felt suddenly cold and started shivering, although it was a warm night. Her head felt funny.

He noticed her discomfort. "It will pass. Thanks to your friends, all of you that still was partly Moosic, and Alfie, and Neumann, has gone. Your friends just saw to that. You won't miss it. It will just make you more . . . passive, more gentle, more dependent, and, come your trip point, no brighter than the girl you now are. There—it's passed already."

She *did* feel different, somehow. On the one hand, she

was terrified of him; on the other, she actually wanted
him. "Wh—where are we goin'?" she managed at last.

"You tell me. Where is the belt?"

She didn't answer, and he pulled the car over by the
side of the road, turned, and pulled her violently to him.
He had a knife in his hand, and his face was absolutely
cold, his eyes terrifying to look into, although she could
not avoid his gaze.

"I will ask once more. Then I will put a mark on that
pretty face of yours. Not deep, but it will leave a permanent scar. Then, if you still don't cooperate, we will start
on other parts of your anatomy."

She felt totally helpless. "No, please—all right! It's in
my bag in the back seat of the car."

He let go of her and flung her back. "Get it. Take it
out, turn it off, and hand it to me."

She didn't hesitate to do what he said. He grabbed the
belt and a look of satisfied triumph came over him.

"There—see? I can be a nice fellow when folks are nice
to me. At least I salvage something out of this miserable
debacle of an operation."

She stared at him. "Who *are* you?"

Eric smiled. "Do you know what Benoni means? No?
It's a Hebrew name, very seldom used, that means 'son of
my sorrow.' I chose it because it was appropriate. A better
way is to turn the tables a bit. I *think* I know who *you* are,
or were. Was your name once Dawn?"

She nodded nervously.

He grinned and spread his hands. "Behold thy unfaith-
ful son, Joseph."

Her jaw dropped, and her mind reeled, unable to accept
it.

"It really is, you know, Mother. And that girl playing
Karen Cline is Ginny."

"That ain't possible!" she protested.

"In *this* crazy universe? Let me tell you what happened
to us, *Mother*. They kept us back there in that Safe Zone

of theirs for five years. Five lousy years, undergoing
dozens of lives, growing very old very fast, while you
never came back. And then, finally, they tired of us when
we didn't do their bidding, become their version of the
savants, doing things just so, and they ordered us to the
edge. Well, we went, of course, but not without a plan.
We no sooner caught sight of the monstrosities that we
were supposed to join than we acted. Two of us, Ginny and
I, were in time. The other three are up there now, probably
monsters.

"We kept the belts on the edge and simply changed the
location on arrival. They were delighted to see us, since
they had lost much of the knowledge of time travel and
were afraid to try it. We were delighted to show them.
They cut the power to our belts, of course, but we were
there and we were in charge."

He put the car back in gear and continued on down the
road.

"Them and their plans. The Outworlders killed our father,
turned our mother into a common whore, and meant to
turn us into monsters. Compared to that, Earthside was
downright refreshing."

She shook her head. "But—you caused all of it. I
borned you, and you made Ron into Dawn and Dawn into
me. You're lyin'. You're just torturin' me for fun."

"No, Mother, you're thinking wrong. You're thinking
that because I couldn't have existed without the rest, I
couldn't have caused it. But, you see, it all *did* happen. It
really did. History is simply the evidence we leave. Time
doesn't *undo* anything, it just cleans it up so there's no
trace left that it happened. Everything Ron, and you, lived
through happened, and since it was made not to happen
after it happened, we exist, but we exist with no roots. We
are nightsiders. Unpeople, no more real in the historical
sense than the *savants* are in the human sense. And since
we, even now, are in the *past*—only the edge is real—this
is merely acting out what was, not what is. There really

isn't any free choice in the downtime—we choose as we must." He chuckled. "You don't understand a word of this, do you?"

"No, and I ain't sure I want to. But if what you say is true, then why I never came back is because you stole my belt and took me away."

It was his turn to be surprised and a little shocked. For the first time, a trace of doubt came over Eric Benoni's face—self-doubt. Finally, he sighed. "You're right, of course. But what if you *had*? You would simply wind up on the edge with the monsters just like we did. Being made over into a monster but with all the memories, all the knowledge. I'm saving you from that."

She looked out at the dark night. "Where are we goin'?"

"Not much further. My time is running out in this frame. A pity, for I wish I could find a way to save Ginny." There was a small dirt turnout that overlooked the bay on the left, and he pulled into it and stopped. He turned off the ignition and removed and pocketed the keys. Then he got out, and after a moment she did, too. There was a warm breeze blowing, and off in the distance could be seen the lights of big ships in the center channel.

"Joseph—if you *are* Joseph—why? You can't win. They'll just blow up the world."

"Why? You stand there, like that, and ask *why*? As for losing, well, one side always claims it is the ultimate victor, doesn't it? Particularly when it wants you on its side. They lie, or tell half-truths, just as we must sometime. It's another part of war. But I've seen both sides, and I know death is preferable to what they offer." He paused a moment. "Good-bye, Mother. Remain here tonight and with your looks you're sure to get a ride and almost anything else you want." He pressed his "Home" stud and vanished into the night.

She stood there, looking out at the bay, not really thinking, just crying in the wind. Finally she went back to the car, got in, locked all the doors, curled up, and contin-

ued crying in the damp and the dark. Finally, she felt all
cried out and just sat there for a while, not really thinking
at all, yet the thoughts came anyway.

Who are you?

I—I don't know.

Why don't you know?

'Cause I've downtimed the night side once too much.

Who were you?

*I—I was a small child of the streets, and a nun, and a
crucified rebel slave, and countless whores, but mostly I
was Ron and Dawn.*

*But Ron and Dawn were lovers. They were two, not
one. Were you truly both of them, or perhaps neither one?*

Something seemed to snap inside her. All this shit—it
was crazy. It didn't make no sense at all. It was stupid,
like dreams were stupid when you stopped to think on
them a little.

She suddenly sat up in the car. "Oh my god!" she said
aloud. She'd seen it in others, but never thought about it in
herself. Crazy. Around the bend. Looped. She'd seen it
before, in Gloria, among others. Girls who just got sick
and tired of this kind of life and knew they'd never be
anything else. She thought maybe it happened when you
got real old, like Gloria—she was almost forty. Not to her.

But it had. It *must* be. Jesus! She'd really flipped out,
and gone to live in cuckoo-land for a while. No use
figuring out how she *really* came to be down here in this
car. She looked in the back seat and saw her overnight
case, then crawled in back, opened it, and pulled out her
makeup case. Switching on the overhead light, she opened
the case and looked at the face in the little round mirror.

That's who I am, she told herself. *I'm Holly. I never
been nobody else but Holly and I ain't ever gonna be
nobody else neither.*

She wiped away the remnants of the tears and made
herself presentable once more. When she was satisfied,
she packed up the case, unlocked the car door, and got

out, taking it with her. It was still quite dark, but she began to walk up the road. There wasn't any traffic this time of night, but if a car didn't come along, she'd eventually reach a phone, she was sure—or maybe wait until morning. She no longer felt tired, just anxious to get back to town and pick up her life.

A very old Volkswagen came rattling down the road going in the opposite direction, and she paid it no heed. The driver, however, spotted her in his headlights and slowed, then made a U-turn and came back up to her. She grew suddenly frightened, aware of just how much in the middle of nowhere she was and just how alone and unprotected she was as well.

The VW pulled in just ahead of her, and the right door opened. She approached it nervously, knowing there really was no place to run and just hoping this was someone who was just trying to be helpful—or on the make. She bent down and looked in at the driver.

"Get in, Holly," said Doc.

"No! You're not real! You're part of the dream!" She backed away from the car gingerly.

"I won't hurt you, Holly, but I'm afraid I must insist. Don't worry. If nothing else, I'll take you as far as the bus station in Waldorf."

"I—I don't trust you!"

"You shouldn't. But you don't have any choice. Now—get in! I have other appointments before this is over, and, as funny as it sounds, I don't have the time for foolishness."

Holly sighed. "What the hell," she muttered, and pushed her case into the cramped back seat and slid into the front passenger side.

As soon as she closed the door, Doc was off into the night.

A QUESTION OF HUMANITY

"It wasn't a dream, you know," Doc said at last. "It all really happened."

She sobered a moment. "I know. I just don't want it to have."

"Understandable. I assume Eric got your belt?"

She nodded.

"That's no catastrophe. He's about to use it to go back to the old home setting, then attack the base. That'll cause us to move and you to jump forward, and the loop will be complete."

"Is it true what he said? About him bein' Joseph and all?"

He was startled. "I hadn't heard that." He thought for a long while. "Well, it would make everything else have some sense out of human actions, although it raises a bunch of those wild cards in time I told you about. If it's true, then we have a couple of laws to unlearn and a couple of new ones to discover, but that's par for the course in something this complicated. You get used to it. Or he might have been lying, and our laws are correct. Only—pardon me—time will tell."

"I ain't sure I want to know. I only understood a little of what he was sayin' anyways."

Doc nodded but said nothing for a while. Finally, he asked, "Are you hungry? There's a Howard Johnson's up here that's open all night."

"I thought you said you was in a hurry."

"No, I said I didn't have the time to fool around back there. I'm on a schedule, and this is part of it."

They pulled into the parking lot, then went into the restaurant, which was mostly deserted. The few there obviously drew conclusions from the sight of the young sexpot and the older professional man there at this time of night, but they were pretty worldly and served this sort of duo quite often.

Doc ate heartily, but Holly just sipped her coffee and picked at her eggs. Finally, she asked, "What now, Doc? What's next?" It was said with weary resignation, not true curiosity.

"I know what you're thinking. You've tripped. O.K., you've tripped before. I must have tripped a thousand times. It's no big deal anymore."

"Maybe not for you. You'll still Doc, no matter what. You got brains and a real job. I guess I had brains once, but it's all gone now. I can't even remember what *he* looked like, you know that? Every time I do this, I know a little less and think a little slower. I think that's what gets me most. It ain't not knowin' what I once knew so much as bein' real slow about what I still know now." She picked up a card on the table. "Clam . . . back . . . every . . . Friday," she read, pronouncing each word carefully and individually as if separated. "All . . . you . . . can . . . eat . . . just. . . . Oh, hell, you see? I can't read no better or faster'n that, and them's simple words. I can't cook or sew or nothin', 'cept some mendin'. How's that for somebody who went through all that college?"

"Nothing is permanent. Surely you understand that now if nothing else. What's forgotten can be relearned."

"C'mon, Doc! Don't kid me! Every single time I get a little dumber. I ain't got much left, Doc. I'm near retarded now. I'm too damn scared to do it again."

"I think you underestimate yourself." He finished his coffee and looked out the window. "It's getting light out now. Looks like a nice day.'' He looked at his watch. "Let's go.''

They drove several places in the area, with Doc stopping now and then to talk to various people and make some phone calls. She fell asleep for a while and paid no attention to the activities, nor did she feel any curiosity about what was going on.

Doc shook her awake. She stirred uneasily, then opened her eyes and looked out the windshield. They were in some kind of public parking area, with another area slightly below them and fenced off. She looked to one side and saw the huge cooling towers of a nuclear power plant. She yawned, stretched as well as she could, and asked, "What're we doin' here?''

"Waiting. Not much longer now, I hope. Ah! There!''

A small blue car pulled into the lower lot and drove to a marked section. A woman dressed in whites got out, locked the door, and began to walk toward a lower entrance to the building. It was one of literally dozens of cars pulling in while others pulled out, but Doc drew Holly's attention to that one in particular.

"Recognize her?''

"Nope. Not from this distance, anyways. I guess I should get glasses, but it don't seem worth the bother.''

"Dr. Karen Cline.''

She sat up. "Huh? That her? You mean she's still comin' in to work and all?''

Doc nodded. "It means success. Cline, or whoever she really is, is going in with full knowledge that there is going to be a terrorist raid today and that the facility is going to be taken over. We achieved complete surprise.''

"You mean she don't know her friends got knocked off last night?''

"No. Eric couldn't risk contacting her, and nobody else dared, not this close to the operation, anyway.''

"So what'll happen to her?''

"Nothing. It'll be a normal, uneventful day. She'll

know something went wrong but won't dare try to contact her friends, for all the good it'd do her. She'll finish her shift and go home and make a time jump—she thinks. Only it won't be there.''

"Her belt?"

"Her apartment. In about ten minutes a blaze will start in the apartment under hers and it will be impossible to control. Every fire department within twenty miles will be needed to contain it. The place will burn to the ground, although hopefully with no loss of life. Cove's a pretty isolated little village. The right help just won't be able to get there in time.''

"And you figure she has the belt in the apartment?''

"We figure. It still might not get the belt, but she won't dare go near it because she'll know we'll be watching and she'll hear about the shootout with the radicals. She'll have no choice but to keep doing what she's doing and hope she's picked up. She won't be, because we'll be on her every second. She'll be assimilated. Why?''

"Eric said she was Ginny.''

"Indeed? Well, is that so bad a future? A career woman? A Ph.D.? An aide to valuable research? Isn't that better than almost anything we might have expected for her otherwise?''

"I—I guess so.'' She paused. "Why're we still here? Ain't we gonna go to her place to make sure?''

"In good time. Here—I'll stick this lousy radio on and get some music.''

They waited in silence for some time, and Holly began to drift off once more, but Doc suddenly switched off the music and she came awake as he started the car. They went down to the second parking area, which had a gate with a magnetic card pass required to raise it. Doc reached into a pocket, pulled out a card, and stuck it in. The gate went up, and they rolled into the lower lot and parked as close as possible to the door.

Almost immediately, a second car pulled in and after

driving up and down the rows it parked very near them. A man got out and looked around at the setting, then locked his door.

Holly stared at him, and her jaw dropped.

"I see you still really *do* remember what he looks like," Doc said gently.

"But—that's *Ron!*"

"Indeed, it is. Ronald Moosic, on his way to discover the secret of this installation and be given the tour. He's to be the new director of security. And because he will have a quiet and peaceful day, week, and month, he'll take over smoothly and do a fine job, and he'll never go downtime himself."

She sank back into the seat, feeling totally lost and confused. She watched the tall, handsome, confident man enjoy the new day before going into the hidden installation.

Finally, she said, in a voice so small it could hardly be heard and a tone almost tragically plaintive, "But—I started out as him. I know I did. Then I got turned into Dawn and all the others and finally I come to be me. But if he don't go back, he don't become all them people. They never lived. It all never happened. *But I'm still here!*"

"Yes."

She turned and looked squarely at Doc. "Then how am I here? Can you tell me that, Doc? How's Eric and Ginny and all the rest here when he never went back to father 'em or bear 'em?"

"It all happened. Every bit of it happened, and is recorded back in time in our master computer and in our own memories. The unmaking of it also happened, Holly. That's why you're here. As to who and what you are, though—you're a nightsider, just like me and the others. We're the leftovers from this mess. All those people that you were lived, and lived their lives out. Time has rippled them into existence, even as it has rippled all records, all signs, all memories of what happened out of the main time

line. Ron was gone, swallowed in time, but now he lives
again and will live out his life. That's a plus, isn't it?''

"I—I guess so. But if he's still here, and he's *him*, then
I'm just what I am. Holly, nothin' more.''

Doc started the car, put it in gear, and drove out of the
parking lot and back up onto the road and accelerated
north toward Cove.

"You're nothing *less* than Holly," Doc said at last. "Right
now you are the accumulated record of this whole thing.
They're all still there, inside you, somewhere. And you're
not as dumb as you think you are, either. You've followed
my entire conversation this distance after the trip point.''

They made the drive to Cove in a few minutes, but saw
the location long before they hit the town limits sign. A
huge column of thick, black smoke rose from the horizon,
and more than once they pulled over so one or another
volunteer fire department could pass.

State police prevented them from driving into the town
itself, but it was small enough that they could tell that the
incendiary had done its work with the team's usual precision.

Doc backtracked to the junction and went over to the
main highway, then headed north.

"Where to now, Doc?''

"Not far. There's a turnoff up here with a van parked in
it which has the time belts. This part of it is now finished.''

There were several men and women already at the turnoff,
and a number of cars were parked around. Holly knew that
most of these were members of the team she might recognize in other circumstances.

Doc got two of the small time belts from the back of the
van and put one on, handing the other to Holly. She shook
her head and didn't take it.

"No, Doc. You said it yourself. It's done. Finished.
Ron's here and alive, and I ain't nobody but Holly, the
best damn fuck in the east. I ain't got no place and no time
else to *go*, Doc. I *belong* here.''

"There's still the kids.''

Holly laughed sourly. "And what kind of Mama would I make now, huh? I don't look or act like her—'cause I *ain't* her. I'm a fucking ignorant *whore*, Doc!"

Talking by the others had stopped at this scene, and all attention was on them. Doc looked around for support. A big man beckoned him, and he went over and they briefly conferred; then Doc returned, still holding the belt.

"You know what happens to nightsiders, don't you Holly?" he pressed, yet maintained a calm tone. "They make no mark and die young. You know what happens to young whores who don't die young? They get old, and some new little chickie becomes the favorite. They get bought and sold by their pimps and wind up washed-up addicts wallowing in filth. You know that. You've seen it. You *want* that kind of life?"

She sighed. "You know I don't. But if I die young, all the better. I won't go that route, believe me. I'll kill myself first."

"So that's your future, huh? A decade or two of whoring until one day you're just so foul and so sick of yourself that you slit your wrists or jump off a roof or something? Unless one of the pimps or johns kills you first."

"Stop it! Damn your fucking soul! *Stop it!* There ain't no choice!"

"Yes, there is. You got one chance, but you have to take it now. Every hour, every day, brings you closer to what you think you now are." He held up the belt once again. "This is your way out. Take it. Use it now. Go where it sends you and listen to the other side of your life. I swear to you that, while I've preset it, it's a free and clear belt and it won't be taken from you without your permission. Just *listen*, for Christ's sake! For your own sake!"

She was more Holly than any or all of the others she had been, but even Holly wanted a way out, if she could only believe in it. She hesitated, then took the belt and strapped it around her slender waist. "Where will this take me?"

"To your future," Doc responded.

Hesitantly, her thumb went down to trigger the belt. It was probably going to be more misery and more lies, she thought, but Doc was right, as usual. When the known was unbearable, choose the unknown.

She pressed the stud and was suddenly falling into time.

The place was familiar. The same rock-like plastic walls, the same furniture, pretty much the same as when Ron Moosic had first seen it so many lifetimes ago. The only difference was that there seemed no one about; the computer complex far back in time was deserted.

Or was it? She stared, once again cursing her near-sightedness, and focused on a high-backed chair across the room. It was turned away from her, but there was the unmistakable smell of cigarette smoke in the air and it seemed to be coming from that direction.

"Hey! Anybody here?" she called out, her voice echoing.

A man got up from the chair and came over to her, smiling. He was middle-aged, with a deep tan, and had bushy contrasting white hair and a thick white moustache. He was rather handsome for one his age, and in obviously good physical condition. He wore casual clothing—a plaid work shirt, a pair of new-looking jeans, and boots. He towered over her.

"Pardon me, but I hadn't more than a rough estimate of when you would arrive," he said in a deep, rich baritone. His accent was some British one, but it had a slight additional sound of some Latin intonation. "My name is Ramon Cruz."

She just stared at him, not knowing what to say or do next. "Are we . . . alone here?"

He chuckled. "Oh, yes—quite alone, except for the omnipresent computer, I'm afraid. Come. Sit down over here and get comfortable. Remove the belt if you like—I will not try to take it from you, I swear.''

There was something in his tone and manner that made her want to trust him. Against her better instincts, she removed the belt and put it on the floor, then sank tiredly into a chair.

He looked suddenly concerned. "Please forgive me! You are very tired, I can see. Would you prefer to go back to one of the rooms and get a good sleep? I can wait.''

She didn't want to go to sleep in this place, at least not until she knew the score. "That's O.K. I'll live.''

He sat back in another chair, facing her, and took a cigarette from a pack. "Do you mind if I smoke?''

"Naw. In fact, I'll take one myself.'' She wasn't hooked on them, but she smoked occasionally. He offered her one, then lit it for her in courtly fashion. "Now—what's this all about?''

"Your welfare—and closing the last little bit of the noose on our targets.''

"I figured it was more *their* game than any feelin' for me. What's left to do?''

"Undo a terrible thing we have done to people who simply didn't deserve it. That is the easiest way to put it. Think of the permanently nightsided. You are one such. When the *cause* of the condition is closed, the ones who are left, the leftover flotsam and jetsam from the shipwreck we prevented from happening, are thorns in the side of time. It wants to be rid of them. It often manages to do so gently, as in the case of your Dr. Cline, but if it's up on the edge, there's not as much leeway. You don't assimilate on the edge any more than you do back here. Eliminate the cause of the nightsider on the edge and time will arrange to eliminate him from future consideration.''

"You mean he *dies*?''

"Usually. But consistently. I think, if indeed you are not too tired, that I might explain the last that you do not know.''

"You might say who *you* are, for a start."

He looked apologetic. "Ah! I'm so sorry! I am generally called Father Ramon, although I am actually an archbishop—without portfolio from Rome, I fear."

"You're a *priest*?"

"Yes. Does that bother you?"

"Yeah. It means I can't even get a good fuck—and boy, do I need one now! Sorry, Father—but I am what I am and I ain't Catholic anyway."

He shrugged. "A few of your lives were, including your origin, if I recall correctly. It does not matter. My branch of the Church is a bit more liberal and less orthodox than the one you know, in any case. You see, my church is on Mars."

She was suddenly wide awake. "Huh?"

"You understood me correctly. Mars."

"But—that's nuts! I know for a fact that them Outworlders are monsters—horrors."

"That's quite true, in a physical sense and from our vantage point as what we call 'human beings,' but it is only physical. Inside, they are humans, and so am I and so are you. Even outside, some have great grace and beauty, and can do many things that you and I cannot, as well as everything you or I *can* do."

"You couldn't live on Mars," she said skeptically. "Hell, I may have forgot more'n I can ever learn, but I know there ain't no air up there."

"Not enough air, and not in the right mixture, but, nevertheless, it is true. I am a Martian. I was born and raised there."

"You downtimed," she guessed. "You tripped over before comin' back here."

He grinned. "See? You aren't so dumb as you think you are. It *is* true that this is not my natural form, although I *am* a priest—and I'm fated to be a priest, no matter when in time I stop. I am certain I don't have to explain that to you."

"You can say that again."

"So, Holly, tell me—am I human or not?"

"You are *now*."

"So, tell me, Holly, what makes a human being? Is a human being this physical flesh or what is inside the head?"

She shook her head in irritation. "I don't know. I ain't smart enough no more to figure that one out."

"Well, I have seen the future of the human race. I have seen *both* futures of the human race. I have seen the Earth sink into a horror of misery and degradation, a humanity enslaved whose very souls are captive from birth to the dictatorial whims of a government elite, its resources depleted, its air fouled almost beyond redemption. The Earth of the future is death. The elite live over three hundred years, on average, in technological comfort. The slaving billions of the future have an average lifespan of less than thirty years—worse than in your own time by far, and live in a wasteland of medieval primitiveness. There's no power, no unspoiled vegetation, and few animals, except on the elite's preserves, where even human beings are hunted for sport. I can prove this. I have many pictures of this future Earth, or you could be taken there to a far corner to see for yourself."

She sighed. "I believe you. So the shits will inherit the Earth. What else is new?"

"*We* are," he replied softly. "Listen, my ancestors came to the New World and found great civilizations there. We did not try to integrate them into our society—we destroyed theirs. A priest of the Catholic Church burned the entire master royal library of the Mayan people in the Yucatan, and others of the Church and the Spanish state destroyed much of what was left. We destroyed their culture and reduced those proud people to slavery, and we were proud of it. They had a different culture, a different religion, and they looked and dressed wrong by European standards. They were, therefore, not human to my ancestors, but subhumans, intelligent but not ever equals.

"When this old world began to run out of its exploitable resources, the fuels and minerals that made civilization good for everyone, they had to go out to the planets to find more, and find them they did. The trouble was, they were in places Earth humans could not live without expensive and extensive life support. Mars had much value beneath its rusty soil; many of the asteroids and moons of Jupiter and Saturn had even more. To change those places to the type on which humans could live and work easily would take a fortune—and centuries. Earth did not have centuries, and the amounts it needed from its planetary sisters was far too great and too expensive to be economically feasible. The only solution they had to this was to make humans into creatures that could live in such places as easily as men could live on Earth. Not easily—but at least as easily as men lived in the Antarctic cold and the desert wastes of the Sahara. Do you follow me so far?"

She nodded. "I think so. They got a bunch of people and changed them into monsters."

"Not exactly. There was no shortage of volunteers. Skilled technicians and scientists were lured by the challenge and the romance of it. Workers were drawn from the poor and the dispossessed who saw a chance for becoming something great. It was a new frontier, and it was tamed, in a way, by such a breed. Scientists, romantics, and both losers and criminals—the same mix that colonized the Americas. And like the colonists of the Americas, they were taken for granted, used, and abused by an Earth grown fat and dependent on their labors. Cultures which had no trouble destroying the Mayas or oppressing the American colonists found even less of a moral problem with the Outworlders. They did not look human at all, but in many cases like strange beasts. They gave the Earth what it craved in abundance, and the Earth accepted magnani-

mously. But they were human *here*—inside their bodies"—
he tapped his chest—"and they found themselves regarded as animals and treated as property."

"And they're gettin' even."

"Perhaps. Being human, I'm afraid that's a part of it.
But they will not be the new Mayans. Earth was totally
dependent on them. When individual employees of a key
mining company staged a major strike, they were ruthlessly rounded up and put to death by the Earth authorities.
That began a massive revolt that swept through the solar
system like a fire. Earth was ill prepared and ignorant of
history. The Outworlders were too angry to be afraid, and
so, at great cost, they seized control of the most vital thing
in the whole system—the transportation network. The supplies stopped, and Earth was strangled. Within weeks
things began to break down. Within months they were in a
crisis state. Within a year they were reduced to a horrible
situation, with mass starvation and the collapse of the energy
which was never very cheap and was now very dear.
Most humans had taken such things for granted. They
didn't know how to work the land without machines, nor
could a non-mechanized civilization feed, clothe, and house
its people. Governments by necessity were forced to act
brutally and ruthlessly. What was left, in the end, was a
terrible, crushing military dictatorship which created a min-
iature of their old world, in which they alone got the
resources and comforts that were left from the masses who
slaved for them or died."

"Seems to me it'd be easier to make a deal."

"That's what *we* thought, but the collapse was so swift
and sudden, the military authorities so absolute and
doctrinaire, and nations which had hated each other for
centuries merged their ruling classes out of common need.
They are sixteenth-century Spain faced with a Mayan revolt in which the Mayans have superior arms and position
and all the resources. They will not deal with the subhumans,
even though they need them, and their own fears and

terrors and prejudices see only a domination by inhuman
monsters. They see themselves as saving humanity, and
will fight to the death for that ideal. And it is a terrible
tragedy, for the inhuman monsters they so horribly fear are
their own children.''

His face and tone took on a distant look. "See me. Am
I not a human being? Yes, I am that—and more. I am the
future. I am the way man broke with his follies and his
wastefulness and spread to other worlds. I am the path to
human survival, for through me humanity will continue to
grow, spread, and thrive, to explore and experiment and
wonder about the next hill, the next ocean, the next star.
And if my skin is white, or black, or yellow, or a chitinous
exoskeleton; if I breathe oxygen or methane—I am still a
human being. I have *seen* the currents of air rushing down
the great valleys of Mars, and I have stood upon the shores
of great sand seas and watched a thousand colors reflect
the pale sunlight. While my brothers grovel in the filth of
ancient Earth, I have the freedom of the stars and know the
wonders of God firsthand.''

She was impressed in spite of her tiredness and confusion,
but Doc had been right. She had followed it all, and still
had thinking doubts.

"Eric said you would destroy the human race."

"We can't destroy it without destroying ourselves. Our
fight is for many things, but it is not to destroy. One day,
God willing, we will go to the stars and sow our seed,
perhaps meet other of God's creations. We wish to save
the people of Earth. Their own rulers wish to destroy what
they cannot control, not us. We could have destroyed all
life on Earth years ago. We are a rescue mission, a
liberation movement, and a vision of man's future. For my
part, I have a more personal motive. I am a priest of the
Holy Roman Catholic Church, yet I am denied ever visiting Rome as myself, ever seeing the great dome of St.
Peter's or the wonders of the Sistine Chapel, if, indeed,
they still exist in my time. I wish to walk the streets of

Campeche on the Gulf Coast of the Yucatan, where my great-grandfather was born and generations of my family before that. I cannot be denied the present or my future, but I am still robbed of my past which is my birthright.''

"Why are you telling me all this? What is your fight to me now?"

"Because we are the cause of your problems, and you are the solution to the last of ours. We have been buying time, as you might remember. Time to make certain that when Earth's last defenses collapse, they will not destroy this world which is my parent and my birthright and all its people. Earth was so weak it was difficult not to win. Our computers examined the time lines and came up with the pattern which has proven invaluable in staving off that collapse. We bore in on the children, but particularly Joseph and Ginny, after you were gone. We filled them with fear and showed them horrors as the Outworlders' legacy, while concealing that which was good, beautiful, and even great. We convinced them that we were the greater evil, and then allowed them to escape below.''

She sat up and stared at him. "You *allowed* them to escape?"

"I'm afraid so. Joseph, as Eric, reopened the time project, and created quite a mess for us to straighten out. The edge continued on, and his and his sister's efforts greatly lengthened the war. All but a few of the great stockpiled weapons of planetary destruction have now been neutralized. Depending on the skill of our extraordinary team, it may soon be over. Then we will come down and liberate the Earth, not as conquerors but as children returning to aid their elderly and infirm parents. The leadership will pack up and escape to their rear time base, while giving the commands to destroy the Earth after they leave. They will go. It is too difficult to stop them. But the Earth will survive and they will not know it.''

She did not *feel* like Dawn, and she certainly didn't feel like anyone's mother, and so it was a great surprise to her that she felt sudden anger well up inside her at what he now said. "You deceived my children and turned them to evil? *My* Joseph and Ginny?" She half rose from her chair in anger, and only a steady gaze from his sad, dark eyes stopped her from going any further.

"Yes. Two lives dirtied so that millions, perhaps billions, may live. It is a sad choice of war. Our Lord went to the cross to save even more."

"Yeah, but he could get up and go again stronger than ever!"

"And so may you and those children. Get some rest here, relax, get your mind and heart clearly in order. When you are ready, we can rejoin the children not long after you left. When the time comes for final victory, you will all go forward to join the future—human, if you wish, helping in the massive job of rebuilding the Earth, or the other kind of human, going out to explore and learn and claim the stars."

She stared at him, and wanted very much to believe him, but she just wasn't sure. And, of course, there was another problem. "You're forgetting who and what I am now."

"What are you? Nothing that Mary Magdalene was not at one time. She chose correctly and achieved greatness and eternal salvation."

"But—them kids! They won't take me as their mom! And I sure as hell don't feel like no mom!"

"You are still very much their mother, and that love and bond is still within you. You have just proven that. The rest is cosmetic, and that is a trivial matter. Have I not just been saying that this is at the heart of that great and terrible war? If you knew what a Martian human looked like, you would not worry. Physical adjustments as minor as yours, using our biology or the old-time method meticulously controlled by the computer, are too minor to even mention."

She had to grant him that, and for the first time felt

some real hope. "But if I go through this last thing, if I close this last loop, then Eric won't ever have existed. Won't that screw up the plan?"

"Ron Moosic exists, and so do you. Eric will be cut off, a leftover at the edge of time. Remember, all that has happened so far actually happened. We wipe out only the record, not the event. What will happen to him, only time can tell, if you'll pardon me."

She felt suddenly very weary and very old, more accepting his proposition than understanding, let alone embracing, it. What was truth and what was lies? Who was real and who was just downtiming the night side?

Only time will tell, she thought, drifting off in the chair. *If they let it.*

EPILOGUE
LEADING EDGE, MAIN TIME LINE

It literally looked like Hell in the Party's headquarters; half the place seemed to be on fire. Actually, dozens of frantic aides were rushing about pulling and destroying files, computer records, and all the basic control machinery that had managed Earth for so long a time from this tiny spot. Of particular import were all materials in any medium referring to time travel, the time project, or the master computer far downtime.

These were the lucky ones—the one hundred men and women who would be allowed to go back. There might have been more, but there were only one hundred time belts available and the prehistoric complex could comfortably house and provide for no more than a few hundred anyway.

A dozen were the Central Committee, of course, and that was to be regretted, but no project like this could go through to completion unless they were included, even if they were far older than would be useful. The rest were family, close associates, trusted aides, and their families.

Most of the complex of several thousand thought they were going, too, and awaited the transfer of the first hundred with nervous anticipation. The belts were then to be homed back to the time control complex and be used again, and again, a hundred at a time, until all were safe.

They didn't know how limited the facilities were downtime, and never suspected for a second that those belts would never return.

Nor did they know that Chairman Shumb had already

read in what were known as the Armageddon Codes into the master computers worldwide that would explode within an hour of the Chairman's own farewell with such monstrous force that they might well shake Earth's orbit and blow so much radioactive debris into the 'air that the world would be plunged into a horrible, cold darkness for years, while radioactivity scoured the planet of even the hardier forms of life.

They didn't even know about the massive superbomb sitting underneath this very complex, which, when it went, would make their silly scramble to destroy all records and controls an exercise in childish futility.

Max Shumb sighed, looked at his watch, then got up from his big desk and looked around the office he'd occupied for so many years. He didn't want to leave, didn't want to give up what had become so much a part of him, but it was either do so or perish with the Earth. He had no intention of doing that. One of these days they might work out a way back there in the great prehistoric wasteland to keep this from happening, to prevent what was now inevitable. He liked to think so, if only because of the great art and great works of literature he would lose here.

The death of the population of the Earth did not trouble him in the slightest. Only a few human beings really mattered other than himself. The rest were mostly cattle, easily replaced if you had enough time and enough women.

General Kolodin entered and saluted smartly. "Sir, we are ready to transport and time is getting short. I must insist that you come with me immediately."

Chairman Shumb nodded and sighed. "Yes, you're right, Alexei."

The general looked around the room and read his leader's thoughts. "It's not really gone, you know. Not so long as the belts work."

Shumb grinned. "You know just what to say every time."

"The Russian is a pragmatist at all times. It is the

climate that does it." He paused a moment. "There is still the matter of Eric Benoni."

"Huh? Second Wave, isn't he? Won't that take care of itself?"

"Sir, he's quite clever and he thinks well ahead for self-preservation. He is insisting on First Wave priority."

"That son-of-a-bitch is a pushy bastard, isn't he? He's the one who was supposed to bail us out and instead we're riding down the toilet, and now he expects to get a free ride. Where is he now?"

"In the reception area near the time project control center."

Shumb nodded. "Well, come on, Alexei. Time to march forward into the past. On the way down we'll find a squad of protectors and order them to shoot the son-of-a-bitch."

GORDON R. DICKSON

☐ 53567-7   Hoka! (with Poul Anderson) $2.75
    53568-5   Canada $3.25

☐ 48537-9   Sleepwalker's World $2.50

☐ 48580-8   The Outposter $2.95

☐ 48525-5   Planet Run $2.75
                 with Keith Laumer

☑ 48556-5   The Pritcher Mass $2.75

☐ 48576-X   The Man From Earth $2.95

☐ 53562-6   The Last Master $2.95
    53563-4   Canada $3.50

Buy them at your local bookstore or use this handy coupon:
Clip and mail this page with your order

TOR BOOKS—Reader Service Dept.
P.O. Box 690, Rockville Centre, N.Y. 11571

Please send me the book(s) I have checked above. I am enclosing
$_____ (please add $1.00 to cover postage and handling).
Send check or money order only—no cash or C.O.D.'s.

Mr./Mrs./Miss _____

Address _____

City _____ State/Zip _____

Please allow six weeks for delivery. Prices subject to change without notice.

POUL ANDERSON
Winner of 7 Hugos and 3 Nebulas

FRED SABERHAGEN

NEXT STOP:

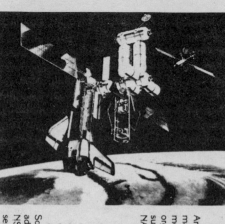

SPACE STATION

"... I am directing NASA to develop a permanently manned Space
Station, and to do it within a decade." ... *President Ronald Reagan,
State of the Union message, January 25, 1984.*

Are you a person of vision? Are you excited about this next new stepping stone in
mankind's future? Did you know that there is a magazine that covers these developments better than any other? Did you know that there is a non-profit public interest
organization, founded by famed space pioneer Dr. Wernher von Braun, that actively
supports all aspects of a strong U.S. space program? That organization is the
NATIONAL SPACE INSTITUTE. If you're a member, here's what you'll get:

- 12 big issues of Space World magazine. Tops in the field. Follow the political,
  social, and technological aspects of all Space Station developments—and all
  other space exploration and developments too!
- VIP package tours to Kennedy Space Center to watch a Space Shuttle launch—
  the thrill of a lifetime!
- Regional meetings and workshops—get to meet an astronaut!
- Exclusive Space Hotline and Dial-A-Shuttle service.
- Discounts on valuable space merchandise and books.
- and much, much more!

So if you are that person of vision, your eyes upon the future, excited about the
adventure of space exploration, let us send you more information on how to join the
NSI. Just fill in your name and address and our packet will be on its way. AND, we'll
send you a FREE Space Shuttle Launch Schedule which is yours to keep whatever
you decide to do!

Name _____

Address _____

City, State, & Zip _____